A *Light* IN THE DARKNESS

RIAN MCMURTRY

This is a work of fiction. Names, characters, places and incidents either are the product of the author's imagination or are used fictitiously, and any resemblance to any actual persons, living or dead, events, or locales is entirely coincidental.

ARPress
45 Dan Road Suite 5
Canton MA 02021

Hotline: 1(800) 220-7660
Fax: 1(855) 752-6001

Ordering Information:
Quantity sales. Special discounts are available on quantity purchases by corporations, associations, and others. For details, contact the publisher at the address above.

Printed in the United States of America.

ISBN-13:   Paperback   979-8-89676-219-5
                 Hardcover   979-8-89676-221-8
                 eBook   979-8-89676-220-1

Library of Congress Control Number: 2020913251

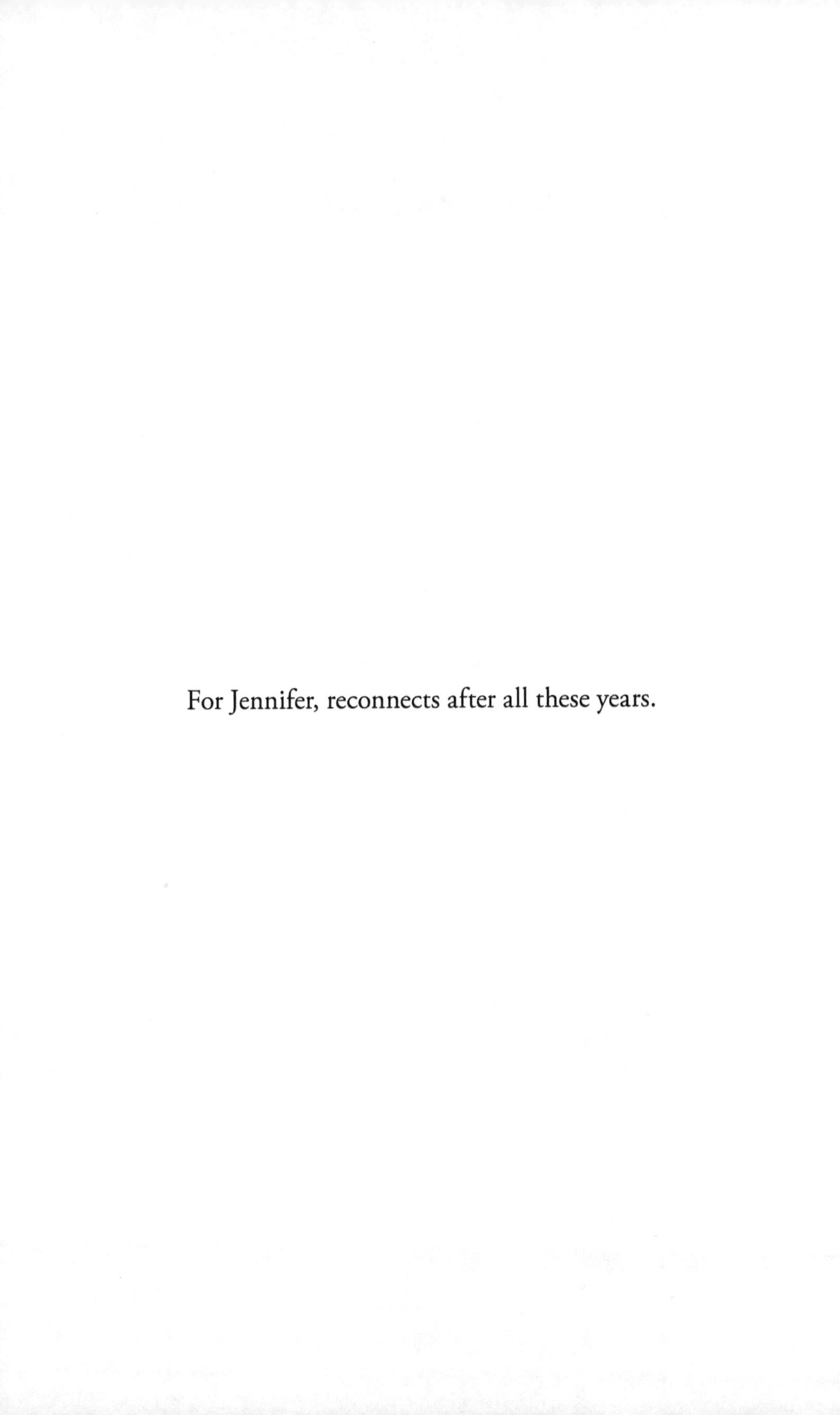

For Jennifer, reconnects after all these years.

CHAPTER

1

Winds whipped around the high headland in the darkness, lit only by the stars, the lights of the city to the south, and the lights on the great red-orange bridge connecting the two peninsulas. The round metal and concrete structure had been abandoned for decades, and it stank of the abandonment and urine and other substances mixing with the sea breezes. No one was present to see a boy and girl appear impossibly out of thin air.

The girl shivered. "Where are we?" Angela Fujiwara asked as she dropped Seth's hand.

"Battery Wallace," Seth Dupree replied, as the wind billowed his trench coat out behind him. "In the Headlands." He gestured towards the city. "San Francisco is over there."

"Neat," she replied, shivering some more and regretting the light jacket she'd grabbed when Seth showed up at her window. The winds here were cold, and were raising goose bumps all over her skin. The t-shirt and jeans she'd been wearing weren't much help, either. "Why are we here, Teach?" It had been only about a month since she'd asked him to start teaching her the magic he and his friends had stumbled upon, and she wasn't very good at it. Certainly teleportation was beyond her abilities at this point, but she still remembered when with nothing but concentration, determination, and a couple of words she'd made a ball of light. They'd been refining that, and she could send it through the rainbow. She couldn't quite manage black light yet, but she was making progress, and she was able to heal herself. That was exhausting, but she still grinned remembering the smokers' faces when she extinguished their cigarettes.

He started walking towards the concrete steps. "Because I wanted to make sure you had your bearings. I could be teleporting us even farther, or directly into the room, but if you see the City from here you've at least got the basic idea of where we are."

She nodded as the wind whipped her hair around. That was the Seth she'd come to know. Considerate, but not the consideration she actually wanted. If he'd just teleported them straight there she wouldn't be freezing now, she thought as she hurried after him. But, no, he wanted her to be able to see and verify where they were so she didn't think he was kidnapping her to strange locations. Just as well her parents thought she was studying at Bridget's. They didn't even know she'd made her peace with Seth over the bus incident last year. The one where he'd put his hand under her bra.

The one where he'd healed her death.

She'd complained loudly and gotten him charged for touching her. But in reversing her death, he'd inadvertently made killing her the obsession of Reverend Johnson. Seth had foiled three more attempts, and she was sure the others had stopped more… without her knowing about it. She understood why, now. She wouldn't have believed Seth a year ago that he had brought her back from death, or any of the other things, without seeing actual proof with her own eyes… and they were being very cautious about who they told. Their parents didn't all know.

Reverend Johnson had turned out to be a vampire. He'd had her kidnapped out of her bedroom, and he'd been biting her neck when she finally reached out to Seth, pleading for his help. He'd given it, and his necromantic power had ripped the vampire to shreds.

Now, she had asked to learn the power that he and the others had. He'd asked if she really wanted to learn it from him, given his concentration on death. She did. Seth was the deadliest of them. She didn't want to ever have to rely on someone else to protect her again. Even with Johnson dead, gone and completely destroyed.

Seth led the way into a round room. "Where's the door?" he asked.

"You don't know?" she glared at him.

"Of course I know. You missed the point of the question," he said as he looked back at her blandly.

"Oh, right." This was a test. At times like this she sort of wished she'd asked Bridget instead. Seth made a fetish of not noticing the cold. That she didn't have that fetish hadn't crossed his mind. She closed her eyes in concentration. Sensory enhancement was one of the things they'd been working on. As she reopened them, they had gone from brown to teal, and glowed. She peered around, taking in the concrete, the graffiti, the steel… and there the door was, between two sections of concrete. She concentrated further, and looked at all the myriad protections on that door, making sure it STAYED shut… Seth's black, Bridget's green, Alex's purple, Keisha's orange, Teddy's blood red, Dawn's yellow, Malcolm's blue, Jennifer's indigo, and Solly's brown. No one not using techniques like these would even be able to find the door, and they obviously didn't want such a person entering without permission. She used her own fledgling abilities to highlight the door, and then stepped back. "There it is, Teach. But I'm not going to be able to open it."

"Oh?"

"You all worked on protecting and sealing that door," she replied. "I wouldn't even know where to begin."

"Wise choice." He stood before the wall, said something in a foreign language, and held out his hand to her. She took it, and they stepped through the wall.

"What language was that?"

<Coptic>, he replied in her head. *<We all picked old or obscure languages, and none of us use the same one. It identifies WHO is entering. When you reach the point where you join the rest of us, you'll need to pick a language to use for your entrance.>*

<Oh?> Seth always spoke of when she would achieve equivalent power; he never evinced the doubts she harbored about her ability to do so.

<Yeah. I use Coptic. Bridget uses Gaelic, Alex uses Nahuatl, Teddy uses Aramaic, Solly uses Hebrew, Jennifer uses Cornish, Dawn uses Tsalagi, Keisha uses Cushitic, and Malcolm uses Phoenician.>

<Tsalagi?>

<Cherokee.>

<Why does Dawn use Cherokee? I don't see the connection.>

<There isn't one. She thought it would be a cool language to know, but it's hard to learn even with our mind-to-mind techniques.>

"Damn, Seth, haven't you taught her thermoregulation yet?" Bridget Sullivan demanded. The huge black maned lion at her feet raised his head to regard the newcomers, shuddered when he saw Seth, and dropped his head back down. She was wearing a striped sweater and comfortable looking green jeans.

"Hmm?" he said.

"She's shivering!" Jennifer O'Neill replied. Jenny was a diminutive redhead in an indigo dress and white leggings. Dawn Takugawa, another redhead dressed in yellow slacks and a red coat, shook her head, motioned, and a large steaming mug came floating over to her.

"Thanks," Angela said as she sipped the cocoa with gratitude. She'd started drinking coffee, but Dawn had a sweet tooth. As she sniffed the air, she realized that they all had sweet teeth. Tea and coffee weren't in the air, just cocoa. And root beer.

"Angela, come on over closer to the heat. Thantoris," Dawn glared at him good-naturedly, "not only forgets other people don't do that, but he takes that 'chill of the grave' thing a little too seriously sometimes."

"She never said anything, you know," Seth said defensively as he took his black seat. The large round table was a slab of petrified tree trunk, the softly upholstered wooden chairs around it each a different color as befit their occupants. The large room was a few degrees warmer than outside, but that seemed to be more a lack of wind-chill. "The heat," though, came from the center of the table, ensuring the pizzas didn't get cold. Angela was still standing, and gently thumped the back of his head as she took her teal chair next to him.

"You're the one who was telling me we have this strong, powerful bond that lets you know all sorts of things about me. How could you NOT know I was cold, Teach?" Angela asked.

"I don't use it much, you know. Your privacy is something I try to respect." Actually she knew that. It was one of the things she'd found she liked about Seth. Between them, the power was almost all on Seth's side. Their bond, formed when he raised her from the dead, was far more under his control than hers. They had already demonstrated that he could physically make her do things whether or not she resisted through it. He'd just made her eat one of Malcolm's sardines, but that was enough. That had been when she was expecting it, with the others standing by and able to intervene if he tried to do something else. His conscientiousness about respecting her personal boundaries—he always asked permission to actually enter her mind, and he'd recommended she work with Alex or Bridget on mental defenses—made her trust him more. She used the bond more than he did, and what he did use it for was mostly telepathy.

"Yeah, I know. What's with the meeting tonight, anyway?"

Solomon Levison spoke up. "We finally traced what the Reverend was up to. It's not pretty." Solly was wearing a brown and copper Sacramento Amazons sweatshirt and a pair of tan dockers.

"That's saying something," Teddy Pope put in. He was wearing his usual white dress shirt, dark red sweater, and black slacks. "Selling kids to rich freaks?" he shook his head. "We need to put a stop to that."

"That was the plan?" Angela asked, horrified. The thought of what she'd escaped because Seth chose not to leave her to her fate chilled her. She looked over at Seth. "Thank you again, Teach."

"I never thought I'd be placing you in danger by raising you," he said. A wry expression crossed his face as he sipped his tea. "Of course, I also didn't expect the reaction you did have." A chuckle went around the table as Angela blushed. "But you were saying, Solly? I got lucky with Reverend Johnson. It might not be so easy if there's a group of practitioners."

Angela considered that. She was still horrified at the plans for her and the kids rescued from Johnson, but Seth had been urging her to detach, to consider what was happening and being said. Seth had ripped Johnson apart before her eyes, and had made it look easy. Would it have been as easy… If Seth weren't the necromancer… Johnson had been expecting Alex, and while Alex was just as powerful as Seth, he did things differently. Alex got people to do what he wanted them to; he was a highly charismatic leader. If Johnson had already gotten control of their minds, Alex would have had a far tougher time.

"We don't know about that yet," Keisha Johnson replied after she swallowed a mouthful of pizza. She was dressed in a West African style, an orange scarf over her curls and bright blue, yellow and white blouse and pants. She wiped her mouth with her napkin and continued. "They might just be criminals, with no power at all. In which case an anonymous call to the Sheriff will work perfectly well."

"If they are practitioners?" Angela asked.

"Then we act." Alex Menendez was definite about that. He was wearing jeans and a purple and gold Berkeley Avengers sweatshirt. The others nodded. He looked at her. "Ange, whether or not you act directly with the rest of us depends on what you can do at the time. Right now, we'd have to protect you."

"It won't be like that for long. You're learning fast," Jennifer put in.

"Faster than we did, really," Keisha said. She smiled wryly. "It undoubtedly helps that you have someone showing you the way. We basically had to figure it out by ourselves."

"As interesting as this is, I'm going to have to modify my parents' minds if we spend much longer." Teddy was checking his watch again.

"AGAIN?" Malcolm Muir asked shaking his head. He was wearing a sea green turtleneck and blue jeans, and his hair was green tinged from chlorine. "I know it's our choice whether to tell our old folks, but how much of what they think is happening actually is, Teddy?" She'd met Malcolm's parents last year, just before he and Bridget told her the truth. They not only knew about his magic, they relied on it to keep the three of them safe on—and in—the sea.

"Not much, to tell the truth, Malcolm," Teddy admitted. At her expression, he continued, "My parents are religious nuts, Angela. They would regard it as their holy duty to do something about me to protect my brothers and sisters from the "witch" I've become. Probably in my sleep. It wouldn't work—I've got enough protection spells active at any given time to keep me safe, including ones that alert everyone else to what's happening—but they'd probably try. And much as they infuriate me, I love my family. I'd rather keep myself safe this way than with something more permanent."

"By the way, Teddy, I haven't seen you guys at the flagpole this year, it's always Patti's group. Where do you take yourselves?" Dawn asked.

"Oh, you know that cement stage? We got too big to be at the flagpole. We were starting to spill into the parking lot. So we moved there. So what's next?" he asked, in a clear let's move on voice.

"Speaking of your loving parents, how was Canaan, Teddy?" Dawn asked as she finished a slice.

"Hot. Dusty. Hysterical. Violent. I kept protection spells up the whole time. I'm very glad to be home."

"Did you find anything this time?" Solly asked.

"No more than you did, Solly. Some old or ancient traces of power. Nothing recent, and even the traces were of things I could fairly easily accomplish on my own. I disguised myself with illusions and went into Gaza and the West Bank, we visited Jerusalem, Nazareth, Bethlehem. Nada. I took pictures. They're on the Wizard Wide Web, if you want to take a look, and I was using the app Alex and Keisha came up with, so if I missed anything it should be there. Anything else on Canaan?"

"Why are you guys calling it Canaan?" Angela wanted to know.

"It avoids the Israeli/Palestinian dispute over whose land it is."

"Okay, so far that's Delphi, Rome, Salt Lake City, Moscow, Istanbul, Athens, Mexico City, London, Anglesey, Stonehenge, the Black Hills, Boston, Canaan, Alexandria, Djakarta, Japan, Hawai'i, Mumbai, Delhi, Paris, Haiti, New Orleans, Giza, Luxor, Rio, Chichen

Itza, Macchu Picchu, Timbuktu, the Ethiopian cities and shrines, Abu Simbel… nothing. I mean, Keisha finding those hominid fossils at Olduvai was great, but not what we were looking for. Should we still go to Mecca and Iran? Check out Australia and New Zealand? Keep checking smaller sites?" Malcolm asked. "We're starting to get to the point of why bother."

"I think we should," Keisha said. "We're still at "what" and not at "why"."

"I agree," Jennifer said. "Even if our hypothesis is correct and we're not finding evidence of divinities because there is none to find, we can refine our techniques a bit more based on what they actually did." There was a murmur of agreement from most at the table. "Next…Angela?"

"Are we asking the right questions?"

Seth answered. "We don't know. My mom likes to make the point that "absence of evidence is not evidence of absence", but we've been a lot of places, and as far as we can tell, there's nothing to indicate that there is anything. So far, I don't think we've really found any trace we haven't already surpassed. If you have a different question, by all means ask it. Anything else?" She shook her head. She still went to church, but the parade of nothing was eating away at that.

"Mars, then, I think. Bridget, Malcolm, and I have made the Castle comfortable, and the teleportation chamber is functioning. Teddy, can you soup up the illusions we've got? No need for some telescope or camera to notice what we're doing… or see us on the surface," Alex said.

"Why are you calling it 'the Castle'? Didn't you tell me it was a cave?" she asked.

Solly grinned. "It is a cave. But half the school knows we play old school Dungeons and Dragons. We can refer to things like castles without anyone else knowing what we're talking about. We call the base cave on Venus "the Temple". Speaking of which, Jennifer, isn't it about time for her to roll up a character?"

"She and I can talk about that, if she wants. Anything else on Mars, though, Solly?" Jennifer replied.

"We haven't really talked about this point, but I think it's something to keep in mind. When we start actually changing the planet, it WILL be noticed. What do we do at that point?" They looked at each other.

"We'll be ready to do Mars by the end of junior year, I think," Keisha said. She consulted a tablet computer. "I'm not sure about Venus. We've still got a number of problems—not the least of which is that slow rotation."

"Why just Mars and Venus? What about the Moon? Or…" Angela asked, confused.

Alex responded, "Atmosphere. Mars and Venus have atmospheres we need to—and can—alter. Luna's might as well not exist."

"We could probably change that," Keisha said. "I think we could, if we wanted to, put atmospheres and Earth-normal gravity on most of the asteroids. But it would be a lot of work."

"We might as well go looking for another solar system to play with," Malcolm said.

"Yeah, probably," Jennifer put in, "but let's not get ahead of ourselves. We've got plenty of work to do on these two. Or three, if we decide we want to play with Luna as well. And fixing the problems here on Earth will be tricky."

"What makes Earth trickier? I've heard that before, but I'm not sure I get it."

"Mars, Venus, and Luna are dead worlds. We don't need to worry about the life on the surface. And, truth to tell, what we do there the authorities here can't interfere with anyway. They can bluster all they want, but no one's been to Luna in decades and there's never been a crewed mission to Mars or Venus. On Earth, we face the constantly changing problems they cause," Dawn said

"And while we considered taking drastic action, we all voted against it," Teddy chimed in.

"What do you mean drastic?" Angela asked a little fearful of the response.

"Trigger an apocalypse for the human population," he replied. "Global pandemic looked like the best option, although there was some talk of zombies."

"We could arrange to spare regions, peoples, whatever. But we don't want to kill that many people," Dawn said. "If we can avoid it, we will."

"Okay, that's a morbid conversation."

"Well, maybe this will help. Dividend checks for everyone. Ange, I can reinvest it if you want. I've got my eye on a number of things. Most of us reinvest most of it."

CHAPTER

2

When the meeting broke up, most of them teleported away. Seth said, "Keisha, could you hold up a minute?"

Her brow furrowed in sudden worry, but she said, "Sure Seth. What's wrong?"

He sighed. "I wouldn't be bringing this up if I wasn't sure, Keisha. But Mike has only a few months."

"What?" she asked, the blood draining from her face. "How? Can we fix it?"

"Cancer. I'm not sure what kind," he replied grimly. "As for curing it, it's too advanced for me to do it. Bridget might be able to."

"Will you…"

"We'll have to see. Best I can suggest is that you stay near him."

"Okay. Thanks for the warning," she said, then disappeared.

"Did you just say…" Angela asked as she and Seth were left alone in the big room.

"I'm afraid so. Mike Wu will die sometime in the next few months." Seth was calm, grim, and spoke with absolute certainty.

"How do you know?"

He sighed. "The approaching death is something I can sense, if there's a developing cause, or supernatural menace. Disease, suicidal depression, something like that. I'm not picking up on accidents or deliberate murder; there's nothing in something like that to indicate an approaching death. I'll be able to pin it down closer as we get nearer to the time. Remember your grandmother?" She nodded, remembering how Seth had predicted her death…and arranged for Bridget to be present when she learned of it.

"The only way I could deal with Mike's cancer now would be to kill him, destroy the cancer cells, and then resurrect him. I'm just not precise enough in a living body. I'm fairly certain that Keisha would rather find a different solution, but that will take Bridget."

"Why wouldn't she agree?" she asked, bewildered.

"I have no idea, but that's her call to make, not mine." She nodded. Something else occurred to her.

"Seth, why does everyone use *fiat lux* for light? No one uses Latin as their language for casting."

He smiled wryly. "First thing we did, actually. Jennifer was turning the lights on for game night and we said it as a throw away dramatic gesture. Her mom came in a few moments later. The power was out, but we still had light in the game room." He paused for a moment as they waited for Bridget to take Leonard home. "It was the normal light of the bulb, too. Shifting colors came later."

"Now we normally do our own color," Bridget put in as she reappeared in a swirl of greens. "You know, Angela, you might want to tell the old folks that you've made friends with Seth. Your choice, of course, but it would make this easier."

"I know, I'm sorry. It's just…"

"You're embarrassed about the way you talked about me last year?" Seth suggested with a small smile.

"Something to that," she replied, smiling back at him. Seth disappeared with the deep tolling of a bell.

"Show-off," Bridget said, smiling. "Ready?"

Angela nodded, took Bridget's hand, and was overwhelmed with the scents of wildflowers as they teleported to her kitchen. The kitchen was huge, with her father sitting at a large oak table in the breakfast nook.

"Hi honey, Angela," Bridget's dad said, looking up from his laptop. "Good meeting?"

"Yeppers!" Bridget replied. "You don't mind Angela staying over?"

"Of course not. Chocolate cake in the fridge is up for grabs; so's the peppermint ice cream in the freezer. Have a good night, girls."

"Thanks, Dad. We may come down for that later." Bridget shifted them to her room.

"He's not the ONLY show-off."

Bridget shrugged, grinning. "Nope. We're all sort of like that, when we're with someone we can show off to safely."

"Which would be me, I suppose."

Bridget gave her a hug and smile of encouragement. "Hey, you're coming along quickly. We aren't joking about that. You asked Seth for training in mid August and it's only mid October. Yet look at what you can already do, reliably, every time. Besides, we all know Alex shows off for Dani."

"Does she know?"

"About Alex? Yes. Since they started going out last year, Alex took charge of protecting her personally, and had to use his power before her openly more than once. About the rest of us? I don't think so, but I haven't checked."

"I knew she was aware of Alex. But I guess I still need to keep my mouth shut around her."

"Not if you want to tell her about you, of course."

"Knowing about me and about Alex, she can probably figure out the rest of you."

Bridget nodded. "I wouldn't be surprised if she already has. Which is something of a problem, but… it's Dani. Alex is the first of us with a steady boyfriend or girlfriend. So she's his responsibility in terms of the secrets we need to keep. If there's a bad break up, we may need to intervene."

"Wow. You almost sound like my parents," Angela said.

Bridget nodded, grinning. "Yeppers, I get that a lot. And I'm not the only one, either. But, as Mom told me when I demonstrated what

I could do, we're just too powerful to not grow up fast. What she told me was 'No one else can decide to use your power. No one can make you choose to use it, no one can make you choose not to use it. I'll help you as much as I can, but in the end it's your choice.' The same applies to you, to any of us. My powers have to do with life and living things, with evolution and one thing turning into another."

She paused and looked directly into Angela's eyes. "All of what we can do depends on the three things Seth told you—will, knowledge, and imagination. Some things are more draining on us than others. There's some additional part, we're not sure what, that makes magic possible. Jennifer's done the most thinking on that; she seems to have a bit more of it than the rest of us.

"Now that I've been pretentious," she grinned merrily, "Whadja think of last week's episode of New Worlds?"

"Marvelous. Can you believe that Captain Blackwolf is Shevaun's *dad*?"

CHAPTER

3

The school bus for Lucas Valley High was crowded as usual the next Monday, but Angela had secured a seat next to Carmen Burns and therefore the ride wasn't that bad. The olive drab seats weren't very comfortable, the seatbelts were even uglier. She could smell the odors of old sweat and shoeless feet, and the morning was chilly enough that she didn't wasn't to open a window. Forgotten gum lingered under the seats. Her fellow students were loud with their complaints about the early hour. Perfectly normal on a Monday morning.

Carmen welcomed her with a cheeky grin. She had other friends on the normal route, too, but it was good to spend time with Carmen. She didn't get to as much with all the extra studying.

"What do you think of the writing assignment from Ms. Chong? 'Write a scene in your year story of at least three pages that satisfies the Bechdel test'?" Carmen asked her.

"Three pages! That's gonna take forever!" she wailed. "And it's due next Friday. I've got practice, not to mention the game that night, plus tutoring, when does she imagine I have time to do three pages?"

"Three pages isn't that hard," Naomi Ulrich, a senior said. "Adjust the margins a bit, tweak the spacing, and you're golden! Assignment done, and you can go back to something interesting."

"Easy for you to say," Angela griped. "I pull shit like that and Bridget will never let me hear the end of it. She'll teach my cockatiel to speak just so she can call me a lazy cheater."

"I don't think cockatiels can speak," Naomi replied.

"Hah! You don't know Bridget, obviously. She has a way with animals. If Kiku physically can speak, Bridget will be able to get her to say whatever she wants her to," Carmen answered. Jennifer caught Angela's eye, smiled, and shrugged. Bridget did have a way with animals, after all. That she augmented it with her power was another matter.

"Oh, she can speak just fine, calls herself 'pretty bird'. But really, three pages! Might as well be a hundred!"

"Oh, relax," Jennifer put in. "It's not that bad. Besides it puts us that much closer to the year end assignment."

"And you can crank that out in an hour of study hall, I bet," Carrie Ramirez said.

Jennifer shrugged. "Of course I can. So could you if you didn't spend so much time whining about it. It's pretty simple."

"Easy for you to say! How long is that novel you're planning on turning in?" Joy Ning asked.

"A fairly short one," she replied evasively.

"Hmph. How many hundreds of pages?"

"Just one thirty or so. I'm aiming for fifty thousand words."

"A hundred and thirty pages. Fifty thousand words, and she makes it sound like nothing! Jennifer, has anyone ever told you you're a serious fucking overachiever?"

"They're not usually that polite about it," she replied. "There's usually some complaint about me wrecking the curve."

"She only asked for twenty thousand you know!"

"So it'll be a bit longer. I already got permission."

"What's it about?"

"A sorceress encountering amazon society. A fantasy story."

"Cheater!"

"Wait," Traci Kellogg said, "What's the Bechdel test?"

"In a story, two female characters have a conversation about something other than a guy. Which is why Jenny's cheating."

"That's what the story was already about, Carmen!"

"Yeah, right!"

"She's telling the truth, actually. She let me read the first few pages. It's pretty good," Angela said.

"Three pages, though! Do you have any idea how bad I am at writing dialogue?"

"You can't be worse than me," Carmen said.

"Hah! And let me tell you how sympathetic my mom's being about the whole thing!" Joy burst in.

"Bad?"

"She said anyone who can rack up a cell phone bill like mine and still tie up the landline twenty-four seven talking about nothing shouldn't have any trouble filling up a mere three pages of dialogue! I am NOT on the phone that much!"

"That is bad," Jennifer said.

"By the way, Carmen, did you get the chem homework?" Traci asked.

"Yep."

"Can I copy off you?"

"Not unless you want to get caught," she replied, angling her head at Jennifer.

"But I didn't understand any of it!"

"Do you have first period free?" asked Jennifer.

"Um, yeah…"

"So do I. Meet me in Study Hall 8, and I'll help you"

"YOU'RE letting me…?"

"No. I'm going to make sure you understand it so you can do it yourself. Don't copy someone else's work, Traci. Do your own."

"That's what you're going to get out of Jenny. Might as well take advantage of it now," Jessica McEogan said. "Before she turns you in."

Jennifer gave them a crooked grin, but Traci smiled in relief and started going over the problems. Jenny didn't actually tell her anything, but was restating the questions, pointing out where she could find the answers in the textbook from memory… pure Jennifer. Angela and Carmen listened in, and Carmen went fumbling for her own homework and made some changes based on listening to Jennifer. Angela didn't bother; she'd done the homework with Dawn and Keisha. All too soon, though, the bus pulled into the parking lot, behind the buses from the other end of the valley. She spotted her friends and headed over, passing Patti with her "prayers at the flagpole" and almost no one else in attendance. Another day. Time to get to class.

CHAPTER

4

Angela was surprised to see Seth writing on the blackboard in the team room when she and Dani trotted in suited up for practice. The only other people there were Alex and Mike Wu. "What gives, Creepo?" Dani asked. Angela and Alex grimaced.

"Nurse Rietzoon asked me to put up an announcement that your practice is cancelled. Somehow the entire rest of your team had to go home with, and I quote, "flu like symptoms". But the only ones who didn't get it are here, so I won't bother finishing. Most of them will have their weekend ruined and be fine on Monday. Three of them will be quite miserable for two weeks, and, again, be perfectly fine on the next Monday morning," Seth said with a hint of anger in his voice.

"Oh, fuck." Alex said, paling as he put his arm around Dani's shoulder and catching Angela's eye. She felt the blood rushing out of her face.

"How do you know…" Mike started, then flinched, staring at Seth. The color in his face drained away, too. "Oh shit. Those idiots."

"Why is it the three of you seem to know something?" Dani asked.

"Was that stench coming from your locker, Seth?" Alex asked. Dani poked him in the stomach for ignoring her question. He caught her hand absently.

Alex's eyes bored into Seth's. Angela caught the edges of telepathic communication passing between them. She put her helmet down on the chair.

"What the hell?" Dani asked.

"If you want to ask Seth that question, he might have more info," Mike said. "I suggest asking him very politely. But if we're not going to practice, I'll go find Keisha." He racked his helmet and headed to the locker room.

"Fuck. We have Rafael High on Friday. This really sucks, Seth."

He shrugged. "There have been flu warnings plastered all over school for weeks, and your brain-damaged morons apparently decided to ignore the warnings. Enough of the idiots get sick and it might just spread. Why, you might even have the opportunity to tend Dani with all the tenderness she could possibly ask for."

"Hey, I get it, I get it. I'll make sure she doesn't get sick. And do what I need to do to vaccinate the rest so it doesn't happen again. C'mon. We can go for ice cream, my treat, talk about it there." Dani looked a bit confused, but they headed off to the locker rooms, Dani still asking for an explanation.

"What did happen? It's no coincidence that Alex, me, Alex's girlfriend, and Keisha's boyfriend were the ones who didn't get sick," Angela asked once Dani and Mike were away.

"You're right. It's not. And as I told Alex last year, I'm not putting up with any more crap. This time they get sick and will recover. Not in time for the game, but they will get better."

"I thought you'd sealed your locker."

"I did. Keisha let us know there was going to be a random search today, so I took the defenses off., and Kevin Abruzzi, Ben Wong, and Zeke Darden decided to set off a stink bomb. In my locker."

Angela bit her lip. They were linemen, the first two on offense and Zeke on defense. Kevin, Ben, and Zeke were messing with far more than they could handle and didn't know it, playing with fire while sitting on barrels of gunpowder. If Alex hadn't already talked Seth down, there wasn't much she could do to keep it from spiraling out of control.

She nodded to Seth, returned to the girls' locker room, and got changed. Her copy of Poe fell out of her locker, and she suddenly realized a way she could defuse Seth. It would hurt the team. But not as much as Seth could hurt those guys if it came down to it. Hurt? Seth could kill.

She walked out of the locker room and went looking for Bridget. She found her going over Spanish with Teddy. "Hey Ange!" she called, "Aren't you supposed to be dodging sweaty boys trying to hug you?"

"Yeah, but three of them decided to put a stink bomb in Seth's locker. With four exceptions, the whole team was sent home with the flu."

"Four? Oh, fuck. He's not messing around, is he?" Bridget said. "We've got to do something."

"Absolutely," Teddy said. "The question is what? Simply restraining him is no good, not if he's furious enough to kill."

"I was thinking on my way over. We not only need to stop it, we need to let Seth know we've got his back and the idiots know they're not just dealing with him. If Seth thinks he's not alone he's more likely to restrain himself."

They both nodded. "You're right about that. Sounds like you already have a plan," he said. "Do tell, I pray."

She smiled. "We've got two weeks."

"How do you figure?" Teddy asked.

"Seth said most of the team will just be miserable for the weekend, but that those three would be out two weeks."

"He's that precise?" Teddy asked. "How much time has he been spending with you?" he asked Bridget.

"He released the virus, he can kill it," she replied, "Or he already had it programmed to die in a specific time. He could also have set it up to be definitely lethal, so he's still staying his hand."

"Some stay. OK, Angela, what evil shall we do?" They talked and plotted until the shadows fell. Bridget got her home.

CHAPTER
5

$\mathcal{A}$ngela came to in a fog with Bridget lifting her eyelid. "Angela, can you hear me?"

"Hunh? Wha happened?"

"STAY PUT, TORANOS! You help no one by flying off the handle here!" That was Jennifer. What was Alex mad about so much?

"Someone put roofies in the Sportyade. We caught it, but not before a bunch of people were affected," Bridget said sotto voce. "Malcolm's helping Jennifer and Solly sit on Alex. He's ready to fry whoever did this." A roll of thunder rattled the windows. "We adjusted it to a tranquilizer."

"Whoa. Trippy." She giggled.

"Now that you're back with us, I'm going to purge your body of it." Lightning flashed.

"She is going to be fine, Alex. Get yourself back under control, or do we need to knock you out too?" Solly said.

"Okay. Groovy." She felt Bridget's power flow into her, making minute adjustments to her, and her mind started to clear. The warm, nurturing feeling helped her sit up. "Are my parents…?"

"We all channel fury differently. Alex is pissed enough that there's a major storm going on outside," Keisha said. "Everyone's supposed to stay where they are until it passes. I don't suppose you're any good at weather?"

"That "stay where you are" is from Alex," Malcolm said. "When he hasn't been a wreck over Dani he's been barking orders. We've got the capacity to keep our minds clear, but the others don't. Bridget, you'd better purge Dani so someone he'll listen to is telling him to calm down."

"Fuck. OK, what can I do?"

"Reinforce Jennifer, Solly, and Malcolm. Give us the time to trace the problem."

"Gotcha." She got up still in uniform and went over to where Malcolm, Jennifer, and Solomon were trying to calm Alex down. She saw the team and the cheerleading squad laid out on mats; from the multiplicity of colors everyone had had a hand in conjuring them up. Dani was on a purple mat, her friend Karen on a black one with Seth sitting by her, Dave Cleburne on a yellow, Rick on a green. The compulsions and enchantments radiating off Alex were intense, and his hands crackled with electricity. Her cleats scratched and clunked on the cement floor as she got there. "Hey Alex. How's Dani doing?" she asked. She put her hand on Seth's shoulder as she came up and willed her power to join theirs. He looked down at Karen again before getting up to join her.

"Unconscious. We still don't know how she is because she can't tell us."

"Alex, that's bullshit and you know it. Chiomara's better able than anyone you care to have examine her. She'll pull Dani through safely. And she stays asleep until we've figured out what happened. Or do you want Teddy to fog her mind? Are you prepared to be non-committal, non-responsive with her when she starts asking? Or further on, to lie to her about what happened?" Jennifer demanded. "If you're that concerned, examine her yourself. But they're all going to stay asleep until we're done!"

"She's right, Alex. Unless we're all on board with someone knowing who we are and what we can do, we don't let her know. Or have you already betrayed us again?" Solly said. "Chill your butt out."

Alex's nostril flared. "What do you know about it, any of you? You don't have a girlfriend."

"Nor am I going to, since I'm far more interested in boys, but you being pissed enough to spit lightning and back your words with inadvertent power isn't helping. We've got four people trying to keep you from becoming a catastrophe. If you want to find who did this, calm down, hold her hand, and let us concentrate on something other than you!" said Jennifer.

Teddy burst into the classroom soaking wet as a loud peal of thunder and flash of lightning made themselves felt. "Will you fucking calm down, Alex? You just took out the goddamn flag pole!"

"Alex. We will find who did this to us. I want their ass stuffed and mounted too. But you're not helping Dani right now. Bridget got it out of me. She'll get it out of her, too. Let's find out who," Angela said with her hand on his shoulder. "You're our quarterback. It's time to be a teammate and not a boyfriend." Another peal of thunder shook the windows and the rain started coming down harder. Alex snarled and stalked back over to where Bridget was tending Dani.

"Dani is fine, Alex," she said as she stood up, accepting Keisha's hand. She glared at him. "If you want to keep control of your guts, see for yourself. She's sleeping and healing through what the drugs did to her. Now let's figure out who to vent your anger on, or do I need to override your storm first?"

He spun, glaring at her, and then Angela noticed the sweat coming off Bridget even as she started to incant in Gaelic. With Bridget actively drawing on her power, she was getting the storm lessened. Malcolm and Keisha seemed to be supporting her, judging by the Phoenician and Cushitic they were speaking. Then, finally, Alex drew in a deep breath and nodded. Angela felt the power seep back out from where he'd gathered it, and he knelt down beside Dani.

"Phew!" Keisha said. "It's been a while since we had to do that. And it's not like weather's even his specialty. He does charms and war." She glanced at Seth. "I'm relieved you stayed in control of yourself."

Jennifer nodded. "We're getting stronger, but his fury was fueling the storm. Bridget's meteorology course seems to have come in useful. With that crisis over, Keish, what say we look at that cooler?"

"Angela, why don't you look, too? Good practice on divinatory uses," Seth suggested.

"Okay," she said, joining Keisha and Jennifer. She concentrated, opening herself to the various residues left behind. As Seth had taught her, she didn't just use her eyes, but increased her sensitivity to smells and sounds as well. She passed a hand over the cooler to see if it felt anything. She noticed Keisha and Jennifer doing much the same thing.

"What did you get, Ange?" Seth asked.

"It was…" Jennifer started, when Keisha elbowed her.

"Let Angela go first, Jenny! It's not going anywhere. She needs the practice. And interrupting Seth when he's instructing the apprentice is rude."

"Oh, right. Sorry, Ange. What'd you get?"

She gave them a nervous smile. "I've seen the standard Sportyade before, so I could remove that. Which leaves these residues," she said, highlighting them. "I'm not sure what they are."

"Did you apply a power detection?" Seth asked.

"I did, but what I got was the transformative stuff you guys used."

"Well, I know what those are. They're the remnants of the roofies put in. I also isolated the fingerprints of whoever put them in, but I didn't have enough to work with to get the actual people. Keish?"

"Good work, girls. Here's what I got." Two holographic illusions took shape of large boys, a couple of years older.

"Hey, I recognize them. That's Mike Richardson and Jeb Young," Angela said. "Seniors. Got kicked off the team when their GPAs dropped below a two-five."

"What?" Alex said, looking up from where he was holding Dani's sleeping hand and putting a cool towel on her forehead. It was purple, which suggested Alex had created it on the spot.

"The two who put the roofies in the Sportyade. Alex, calm. We'll handle this," Keisha said, indicating Bridget and Jennifer. He growled.

"Alex, killing them won't accomplish anything, but will cause you problems. A lot of problems," Seth said. "You've never killed anyone, Alex. I have. I still see their faces in my nightmares. I know you're going to West Point or Annapolis, but let's put off that moment as long as possible. Let Keisha and the justice system work."

Alex crushed a root beer can, and a bolt of lightning struck a tree outside as a peal of thunder rolled over them. But he nodded. "I hate not doing anything, but…"

"We know. We'll get them for you," Bridget said. "I've already put the roofie residue back in, and the cops will be able to get their prints. If that doesn't do it—if they beat the case, or if it doesn't get prosecuted or something—we'll revisit. I'm sure we can make them regret it." Alex smiled grimly.

Seth teleported them to an abandoned building on Angel Island. Now they were working on will and control. He tossed her a football so badly she nearly dropped it. It was an old leather ball, rather deflated. "Let's start with making it glow."

"Alex really needs to spend more time with you, Seth," she said as she took the ball and concentrated on it.

"Because…?"

"You can't pass worth a damn." The ball was now glowing teal.

"Good. Refill it. Watching football is okay, but no one wants me on the team." They tossed the ball back and forth for a while, levitated it. Then he said, "Since I'm so lousy at throwing the ball, take control of it and bring it to you." They did that quite a bit, with Seth tossing it randomly into the air, not even trying to get to her. "Now, fight me for control of it." THAT was a lot harder. Seth barely seemed to be trying but the old ball stayed firmly under his control.

"Hey! What gives?"

He stopped controlling the ball, and she brought it in a lazy arc through the air to her arms. Then she got it. The ball was made of actual leather… dead tissue, and, therefore, Seth's to control. Angela had a mischievous thought. She refilled the football with water and tossed it back to him. "Catch!"

"OOOOFFF!" he caught and dropped it from the unexpected weight. She grinned. She felt him gathering his power to respond, and heard the skittering on the concrete. She looked around and was repulsed. Seth had just animated half a dozen rat skeletons and sent them surging towards her.

"Ugh! That's disgusting, Seth!" She quickly incanted a verse and incinerated the little skeletons one by one.

"Poetry?" he asked.

"Yeah, is that a problem?"

"Not at all. If you want to do poetry, do poetry. It's not necessary, though."

"Yeah, I got that, Teach. What's next?"

"See the scrub jays?"

"Yeah…"

"Don't worry, they're alive. Can you make them sleep?"

She reached out with all six senses, and made contact with the birds' minds. Then she convinced them to go to sleep. At the end, she blinked sweat out of her eyes and Seth tossed her a juice box. "Good job!" he said. "Drink up." When she hesitated, he said, "Angela, we're drawing on our bodies' energy reserves. You need to replenish just like at football or swimming."

"Do you mind a question? It might be a little personal."

"Ask away; I'm supposed to be teaching you. I can always not answer if it's really personal."

"I've noticed sometimes when you're talking telepathically, you speak aloud. Does that help with the energy drain?"

"Oh, that. No, in fact we did some test runs last year and it uses more. But it is clearer for the person on the other end, especially if we're already tired. There's more intention to communicate if we're actually speaking than just using our minds," he explained. "The mind fog effect', we've been calling it."

"Why does it work that way?"

"We don't know. I think I've mentioned that before. We're sort of all still looking. Solly's planning on going into medicine and see if he can figure it out that way. Bridget, as you might have guessed, is looking at field ecology. Jennifer's best hypothesis is that we evolved to communicate with our voices, so when we use our voices it's a bit clearer telepathically." He made a throw away gesture. "But we really don't know."

"OK, what's next?"

"Necromancy." She nodded. He levitated an oak branch and brought it over to them. "Can you restore this to life?"

"It's a plant. I thought necromancy was zombies and killing and stuff."

"I used it to bring you back. This is dead. It is therefore subject to necromantic control. Quit thinking of that medieval church 'hierarchy of life.' It has no basis. If you really want zombies, I can make some more." The branch suddenly started twisting in her hand, wrapping itself around her arm in an impossibly fluid way. She let out a squawk and a fuck and called up her power.

She tried a technique Bridget gad taught her to take control of the branch, but it didn't work. The branch was dead; as a result, Seth's necromancy controlled it. She summoned her power and burned the branch to ashes. As the carbon dust blew away, Seth regarded her with disapproval. "Was that the only way to deal with it?"

"I had a branch attacking me, teach. How would YOU have dealt with it?"

"I'd have tried the first thing you did. The second thing you tried certainly worked, but you've already demonstrated your ability to incinerate."

She twisted her mouth. "Reviving it would have broken your control?"

"Not necessarily, unless Bridget was doing it. What it would have done is put you on an equal footing with me for control. Let's find another branch."

"Why am I reviving branches?"

"Ecology."

"Huh? Oh, I see. A revived branch is living again, but won't produce seeds."

"It might, but that wasn't the point. Left in here, the branch will simply die again. There's nothing for it to take root in, the roof's good enough to keep out water. An animal will go looking for food. The branch can't do that."

"Oh." She thought about the branch, wet and green, fully leafed, and applied her power to making her vision a reality, replacing the water in the cells, getting the biochemical reactions going again. The branch grew heavy with the additional water. The leaves were dark green, almost pulsing with revived life, the chlorophyll vibrant in the afternoon sunshine… and then Seth took control of the oak branch again. This time as she struggled for control over the branch she felt a lot more control over it. Seth wasn't simply brushing her aside to rule over the dead. It was still a struggle—Seth was more experienced at this than she was—but she managed to get the spiky leaves to scrape at him.

"Good job!" he said. "I think that's enough for today."

"What? We're done just like that?"

"Look down, Angela." She was drenched in sweat, her chest heaving with labored breathing, and her t-shirt plastered to her. She blushed at Seth's smile. Next time, a darker shirt.

"The more you practice, the easier it is to control. Until next time, try controlling the plants in and around your house. Go for insects and the like you happen to have in the house, like flies or ants. See about reviving, say, dead wildflowers, or hastening the decay of a Halloween pumpkin, or the leftovers that get thrown out. Or try to bring back something rotten. I can ruin cheese if I'm not careful. Sound good?"

"Yeah. OK, I'll give that a shot during the week. Thanks, Seth. Can you drop me off in the school library? That's where I told Dad I'd be."

"Not a problem, but why don't you try drying yourself off first? You don't look like you've been hitting the books all afternoon in an air-conditioned library." He reached into thin air and pulled out a pair of wooden mugs with cold juice and sent one over to her. She thanked him and drank deeply, downing the cranberry juice quickly. She was surprised when she pulled it away from her mouth to discover it was still full. He grinned.

"What's the point of an ever-full mug that doesn't stay full?"

"Cranberry juice, though?"

He shrugged. "We burn a lot of energy making natural laws conform to our will. Juice is the quickest way to replenish it short of sugar water. I happen to like cranberry. A wonderfully dark shade of red…"

"To weird people out when you're drinking from some crystal skull glass?"

"That, too," he replied.

CHAPTER

7

The confrontation came sooner than she'd anticipated. Kevin, Ben, and Zeke didn't lay a hand on him, fortunately. They hadn't gotten into his locker. They'd spray-painted something in neon green and were crowding around him. Not quite looming over him, but they were linemen on the football team, some of the biggest boys on the team. Angela couldn't quite hear what they were saying as she alerted the others, strode up to Kevin, and spun him against the lockers.

"You have a problem, Ange?" Zeke asked, surprised.

"No, Zeke you do. I told you to leave Seth alone last year. There's no place for petty bullies on the team," Alex said. The other wizards flowed out of the crowd to form their own ring. They weren't quite forming an amplification circle… but it was close.

"Whoa, Alex, whoa. There's…"

"You three are the assholes who put the stink bomb in his locker right before you got sick," Angela said.

Solly chimed in. "You're lucky you got sick and the Lord of Vengeance hasn't had the chance to seek payback."

"Which we all know would be public and splashy while leaving everyone knowing who did it, no way to prove a damn thing, and you probably in traction," Jennifer said.

"We're just having some fun with creepo…" Ben said.

"He's not enjoying it." Bridget said. "He thinks you'd look marvelous in the late stages of Ebola."

"The point is, Ben, you come after one of us, you're dealing with all ten of us," Angela said.

"All for one?" Zeke said scornfully.

"And one for all," replied Malcolm with a smile.

"Make it eleven, Ange," Shevaun stepped into the circle.

"Twelve."

"Thirteen." Julian and Karen joined the circle around the three. Dani, Rachel, Eric, and Mike didn't say anything, but they stepped in as well. Carmen, Joy, Beth, and Trevor noticed what was happening and added themselves to the ring. As she watched, Teddy's minions formed a ring of their own around the wizards. The three boys started glancing around, looking for a way out, when Mr. Culver stepped around the corner.

"What's going on here?"

"These three decided to try bullying Seth," Teddy said. "Thank god we were here to intervene."

"We stepped in to stop it," Keisha said. "Before it could escalate." Mr. Culver nodded.

"Alright you three. Get yourselves to the principal's office. With a dozen witnesses, this isn't going to go well for you." He turned to Keisha, "Good job, Miss Johnson."

Seth stood in the ring, astonished. "Thank you," he said, looking at all of them, even making eye contact with everyone but Rachel who was keeping her eyes downcast. Alex replied in Nahuatl, making Seth grin. He answered in Coptic. Alex smiled back at him.

"I didn't catch that, sweetie, but I'll back you all the way," Dani told Alex with her arm around his shoulders.

"What did they say?" she heard Rachel whisper to Julian, the class president. He towered over her; he was the biggest boy in school not on the football team.

"I have no idea. I don't even know what languages they were speaking," he replied.

"Nahuatl and Coptic," Keisha said. "As for what they said, don't worry about it. Just a joke."

At practice she was running routes against Neil. He was a good defender, very challenging, but he had a grabby tendency. As she caught the ball away from him, she heard the whistle. He wrapped his arms around her upper body to bring her down. Players exchanged spots; she and Dani came off and were replaced by understudies.

Angela and Dani trotted over to the cooler of Sportyade and supply of orange slices. They were surprised to recognize Seth in charge of it.

"What did you do to it?" Dani asked suspiciously as he handed her a cup of the dark purple liquid.

"Nothing yet. Ms. Nguyen told me I should get more involved in school activities if I wanted good recommendation letters, so when Alex mentioned there was a support assistant place open I applied."

"You really want to be this close to the team?" Angela asked, skeptically.

"No. Most of them are idiots. But Alex said he wanted someone he trusted in charge of provisions, especially after that tranquilizer." Seth waved his hand at the cooler and orange slices. "You've apparently got several games against teams with some of those morons from White Hill. They're somehow convinced that LVHS football team is responsible for their de-education facility being shut down."

"I wonder how they got that idea,"

"Don't worry, Danielle. However amusing it would be to see you all in Alex's colors, it's just Sportyade and oranges." He filled another cup for Greg McClain and gave it to the left tackle.

"I don't believe Alex asked you to do this," Dani said suspiciously.

"Ask him yourself," Seth suggested, shrugging.

"Don't think I won't," she responded. Seth shrugged indifferently.

"I can. Set a thief to catch one and all that. Few people in school want to provoke a retaliation campaign from Mister Vengeance here. He'll will keep anything from happening to it and he's one of the best people in school to do that," Angela said, holding out her cup for a refill. "Filler up, please, Seth?"

"Of course, Angela." The purple Sportyade came out frosty cold... much better than with ice. Seth was on the ball with the temperature, anyway.

"Hey, Seth, good to see you. Can I get a drink? Everything working out ok?" Alex trotted up, his hair plastered to his head. He nodded to Angela and Dani; they weren't demonstrative on the field.

"Except that your girlfriend here is being suspicious of me. One faux-grape electrolyte cocktail coming up," Seth replied to Alex.

"Why are you being suspicious, love?" Alex asked Dani

"She thinks the cooler is filled by my failed chemistry experiments," Seth answered for her as he handed a cup to Alex.

"You've kept them all these years?" Alex responded with a smile. "Relax, love, when Seth fails a chemistry experiment the results are doom, destruction, and despair, not something you can put in a cooler."

"He has failed a chemistry experiment? When was that?" Erik Montoya wanted to know. "I was hoping to be your lab partner this year, dude, but Rachel Strauss nabbed you first."

"*Seth* the Creepy is in charge of the Sportyade? What sort of twisted idea led you to think this was a good idea, sweetie?"

"It gets the team off his back for that misunderstanding with Angela, should keep any more idiots from deciding he's a good choice for bullying. and puts someone fully capable of making sure nothing happens to it in charge of it," Alex replied. "Relax! Seth was the most likely person in school to use it for a chemistry experiment. It's a point of pride for him to not let anything happen."

"I guess so."

"Cheer up Danielle. I never said anything about not using it for an alchemy experiment." Seth grinned evilly at her. "Would you like to be a rabbit?"

"SETH!" Well, Alex was right to be alarmed. Seth *could* do alchemy experiments. It might be utter nonsense to most of the world, but not to the Nine. OK, Ten, but she hadn't done any yet. And that bland smile…

"No need to worry, my good man. I don't need the gold any more than you do. See you at the owners' meeting?"

"But of course, dear fellow!" Alex downed his drink. "Oh, I've been talking with everyone. Can Dani sit in with me?"

Seth pulled out his phone and checked something. "Sure. Nothing on the agenda an outsider can't hear. I would prefer to limit the distractions, though, and keep it to just us."

"That's rather offensive, Seth," Dani informed him.

"Why? This is a business meeting, Danielle, not a date night. We're reviewing revenues and costs, safety rules, and getting ideas on what to do this year. There are questions and topics at other meetings that I'd rather not have made public. And yes, in this instance, YOU are "public." If you don't like that, if you want to come to all these meetings, Reno doesn't have a team."

"I am NOT a distraction!" Dani burst out.

"You guys are expanding the league?" Angela asked.

"We've always planned to," Alex put in, with a glare at Seth. "But you know perfectly well she doesn't have that sort of money."

"We're thinking about it. Actually, Alex, I have no idea what sort of money she has; she doesn't exactly talk to me much. Who gets to start a franchise is subject to the vote of the current owners, and if she had the money I think she'd have the votes," Seth replied. "Danielle, you're not an owner, or a trustee, or a lawyer. Your presence would be a distraction." He turned back to Alex. "I get you have no secrets from her, Alex. That doesn't mean I don't. Clark's free to tell Lois everything about himself, but that doesn't mean filling her in about Bruce."

"Seth…" Dani started angrily.

"Dani, he's right," Angela put in. A fight between Seth and Dani would be a bad thing. "Do you want Alex telling Seth everything about what you're doing?"

"That's different…"

"Not really, not to him. But if this is a league business meeting, it makes perfect sense that only the owners are present, not their boyfriends and girlfriends. As far as I know Mike's still in the hospital, so he won't be there. Quit being possessive and recognize that Seth's being nice in saying you can be at that meeting," Angela said. "He could have said no."

"Why are you siding with Seth, anyway?"

"I think she's trying to stop a quarrel, love," Alex said.

At Alex's comment, Dani stopped with her mouth open. "Yeah. Sorry," she said.

"You don't owe me an apology, Dani," Angela said. "But everyone in school knows not to start a feud with Seth. It wouldn't be pretty." Worse would be an open split between Seth and Alex.

She opened her mouth, closed it, and then said, "Sorry, Seth." She got her cup of Sportyade and went off with some of the other linebackers.

"I know it's your choice, Seth, but maybe if she had a better idea of what you can do…?" Angela suggested tentatively.

He shook his head. "She doesn't need to know. Relax, Alex, she hasn't pissed me off enough for me to do anything to her. Although I will keep the rabbit idea in reserve. I'm sure there's an endangered species of rabbit somewhere that could use another member."

CHAPTER

9

$\mathcal{A}$ngela was sitting with Karen MacLeod in the study hall when Keisha walked in. She waved to her friend, and Keisha walked over. "Salutations, Ange! What are you looking so worried about?"

"History. Mrs. Parker. I'm not sure where to start."

"Really?" Her brilliant smile peaked out. "I've got Ms. Reed. But I'll be your Clio. What's…" Karen was looking baffled. "The Muse of History." Angela's tongue found her cheek quite firmly.

"Thanks, Keisha."

"No problem," she responded. In her mind, she heard Keisha say, *<Karen doesn't know, does she? Then let's leave it like that.>*

<Gotcha. History only.>

"So what's Mrs. Parker's assignment?"

"It's a major project," Karen said. "Our semester paper, and we're almost blanking on what to do. We can do it together, but we need to present after New Year's, and with Ange's practice and game schedule…"

"Naturally. What are her basic parameters?"

"Civil War," Karen responded. "What we don't want to do is a general rehash of the battles and such. Half the class is going to do that."

39

"You know, last summer I read a book on women who disguised themselves as men and joined the armies. Would that work for you?" Keisha said.

They looked at each other and grinned. "Sounds awesome!" Karen said. "Thanks, Keisha. What was the name of that book?"

"<u>Blue and Gray Amazons</u>, by Edwina Blendle." She sat down. "I can loan you my copy this afternoon, it's in my locker." Angela suppressed a smile. That book might be in her locker, but she'd be willing to bet that it was at home.

"Cool. My ancestors were still in Japan during the civil war."

"About when great-whatever grandpa MacLeod was stationed in India and brought a local girl home with him," Karen put in. "That side didn't come to the US until after World War II. Mom's family came earlier, in the nineteen hundreds. Central valley farmers. She became an engineer."

"Cool."

"My family was already here, of course. Didn't come west until World War II; we'd been in South Carolina. Got freed by Sherman's march," Keisha said.

"Did any of them fight in the war?" Karen asked.

"Some of my ancestors joined the colored regiments, but none of the ones that did were women as far as I know."

"Well, that's one thing off the panic list," Angela said tapping at her phone.

"You have a panic list?" Karen asked. "Can I see it?"

"Sure," she said passing over her phone.

"History, English, Spanish, algebra, chemistry, literature, football… what's with the Japanese characters?"

"Oh, don't worry about those. Family stuff." *<Keisha, any idea on a better way to hide magic tutoring? Those characters are my homework assignments from Seth, and all too many people can read them.>*

<Can you put them in another language altogether?>

<They're currently in Japanese.>

<Go more obscure. There's a reason I cast in Cushitic.>

"That's cool. Mom's after me to take extra Spanish classes over the summer. Groan. I spend enough time in school learning Spanish. Yeah, it's useful, but I'd rather spend the time on something else."

Keisha gave her a wry grin and said something in Cushitic. Something about everyone needing to do things they didn't like, if she was following well enough.

"What was that? I don't even know what language that was! What's with the obscure languages these days? I 've heard four or five—six now—people speaking really strange languages. To each other, and understanding each other, even when they're speaking different languages!"

"Never mind."

"Can you at least tell me what language that was?"

"Cushitic," Angela responded. "And you speak it, too?"

"Not yet, but I've picked up a few phrases from homework with Keisha." Karen checked her phone.

"Oh, damn, I need to get to English. Meet me in the computer lab to see if we can find some online articles to help with our paper! After school, or do you have practice?"

"Practice. Can you email me the links?"

"Aye, lass. Sayonara, you'd better get to math." She walked off rapidly as Angela gathered her books together.

"While I'm here, hold out your hand," Keisha said. "I'll give you the Cushitic language. You'll still need to practice it, but it'll give you something to build on."

"Cool." She took Keisha's hand and felt herself flooded with information, meaning… a language completely foreign to her. She was a little unsteady as she got up for math.

10

"I'll kill him!" Angela raged on the sidelines, plopping down on the bench next to Dani and dropping her helmet.

"Death is all too easy to accomplish, Angela, and all too hard to reverse." Seth had somehow appeared next to her with a cup of Sportyade. He studied her for a moment. "Is that what he deserves for tackling you? You are playing football, and you did catch the pass. Isn't tackling you exactly what a cornerback is supposed to do?"

"Shut up, Seth! She would have scored! What do you know about it, anyway?" Dani said. She firmly turned her back on Seth to return her attention to Angela. "Where'd he grab you?"

"I don't believe I was addressing you Danielle. Go make out with Alex. I need to speak to Angela," Seth said. He turned back to Angela. "Killing is easy, Angela. Dealing with the consequences is not."

Dani rolled her eyes. "For God's sake, Seth, it was just an expression! Angela's not actually going to put him in a coffin!"

Seth ignored Danielle. He kept his eyes strictly on Angela. *<If anyone knows that, I do. Need I remind you of the church at White Hill?>*

"Yeah, it's just an expression, Seth. Don't be so morbid."

He looked at her for a moment, then she could feel his power gathering, and spoke couple of words in Coptic. "Danielle, would you please go give Alex this cup?" Surprisingly, Dani got up and took the paper cup over to the quarterback. He muttered something else in Coptic to draw a privacy shield around them. "Angela, words have power. Especially ours. This wasn't me being morbid. I just blocked you from killing that guy."

"*WHAT?!!*" she asked, stunned.

"I didn't stutter. I spoke English. Which word are you having trouble with?" He looked intently at her, locking their eyes together.

"I was blowing off steam, Seth! I wasn't trying to kill him! I *didn't* try to kill him!"

"Yes, you did, Angela. Whether you wanted to or not, you tried." He pursed his lips and crouched down in front of her. "You gathered your power and unleashed a deadly blow at him. Lethal is what I do, Angela, and you're learning from me. We didn't learn a bunch of obscure languages few people in the US understand just because we're nerds. We don't use them to marshal our power because we need to use them. The power isn't in the words or the language. It's in us, but pausing to put our thoughts and words in something else cuts down on accidents. It's not foolproof, especially in our specialties, but it helps."

"Should I be learning Coptic, then? Keisha gave me Cushitic mind to mind."

"We all speak all the languages, Angela. I'm a little better at Coptic, but I can hold a Tsalagi conversation with Dawn or a Nahuatl conversation with Alex almost as easily. We can start practicing Coptic this week, if you want. What we did was all pick our own language we wanted to learn, and educated ourselves, then taught each other. Fortunately, we have certain advantages when it comes to that sort of learning, as Keisha demonstrated. Give me your hand and I'll pass you Coptic." Again she felt the rush of information finding a home in her brain.

She considered that for a moment. It made sense. "Would Ainu work?"

"Since I'm not sure what "Ainu" is, probably."

"They're the first inhabitants of Japan."

"Ok. Yeah, that should work. See you at tutoring. Just remember to watch what you're doing. We're as capable of immense damage by accident as on purpose." He got up and headed back over to the cooler dispensing the Sportyade. For the first time, she noticed that Seth—despite not exactly being an athlete—never had trouble lifting it, and that brought a smile to her face. Of course he didn't. He could and obviously did enhance his own strength. He wasn't on the team.

"Bye Mom! Bye Dad! Going horseback riding with Bridget!"

"Ok, honey. Take a jacket," Dad replied as she skipped down the walk to where Bridget and their mounts waited. Naturally, she was already wearing her coat… and sweater, and gloves. Since with Bridget, there was no guarantee they'd be staying in this time zone.

"Hi Angela. Ready to go?" Bridget grinned at her. Two of her team's mascots, decked out in the team colors of the Arcata Unicorns, were calmly browsing on her mother's bamboo. They looked like horses in elaborate costumes. Angela knew the truth about them, though.

"Yeah. Why do I need the special coat, gloves, and sweater, though?" The special coat was something she'd worked on with Seth after he'd ignored the temperatures once too often. It would keep her warm kind of regardless. But it was a nice autumn day.

"Because it's cold where we're going," Bridget winked at her. Obviously this wouldn't be a normal ride up into the hills, which might be windy but not that cold. "C'mon, the boys are meeting us up top."

"Hi Marshmallow," Angela greeted the big unicorn stallion. He nuzzled her neck in response, and then held his head up. She scratched under his chin and stroked his neck.

As they got up into the saddles, Angela noticed that as usual—now that she knew the truth—the reins were purely for show. Bridget didn't even bother with them; they were loosely tied on her saddle horn with a slipknot. The hills were green from recent rains, with oak trees in the valleys between them and deer trails scattered about. The unicorns got them up the hill faster than they should have.

"I don't know why you two are so eager, it's going to be cold," Bridget said to them. "Oh, new place? Well, glad you're going to like going to a new place, because to get this accomplished we're going to be going back quite a bit." Bridget shared a smile and chuckle with Angela.

"Where ARE we going, Bridget?"

"Bering Island," she replied, smiling.

"Where's that?"

"The Bering Sea," Seth replied from atop his great pale gold palomino, Orcinus. "The Russian side, actually."

"What? Why? What's there?"

"It's what's NOT there, anymore, that has us going. Bridget?" Solomon replied.

"Angela, can you create a privacy sphere, for us?" Seth asked. She concentrated, and the sphere coalesced as she drew the air into a very thin, but extremely turbulent bubble. Sound couldn't escape and vision was obscured.

"Got it," she said.

"Impressive," Solomon said. He poked a finger at it and came away bloody. "Ow!" He concentrated a bit and the injury closed. "That's some wind shear."

"We've found sub fossil samples of both the sea cow and the cormorant. Sufficient for revivification. For that we need Seth. Once we've got them, we need to rapidly increase base numbers. That's my job. Solomon, you'll get to prepare their natural increase. Angela, you, Orcinus, Marshmallow, and Snowflake will provide security. Everyone ready? Seth, you know where we're going?" Seth nodded. "Angela, you can drop the privacy."

The green grass around them, product of the late autumn rains, had been flattened in a circle around them by the force of the air molecules Angela had whipped into speed. As the air speed returned to normal, she felt Seth's power, dark and brooding and certain, reach out to shift them to a bitterly cold forest cove, snow on the ground. They could hear the waves crashing on the rocks below them, and Bridget casually motioned to dispel the temporary stones she'd used to hide bones and feathers.

"Damn it's cold!" Angela erupted.

"Yeah, sorry. Best time of year to do this, though. Less chance of being disturbed."

"Will they survive the winter?" Angela asked, shivering even in the coat.

"They should," Bridget said. "Neither is migratory, and they'll be revived with plenty of fat. Got that, Seth?"

"Yep." His long black coat whipped around him in the cold, but as usual Seth didn't seem to notice the chill.

Fortunately, they'd been working on that, too. Angela had learned how to conjure heat as well as light, and summoned up a stable flicker of purple flame to keep herself warm.

It was still cold. The special coat helped, it was mostly the wind—and the snow on the ground. She had her little flicker of flame to keep herself toasty with while she watched the others, and it provided a good point of visual reference for the two out in the water. Bridget was wearing a forest green wetsuit that she'd obviously enhanced. Seth wasn't wearing a wetsuit—hell, he still had his trench coat on!—but the water didn't appear to be affecting him at all.

From tidbits of bone, Seth summoned back the whole animal. In a few cases, other bits of bone Bridget had gathered flew into the restored animal. It was a feat Angela knew would be well beyond her fledgling abilities in necromancy; a fish dead in a tank was more her speed. Extinction reversed, because four teenagers would have it so. Sea cows and spectacled cormorants lived again in the Bering Sea. Then Seth stumbled out there in the frigid water.

Bridget was there in a flash… literally. One moment she was in a wetsuit out with the sea cows and the next she was appearing in a flash of green light supporting Seth. That Seth was several inches taller and a lot heavier didn't matter so much—Bridget was certainly capable of enhancing her strength—but he had been at least fifty feet away, and Solomon was over with the spectacled cormorants. Bridget swept her arm under Seth's knees and picked him up. Snowflake was out there almost as fast, and Bridget put Seth on the unicorn's back. Together Bridget and Snowflake got Seth over to Angela and edged him down onto a bed of moss. Damn, that looked comfier than her bed at home!

Angela had watched Seth cut loose battling Reverend Johnson and his minions. Now she was watching Bridget do something similar. The power roiled off her as a thick woolen blanket took shape out of thin air to cover Seth. The moss bed thickened and deepened, the air warmed. Seth's pallor eased, becoming ruddy with warmth and blood as Bridget worked.

Angela grabbed Seth's wrist to check for a pulse as Solly and Orcinus joined them, the big horse poking his nose at Seth and turning his head towards Bridget. "Don't worry, he just over did it. He'll be fine. Can you take your little spark and expand it to a real fire? I need to get some calories into him," Bridget said. She seemed to do that by creating steaming bowls of something and teleporting it directly into his stomach. "Seth, thank you, but rest."

"I think that's exactly what I'll do." He sat up a bit. "We're out of bits anyway." He took another bowl from her and nodded at where Angela was putting together some driftwood. "Keep an eye on that, would you? That's not fire."

"Huh? It's not?"

"It's plasma. And she's got it instinctively under very, very tight control."

"If it's not burning her hands—or us, this close—that is tight control." Angela felt her eyes widen and dismissed her little heat source. "I was playing with what?"

"Plasma. The fourth state of matter. Heat it until the electrons come off," Bridget said. "You're sure, Seth? I didn't get a very good look."

"I'm sure. I've been getting more and more confident that your personal talents lie in the area of matter manipulation, Angela. Solid, liquid, gas, plasma."

"You think you might have mentioned this to me, Teach?"

"I might have, yes," he replied, as a stick became a wooden spoon in his hand. "We didn't know what our specialties were when we started. Actually, we didn't have a clue. I was thinking that it would be better for you to figure out your own specialty than for me to tell you what I think it is, for you to keep testing at the boundaries of what you can do. Just because I'm good at death and revivification doesn't mean Alex or Teddy can't do much the same thing if he puts his mind to it." It was a point Seth had made many times. Seth continued, "So far, we haven't found anything one of us can do that someone else can't do. It might take a lot out of you—Keisha was home in bed for a week last time she tried to revive something—but I don't want you taking my opinion of where you're strongest as a reason not to try something." He paused to drink more of the soup.

"He's right," Solly put in. "Chiomara or I can do the necromancy he's doing, and you'll be able to, too. He's just better at it than we are." He paused for a moment, then continued, "Either of us, though, would have been wiped out long before now, which of course is why he was doing it. How much material do you actually need, Seth?"

"I haven't tried reviving something from true fossil remains, although some dinosaurs would be interesting. I could probably revive those frozen mammoths, but each would be a day project at least. If you want dinosaurs, it would be simpler to go through a bird, than revivify something from fossils." He sipped some cocoa (where had that come from?), and asked Bridget, "Did I get that right? Living things are your area."

"Yeah, pretty much," she said. "But we're not doing dinosaurs. Not on Earth, anyway. We can talk about Venus, eventually. When you're up for it, though, how do you feel about a trip to Tasmania?"

"Thylacine?" Solly asked. She nodded.

"Better than Chernobyl for the aurochs," Seth said. "Or was the great auk going to be next?"

"I'm surprised that you're not talking about dodos," Angela put in.

"The island of Mauritius is too small to hold a surviving relict dodo population," Bridget said in response. "But there are still random thylacine reports, so why not confirm them? I was thinking the Caribbean monk seal for next, actually, or maybe work with Solly and Malcolm to boost whale populations."

"What about the passenger pigeon or Carolina parakeet?" Angela asked. Bridget's project was interesting.

"They both existed in huge flocks. I'm not sure they could be brought back in a way that would permit the "overlooked" method we're trying. They can wait, at least for now, until we're ready to go public."

"Have you considered turning the rock pigeons into passengers?" Angela asked.

Bridget's smile was slow in coming, but brilliant. "Oh, thank you! That's so much better than killing them all!"

"Can passenger pigeons survive in the modern world?"

"That is a good question. I expect the agriculture industry will pitch a fit."

CHAPTER

12

"Hey, Ange!" Karen walked up to her as she was on the phone. "OK, tomorrow after school, Seth?"

"Yes," Seth replied on the phone. In her mind, he said, *<I hope you'll have finished the books by then.>*

"Yeah, yeah I'll be ready," she said. *<Just have a few chapters left. Gotta go, Karen and I have study plans for history.>* She felt a surprised surge of interest from Seth. Well isn't that interesting, she thought to herself. The Death Goth has something living in him after all.

As she put her phone back in her pocket, she said, "Hi Karen. Just setting up a tutoring session."

"How'd you get saddled with Seth as a tutor?" she wanted to know. "Especially after last year!"

"Wasn't anyone else still free. And I made peace with him last June, so Mr. Edmondson asked if there was a problem with it and I said no. I'm learning a lot from him, actually."

<Are you ever going to admit that you requested me? Bridget or Alex would have been happy to do it.>

<What are you still doing there?> she asked. She'd thought he'd shifted his attention.

<I could tell you that you accidentally sent me a thought, but I really hung around to let you know if you need any references for the history session I'm just at the hospice this afternoon, so feel free to ask.>

"And besides, he's getting A's, in every subject, almost like he's not even trying. I mean, the guy could probably skip a grade if he wanted to." If Seth was going to hang around in her head, maybe he'd answer that. But... silence.

"HE'S getting A's? What about YOU?!" Karen said in disbelief. That made Angela pause for a moment. Since she'd fallen in with Alex's friends, her grades had dramatically improved. Not that Karen's were anything to sneer at. "I mean, it's awesome that you're on the football team and all, but when have you gotten less than an A this year? And I saw that report Ms. Kravitz put up on the bulletin board. Damn it was good, but I also know you did the work in the library. It's not like athletes can buy anything here."

Truer than she knew, actually. News reports of that sort of thing disgusted the brain trust. They'd laid a curse on anyone who purchased or sold a paper or cheated on a test; they would be inevitably discovered. She hadn't known that until it was mentioned in that room in the Headlands once. But even though she knew it now, it wasn't like Karen would believe her....

"Well, having him tutoring me and Bridget as a study partner really helps. Want to join us? Our next session's on Friday at lunch." Bridget wouldn't mind; it was schoolwork rather than magic.

"I thought you two agreed on tomorrow?

Angela grimaced. Karen was more observant than she'd anticipated. Seth might be interested in her, but he had her working on metamorphic spells—in his lair, the Mausoleum. It was her choice to tell someone what *she* could do, but that didn't cover Seth. He might like Karen, but that wouldn't stop him from removing the danger. "That's with Seth. I figured you wouldn't want to be near him."

"Well, if it's helping you that much, maybe I could handle him for a bit."

<Chiomara, I beseech thine aid! How do you modify a mind? Seth hasn't covered that>, she screamed telepathically for Bridget. Fortunately, Seth HAD covered how to telepathically reach the others.

<Calm down, Angela>, Bridget answered her. *<What's happened? Whose mind are we talking about?>*

<Karen's. I accidentally mentioned my study session with Seth in front of her, and she's wanting to come.>

<And it's a secret session, naturally.> Bridget paused, considering. *<Simplest is to contact Seth and get him to cancel, or at least call you on your phone and have it cancelled as far as she knows.>*

<He likes her, though. What if he doesn't cancel?>

<Believe it or not, he's capable of conducting your lesson entirely telepathically, or just reschedule the secret session and cover something for school with her present. But don't worry. He's not going to do anything like that. He's had a thing for her for years, and he's thoroughly convinced she's not interested, so why waste his time?> She felt the mental snort.

<Actually, he doesn't think any girl is.>

<Thanks. I don't know why I was panicking like that.>

<First time you've been caught like this?> she suggested. *<And while you two have gotten a lot better, after watching him in action Seth is pretty scary even for the rest of us.>*

"Ok, ready for the Revolution?"

<Seth isn't very good at modifying minds, which is probably why he hasn't covered it. He tends to take a brute force, forgetful approach rather than build fake memories. Do you want to come over this weekend and learn how?> Bridget asked.

"Yep," also projecting the thought to Bridget.

<Fabulous! I'll let you get back to Karen. We can meet up with Jennifer at Northgate.>

"You know, I've got a study session with Jennifer, Julian Kanekawa, and Shevaun Lone Elk set for Sunday afternoon. You'd be welcome to join us for that one too; we're at the Civic Center library. I will need to check with Seth on tutoring, though. It was supposed to be just us, and he's not big on surprises."

"You've got a thing for Seth? Wow. I never realized. Kind of sick, after last year. You need help, lass."

"What?"

"Hey, you like who you like, but for you to want the guy who felt you up last year is really, really sick."

"No, it's nothing like that. And he wasn't feeling me up."

"Then what was his hand doing there?"

"You wouldn't believe what he was really doing. It took me all of last year to figure it out, and that was with the hints coming at me."

"Try me."

Angela turned to face her, looked her straight in the eye, arched an eyebrow, and said, "Something impossible."

The school trips were an opportunity to get to seriously know someone better… as long as you wanted your own gender. The fall camping trip out to the coast was only available to those with a perfect disciplinary record, at least a three-oh grade point average, and divided by gender. She was hardly surprised to find Dawn, Keisha, Bridget, and Jennifer on the bus with her. Karen and Shevaun were certainly brainy enough, but they'd been getting in trouble a bit more—or at least they had last year.

"Hey, Lassie!" she said to Karen as she found a seat next to where Karen was sitting with Shevaun.

"Hey yourself, lass," Karen responded.

"How've managed to keep your nose clean enough to come?" she asked.

She grinned. "We didn't get caught. Yet."

"Cause cheerleaders can do no wrong," grumped Faith McClendon. Karen snorted. "Maybe in Texas, but we've been suspended or gotten extra work piled on us plenty of times."

"Hey Shevaun. How early were you?"

"Half an hour," she said ruefully. "I know, I know, no sense of time. I have no idea how Dad hits his cues on time so easily."

"Wanna grab a cabin with us?" Karen said.

"Sure! They sleep eight, right?"

"Yeah. I kinda agreed to grab one with Dawn, Keisha, Jennifer, and Bridget."

"Well, that's seven of us. They're not going to insist on doing homework in the cabin, are they?"

"They don't have any." At Shevaun's expression, "I'm serious. We had a major study session over the weekend and finished everything up. So we don't have any to do." She smiled beatifically.

"I hate you," Karen said.

"You love me. You just wish you'd gotten all yours done. But if you need help, you can't ask for better than our cabin mates." She tapped at her phone to email the other girls.

"Thanks for letting us know, Ange," Bridget said, crouching in the aisle. "We were wondering how to fill up the rest of the cabin."

"Some one's gonna get stuffed in there. We're only up to seven," Shevaun pointed out.

"Should we pull in Dani?" Karen asked.

"She forgot a paper at home last week and couldn't get it before class." She must not have remembered in time to tell Alex, since he could have pulled the paper from her home.

"Well, anyone should be fine."

"Yeah. How many girls are on the trip?"

"Three hundred or so. A few less guys, in their buses"

"What are you looking forward to doing?"

"Three days of nature hikes. Going out to the coast. I just hope we see something worth seeing," Shevaun said.

"Oh, I'm sure we will," Bridget answered with a slight smile. She winked at Angela, who smiled back. With Bridget guaranteeing it, she better have the battery on her phone working properly.

"Plenty of wildlife in the area, great redwood groves. Even some teaching on edible plants. Should be a lot of fun," Bridget said.

Shevaun and Karen looked at each other, then at Bridget. "Since you already know all the trees and animals by name, we're gonna stick with you and get perfect results."

"Fine by me," she said, smiling.

"We can give Angela some tutoring while Bridget is introducing you to all her friends in the woods," Keisha said.

"Is it true we have to do our own cooking?" Faith asked.

"Yep," Jennifer replied. "We went last year. Each cabin in assigned a meal to prepare. We'd have won last year, but the guys cheated. They made pizzas."

"From scratch?"

"Somehow, yeah. Game on, boys. We'll win this year," Keisha said.

She looked meaningfully at the other wizards, who nodded back.

"Of course we will," Dawn said. "The numbers are even this year."

<Do I count?> Angela asked Bridget.

<For this? Absolutely. We don't have to hide from you.>

"We'll need to see what the supplies are," Shevaun said. "If they're like girl scout camp supplies, we may not be able to do much. Canned fruit, flour, preserved meats, cheese, canned vegetables. Besides we're still one person down."

"Oh, I'm not worried. We'll come up with something. Something fabulously unexpected," Bridget said.

"And the guys need to come up with some other boys for theirs, right?" Karen said.

"Depends. If they're more interested in winning, they'll kick the others out and just do it themselves," Dawn said.

"They're that good at cooking?"

"If they put their minds to it, they can do just about whatever they want to," Keisha said. "Just like we can."

"Oh. Why are you competing with them?"

"As long as we're split up, we might as well determine who's helping on whose projects first."

"I think we can come up with a full meal rather than just pizza or something like that," Jennifer said.

"Probably."

"Sounds good to me, lass. I hope to be able to get out to the coast and enjoy the sea," Karen said.

"You will," Dawn said. "We got out there last year."

"What else did you do last year? I mean, what's it like? I didn't get to go last year," Faith asked.

"It's mostly a nature education experience, but we also cook our own food, keep the cabins clean, have fires in the evening. It's a lot of fun," Dawn assured Faith. "There are a couple of communal showers. The cabins sleep eight. There's a footlocker for your stuff, a few outhouses. The guys are about half a mile away from our cabins. There's a small amphitheater and several stations scattered about the site. The staff cabins are about midway between us and the guys, and that's where the kitchen, dining hall, and big fire pit are."

"Okay."

"We'll have nature presentations. Pay attention to them, because every class is going to have an assignment when we get back on them. Even Spanish, French, German, or Japanese."

"Oh, wow."

"What we get for missing three days," Jennifer shrugged. "It'll be fun."

Rose Smythe came down the aisle talking sotto voce with people, but bypassed their little cluster. "What's that about?" Karen asked.

Bridget's eyes gleamed. "She's putting together a raid on the boys' cabins."

"And she didn't stop here because?"

"She thinks Dawn is a goody-two shoes who'll spill to the teachers. But Dawn's not the one she should be worried about. We made a deal with some of the guys. They'll warn us if there's a raid on us. Only seems fair to let them know." Bridget pulled out her phone to send the message.

"Oh, come on, Bridget! That sounds like fun!" Shevaun said. "Just keeping them from overreacting," she replied, tapping her phone to text. "Besides, those five are the only ones who can read it, and they won't blab about it." She finished and then said, "Huh. Warnings crossed in cyberspace. That was from Malcolm warning us."

"I hope a teacher doesn't see those texts," Karen said. Bridget smiled and handed her the phone. "What the hell?"

"From Malcolm, Phoenician. Script and language. From me, Gaelic in ogham script. There are nine people in school that would understand it."

"So, you guys can communicate secretly in different languages and alphabets? Just to keep the teachers from understanding?"

"More a matter of making sure the recipient is the only one who can understand it. Works pretty well. We're not going to stop either raid from happening. We're just going to make sure no one comes in our cabins."

The rest of the trip went pretty much the way the girls who'd gone last time said it would. The twin raids went off with only one hitch—some of the girls had the misfortune to catch Alex alone in the shower. He sent them back to perform the Tea Pot Song at breakfast the next morning, even though they couldn't say what possessed them to do it. The guys drew a breakfast slot and made a variety of pancakes, cocoa, sausage, eggs, and bacon. The girls drew dinner and, after making sure Shevaun, Karen, and Faith didn't realize what they were doing, put out vegetarian lasagna, garlic bread, and salad. The guys unanimously agreed the girls won this round.

C H A P T E R

14

"Thanks Jimmy!" Angela said as she and Karen got out of her brother's car. The Renaissance Faire in Golden Gate Park was going to be marvelous fun. They got in line behind a couple of women in full skirts and bodices and hats. "Welcome to the faire! How be you fine ladies this wondrous day?" A tall man with a lute and hair reaching to his shoulders came up to them. They grinned and giggled as he played a ballad with their names in it. "He'll just switch names for someone else," Karen said.

"Yeah." They headed off into the faire. They got past a juggler and some trinket booths to find a large group of people dancing in the street. Not just the performers, either; they saw several people in ordinary clothes interspersed among the dancers. A blond woman in a dusky orange bodice and green skirt noticed them on the margins of the dance and came up to them with a cheery grin

"Good morrow, fine gentles. Would you be wanting to join in? All you needs be able to do is walk, skip and count to four."

"And I was worried we'd need to fly!" Karen said with a laugh. "We'd love to." The dancer called out to a couple of the others; only now did Angela see the slight hitch in her step.

"Flying's great fun. Did some last weekend," she let slip before her brain caught up with her.

"I never knew you had a pilot's license!"

"I don't. I was up with Bridget, and her pilot let me take the controls," she lied glibly. She'd been flying with Dawn and Bridget, and they hadn't needed a plane.

"Oh, cool. I think I need to get to know Bridget better!"

"That shouldn't be a problem," she said to Karen as the dancers guided them to their places.

"Well e'now. First, ladies are always right and always on top." The woman teaching the dance demonstrated by taking position on her partner's right and putting her left hand on his right. "Now, bow to your partner. Starting with your right foot, walk in for four steps, bow, and walk backwards for four steps. Do that again. Now, face you partner. Hop to the right, hop to the left, and turn around to face out with your partner. Take four steps out of the set, turn around, come back in. Hop to the right, hop to the left, and turn around to face out with your corner—the person next to you you haven't danced with yet. Walk out for four, turn around and walk back in.

"Now turn and face your partner. Take them by the hands, and exchange places starting on your right foot, then go back. Do the hopping and turning again. Exchange places again. Hop and turn out to leave the set four steps with your partner, come back in, turn, go out with your corner, return. Now, link right arms with your partner, walk around them. Link left arms with your partner, go around. Hop to the right, hop to the left, turn around and go out with your partner. Hop again, turn again, go out with your corner, bow to your partner, and that's the dance."

They didn't screw up too badly, so they stayed with the dancers for a time, getting repeatedly pulled into the dances. They kept using the same basic steps, although in different combinations. After half an hour, the dancers broke up and they wandered further into the faire.

They ran into Keisha and Mike at one of the clothing booths, where Mike was trying on hats for Keisha. Keisha was dressed like one of the actors, in a noblewoman's heavy fabric, so they didn't recognize her immediately. Mike—other than the plumed hats—was wearing jeans and t-shirt. They sided with Keisha trying to get him to put on faire clothes, and when she bought him a whole outfit he finally agreed.

After getting Mike into his new clothes, they went to listen to some musical acts. They grinned and giggled at the bawdy lyrics. They stood in line for twenty minutes to get turkey legs and lemonades for lunch, encountering Carmen and Grace Minh. They had lunch together and spotted Alex and Dani, who waved but were otherwise just into each other. They went to a jewelry booth and a trinket booth where they picked up bone pins that read, "I only look sweet and innocent" and "Magic is alive". Bridget met them at a comedy show. She smiled at Karen's pin, and winked at Angela's, commenting that at least no one could consider it a challenge.

Later in the afternoon, they watched the dancers put on a performance. Quite a bit more complex than the ones they'd been teaching in the street, but that looked like a lot of fun. They went out to see the joust, and met up with Alex and Dani. They were amused by Alex's running critique of the jousting. It was a full-contact show, complete with the Queen watching and presenting a favor to the winner. After the joust they got more food and sat listening to more music, this time an all-male group singing and playing their instruments.

The final gun sounded to close the faire, and they made their way to the identified spot where Jimmy was supposed to pick them up. It was well away from the entrance, behind a clump of short evergreens that were still taller than them. Karen pulled out her phone and called her brother.

"Hey, Jimmy, we're done. We're at the spot we saw on the way in." She paused, listening. "Well, we weren't done then." She listened some more. "Well, as soon as you can get here." She put the phone away and turned to Angela. "It'll be a while. He hasn't left yet."

"Hey, guys," Alex said as he and Dani came up behind them. "You guys need a ride?"

"No, he's on the way. Brothers." Karen sounded a bit disgusted. "Okay. See you at school," he winked at Angela. She knew he and Dani would be teleporting away as soon as they were out of sight. They stood there talking about the day when a man walked up to them and pulled out a gun. "Hand over your wallets and phones." Karen immediately pulled hers out, but Angela said, "Get lost loser."

"Angela, he's got a gun."

"That cap gun? What'd he do, take it of a four year old? Please! I'm a lot scarier than that thing."

"I know you're on the football team, Angela, but what do you think you're doing?"

"Get behind me, it can't hurt me." She and Seth had covered armoring her clothes, but Karen didn't know that.

"Listen to your friend Angela."

"Fuck you."

Angela ignited the gunpowder in all the gun's bullets at once as she explosively raised the gun's temperature. In the explosion of the gunpowder she'd neglected the one in the chamber as he pulled the trigger... the one that hit Karen in the heart.

<Seth! There was a guy here with a gun robbing us!>

<Ooookaaay. Why are you calling me? You're more than capable...>

<He shot Karen! She's dead! And...>

Death was kneeling beside her. Seth had arrived without warning, no bell tolling, no flash of darkness. He paid no attention to the moaning, unconscious criminal under the trees. He put one bony hand on her head, covering her sightless eyes, while he placed two fingers on her chest, right as the spot of the gun shot, where the blood had poured out of her heart. The black glow of his power enveloped his hands, the rhythmic Coptic poetry emerging from between his jaws. As Karen suddenly breathed in, Seth vanished. She sat up, and the bullet fell down into the grass. Her skin finished stitching itself back together as she watched, and then the hole in her shirt repaired itself, but the blood remained. "Ow."

"Hey lassie. Stay down. You'll be OK, I promise you."

"Did I get shot?"

"Yeah you did. You've got a very tough breastbone. But let me get you cleaned up," she said.

"Oh, fuck, my shirt is ruined isn't it? Damn, I got it visiting my cousins in Glasgow last summer!"

"Then let's save it." She put her hand on Karen's stomach and spoke briefly in Ainu.

"Angela, your eyes, they're glowing… and teal…" Karen said weakly as she sent the blood back into her veins, leaving the shirt completely blood-free. Her eyes flew open wider than she'd ever seen them.

"FUUUUUUCKKKKKKKKKKK…"

"Good as new."

"Thank you! How… What…"

"Don't mention it," she replied. Then she caught Karen's eye. "No, really, don't mention it. To anyone. Not even to me, unless we can't be overheard. That guy had a bad accident with his gun exploding in his hand. I'll fill in what I can later. Here come the cops."

CHAPTER

15

"Why are we here, Ange? I mean, yeah, it's cool we're in this classroom, but..." Karen asked her as the girls sat down. The little temporary classroom wasn't used much for anything but storage, and was usually padlocked. Of course, it wasn't very secure against her anymore. A little concentration, a word, and the wheels of the lock had opened easily. "It's dark as a goth's fashion sense in here."

"We need real privacy for this conversation, and I don't have a space of my own yet. And while I know what you saw, I wanted to emphasize some of it to you, since I probably won't be answering questions I know you have. There are others involved, and I've made promises to keep the secrets I've been entrusted with. As for light, *fiat lux*." A glowing teal ball appeared in the middle of the room.

"Well that's being cryptic, lass. Thanks for saving me. And you won't be answering because...?"

"I wasn't the one who saved you. I just called him in. But telling you my secrets is my option. Telling you someone else's secrets isn't." She paused, cocking her head at Karen.

"I know him or some of the others, don't I? Who... oh, that would be what you meant, wouldn't it?"

"Yeah. The others? I learned some things about them before I was really brought in because my ass was getting saved from repeated attempts to murder me."

"Murder you? What for?"

"I was still alive after the bus crash and the head killer didn't know why. I was a girl playing on a boy's team and that was an abomination."

"What about Dani Serafini? I mean if you were targeted why wasn't she?"

"She was. They failed, loudly, in a way that let the killer know he'd run into far more than he expected. If you want to know more you'll have to ask her," she responded flatly. "More important is that we share something very few other people do."

"Okay. You can do magic, I can't so what… I didn't really survive that gunshot, did I?" she asked.

"No, and I didn't survive the first hit. Death decided not to keep me—or you." She popped open an orange juice. "You're smart enough to figure out who they are, if you put your mind to it. But when I was learning things, there was a suggestion that my mind be wiped, my memories altered, so I was clueless. That hasn't come up yet regarding you, but it easily could."

"By "Death" you mean Seth, don't you? That's why you've gotten so friendly with him? He's not tutoring you in any school class. You're good enough friends with Bridget Sullivan or Keisha Johnson that she'd be doing it, so you didn't have to put up with Seth, if you just needed help with school stuff. He did 'something impossible' you said. He brought you—and now *me*—back from the dead. He's tutoring you in *magic*." Angela grimaced internally. Karen might not be massacring the curve the way the ten of them were—especially the way studying together reinforced their GPA dominance—but she was far, far from stupid, and her grades were more of a reflection of her many distractions. "And 'run into far more than expected' means Alex is one of the others, doesn't it?"

"Karen, I'm not going to tell you who's one of them but you should know that all of my fellow magicians can read minds. It's not easy, and maintaining the read can give us a headache, so we don't do it all that much. If they have no reason to look, there's no need for any of them to find out." Karen made a face. "I'm serious, Karen. One of them was still advocating wiping my mind at the end of the year. Oh, and you'll find some odd occurrences. Resurrecting you created a bond between you and whoever did it. It's not bad; I've got it with him too, and I've done some things that strengthened it."

"Oh, god. What's he going to do now…"

"Based on my experience with him, nothing."

"He's not looking at you as girlfriend material," she shot back.

"I know. When I joined the group, I learned that we don't date internally. I think someone's sister had just had a huge blow it all up break up with her boyfriend, and they decided that breaking up between two of THEM would be even worse. From what I've seen, though, he's well aware that you have no interest in him. He respects my boundaries, so I have no reason to think he'll violate yours." She gave Karen a crooked smile. "He goes out of his way to not cross the line sometimes. Which can be even more irritating when it's cold out and he's ignoring it."

"ARRGGGH!" Seth looked up at her as she screamed in frustration and walked over to sit down next to her. She noticed he drew an opaque sphere around them as he sat down. Well, it wasn't really opaque—most people wouldn't notice anything other than the two of them sitting together in study hall, but that was all they'd notice.

"What's wrong, Angela?"

"Why isn't this working?"

"You'd have had to explain something if it did work, but no, I wasn't actively stopping you. What were you trying to do?" he asked.

"Pull my history book up to the table."

He gave her a crooked smile, and then said, "How?"

"Power! Magic! Will!"

"I gathered that, Padawan. How were you trying to accomplish the feat? Were you altering the air? Using it to lift from below? Or creating a vacuum above to bring it to you? Were you creating a gravitic anomaly that would carry it to you? Altering its atomic structure to make it lighter than air?" He looked mildly at her. "Magnetic field manipulation? What, precisely, are you DOING?"

She looked at him, and realized he had a point.

"The whole reason we've been cramming as much information as we have is that if we know how we're trying to accomplish something, it's the easiest way to actually do so." He gathered his thoughts, and said, "Remember the three elements of knowledge, will, imagination. When we're overriding the laws of physics, it's easiest to work with them, and just alter the point we want to change. Alex even thinks that's why there are so few others… people who don't know the science of how things work make it harder for themselves to adjust things in the first place, so even if they can they don't bother. As we get more practice at using our abilities, working out the science of it becomes less important and the will and imagination get more important. Does that make sense?"

"That's why all the extra studying. How does Alex have time for football?"

"That, unfortunately, is a question for him. You could ask Malcolm about swimming or Keisha about volleyball."

CHAPTER

17

"What's wrong, Angela? You were able to do this last week," Seth asked, stopping the lesson in transformation. They were in an old marble building in a graveyard, covered in ivy, in the middle of a graveyard— Seth's lair, known as the Mausoleum. She'd been surprised he wasn't based in pyramid. Seth had created lights inside, and there was lower crypt in addition to the above ground crypt—but only some of them were in the visible spectrum. Black light was a favorite of his, and he often altered his vision to use it.

"Nothing. I'll get it," she responded.

"Okay. Concentrate on what you want to happen." She flubbed it again three times in a row, the last time not even turning the rock over much less into a golden poppy. "That's enough of this for right now. Tell me what's wrong so we can fix it."

"I told you, nothing's wrong…"

"Bullshit." He tapped his left temple. "Or are you forgetting our bond? I know something's wrong, Angela. I haven't delved into your mind to find out what that something is, but given the forces you're playing around with here, let's not have a stupid mistake. This isn't Hogwarts and we don't have dozens of more powerful and experienced practitioners around to handle problems for us. We're certainly not

70

going on to protection until you can at least blunt what I'll be throwing at you."

"You'll think it's stupid," she said lamely.

"I might, but since I don't know what the problem is I couldn't say one way or the other. But let's get it out in the open. Maybe I can help."

"Never mind…"

"Angela, it's affecting your concentration and your control. We need to keep both. You may have noticed none of us go to those blowout weekend parties with beer? Bridget got really pissed a couple of years ago and half her junior high got sick. You may have heard about it?" She had. A cholera outbreak in wealthy, sanitary Marin had caught the national news.

"That was Bridget?"

"No. That was Bridget out of control. Malcolm lost it one summer and there were thirty shark attacks in a single day. Why do you think Alex finally stepped in to get the football team to stop coming after me last year?"

That chilled her. They'd taken to harassing him after that bus crash. He'd taken his problem to Alex and Dawn, and Alex had told the team to leave him alone…and, though she hadn't known it at the time, backed it with his own power. But if Seth had lashed out with his magic in fury, he'd have killed them. "Death is your domain. You can kill with a word, almost with a thought."

"And I eventually would have. Not striking back with my power was very difficult." He narrowed his eyes and looked at her, his eyebrow raised. "Maybe I'm the problem here. Would you be happier talking to someone other than me about whatever this is?"

She stared at the ground. He sighed. "Felarie, hear me. I beseech thine aid." He paused, listening. "Angela's having some problems with concentration and control, and she's reluctant to discuss it with me. I was wondering if she might consider your ears more sympathetic than mine." He paused, listening again. "Well, yes, she could just consider me an insensitive idiot." Angela felt her lips twitch. "But let's not set off another earthquake, hmm?" He listened again. "I know you didn't intend to. Any more than I intended to kill all those eucalyptus trees. Given what she's best at, though, it's harder to predict what she might accidentally do. If talking to you will help her get her concentration and control back, let's bring you in." Angela remembered that episode as well; her mom loved the smell of eucalyptus. Over one hundred of the trees had simply died, and last she'd heard no one had an explanation for why. She'd thought it had been another part of Bridget's campaign against invasive species. If that had been Seth losing control…

"Good enough," Jennifer said in a flash of indigo light. "What's going on, Angela?" She caught Angela's glance at Seth, and shook her head. "I get that it might be embarrassing for him to listen in, Ange. But as he's your tutor, he needs to know what the problem is. It's easiest if he's just here listening in, but if it's that much of a problem, I'll fill him in later. Your choice."

"Oh, alright, he can stay." At her utterly resigned tone, Seth rolled his eyes, said something in Coptic, and vanished.

"Rather than what's up, *who's* up? Sounds like boy problems," Jennifer said. She leaned back. "If so, I can see why you didn't want to talk to Seth. He's kinda clueless."

"Yeah, he is. But *he* isn't the problem." Jennifer summoned up an indigo beanbag that oddly went with the black furnishings Seth favored for his little hideaway and sat down cross-legged. She then summoned up grape sodas for them and leaned back, cocking an eyebrow at her.

Angela didn't say anything for about a minute. "Ange, I hate to rush you, but I'll be missed before too long. And you still haven't told your old people where you are and who you're with for these sessions, so you'll need to be where they expect you on time, too. So, who's up?"

"Dave. Dave Clebourne. I keep thinking about him, and the way he laughs, the way he walks. That cute smile. I got one dance with him last year, and I know he enjoyed it and he isn't going out with anyone but he acts like I don't exist and…"

"Okay, okay. You've got the serious hots for Dave and he's not even looking at you. Do you know why not?"

"No," Angela replied miserably. "Is there something wrong with me?"

"So that's it," Seth's voice came out of empty air. "What? This *is* the Mausoleum," he continued when Angela started. Right. Seth's lair, where it could be silent as the rest of the graveyard, but Seth was ever present. "Do you want me to talk to him?" Seth asked.

Angela felt her face distort it horror at the idea. Seth and Dave weren't anywhere close to being friends. "No, really, thanks, Seth, that's alright. I'll get it back under control."

"What I'm thinking, Angela, is that Dave has drawn the conclusion from our tutoring sessions and discussions in the hall or at lunch that you're dating *me*, and he simply doesn't know you well enough to know that's not happening, or that our little group—you know, Jennifer, we should probably come up with a name—doesn't date internally."

"That might work," Jennifer said, contemplating. "Given how boys think, getting the message from Seth rather than you might convince him you aren't dating anyone." At Angela's expression, she added, "I've been reading minds a lot lately. Class is so boring. If the "romantic obstacle" reveals himself to not be one, you're more likely to get asked."

"Or you could ask him yourself."

"I don't see you asking anyone out, Teach," she shot back.

"True, but no one wants to go out with me, and we were talking about you and Dave," he said. He finally reappeared in the room. "I can help solve the problem. Do you want me to?"

$\mathcal{S}$econd and ten, behind by four points, thirty seconds to go, twenty-eight yards from the end zone. She took her place in the huddle, and Alex started going over the play. "Alex, *guarantee* I'll catch it and score."

"Glad you're that confident, Ange, but he's covering you so tight I think he wants to slow dance with you." There was a round of chuckles in the huddle. "You are third receiver, though, so get open."

<I know the game's on the line, Angela, but this isn't the place.> Seth's mental voice sounded… irritated.

<Could you not distract me just now,> she returned. She set herself, listening for Alex to hike the ball.

<Then let go of your power. I can sense you've gathered quite a bit to help you with the game>. She was surprised at that, but ran through the calming exercises from karate. Then she heard Alex and took off down the field, dodging around the other defenders with a fluid grace. She got open, but the boys on the Sausalito team converged around her… leaving Rick in single coverage.

Alex got Rick the ball with an easy pass into the end zone. Angela trotted off to get herself a drink. "Thanks, Seth."

"We should have a talk, Angela. At pizza?"

"You're going to be there?" she asked in surprise. "You normally don't."

He shrugged. "I'm not exactly welcome at team gatherings. But I'm not supposed to be in your locker room at all, and we do need to have a talk. That's twice you've gathered your power during a game."

After the game, Angela caught a ride to Salerno's with Jon MacWilliams. Seth—not having to shower and change, and able to teleport without suspicion—was seated at a two person table with a plastic number on it. She ordered, got her number and sat down with him. "I didn't even feel your privacy sphere," she said as she set her own number on the table.

"It's not up yet. There aren't that many people who would choose to sit with me, so I just needed to grab a table." He spoke a word in Coptic to create the privacy sphere, and went on, "One of the things I wanted to discuss with you was you're getting pretty good at the basics. What do you say to some specifics from the others?"

"Um, you're not trying to get rid of me?"

"Not at all," he smiled at her. "We all teach each other when we come up with new techniques and the like. I want you to get the best grounding in everything we do. I've mentioned that we can all do everything. That being said, I've got some weaknesses in what I can do, which makes it somewhat harder to teach. It's very strenuous for me to work in a living body, and I'm not that good at illusions. The sort of illusions Teddy can craft would put me in coma, and Alex's ability to control people is similarly something I can barely do. You might as well get direct instruction in everyone's specialties from them, and Jennifer doesn't have trouble with anything, so some learning from her would help you too."

"Okay, makes sense."

"We'll continue our sessions, but my idea is to get you as quickly as possible up to where the rest of us are. Working with everyone should advance you that much more quickly."

"Seth, one of them wanted me left dead! Or my mind wiped! I'd rather not be one on one with whoever that was."

"I don't think you have anything to worry about. He changed his mind when we brought you fully inside. Now that you're one of us, the threat you represented has dissipated."

"Will you at least tell me who it is we're talking about? The name hasn't even come up at game!"

"Oh, that character died. Tell you what. It sounds like figuring it out will be a good project for you."

"All I know is the secret name and that he's one of you nine!"

"Is it? Can't you eliminate anyone from consideration?"

She paused for a moment. "I guess I can. You're Thantoris, Alex is Toranos, Bridget is Chiomara. For that matter, I can eliminate Dawn, Keisha, and Jennifer since you continuously refer to him as male. Which leaves Malcolm, Teddy, and Solly."

'Excellent. I'll let Angoral, Bestarion, Cuan, Felarie, Grianne and Kara know that you have an assignment to figure out who is who. Good sleuthing." He smiled at her.

She groaned. "You just did by speaking their names." He simply grinned. "But you can scratch Felarie off the list. You bespoke Jenny when I was having trouble concentrating."

"See? It won't be that hard." She gave him an exasperated look as they ate their pizza. "How much do I owe you for the pizza?"

"Don't worry about it. I'm writing it off as a business expense scouting a potential player for the Valkyries."

"I should have dinner with you more often."

"Your parents would pitch fits."

"Not if I'm in line for a job. They've been after me to get one, but I don't have time."

"Want one? We could probably get you something official sounding with the league, and help you cover your tutoring sessions from your unknowing parents."

"How much work would there be?"

"No idea. We'll need to talk to the others. Do they want you earning money, or is it an experience thing?"

"Earning money, but the experience would be good too. College applications. You guys will be able to put managing a pro sports team on your applications."

"Owning. We generally let the people we're paying to manage, manage. I was thinking something in the league's central office in San Rafael. We can easily get you there after school and such."

"Ok. I'll let you get back to me on that. Can you drop the privacy? Or are there still some secret things for us to discuss?"

"No, that was it. If you're wandering away, could you tell Alex I'd like to speak to him?"

"Sure," she said, getting up to rejoin her teammates. Alex grabbed a slice and went to talk to Seth; Dani shook her head at how quickly Alex joined Seth.

*A*ngela looked around to make sure no one else was around—unlikely, out here in the secluded grove of oaks—and levitated herself up into the branches. There was a nice broad branch, she could lean back against the trunk and watch in privacy. She got out her turkey on sourdough and her grape juice, pulled out her phone and activated the scrying app Keisha had uploaded for her. Fortunately the app sent the sound out so only she could hear it, and focused on Dave. He was eating his own lunch—god, was that peanut butter and jelly?—at a courtyard round table. One of the sea green ones, next to the cement Manzanita planters.

"Dave?" He looked up to see the black clad boy put his tray down at the next table. A red one, which was oddly clear of people. Oh, shit.

<Seth, what are you doing talking to Dave?>

<Making sure Dave knows I'm not in the way. Chill, Padawan. I already scanned his mind—or what passes for one--and yes, he does want to be with you.>

"Seth." He took another bite of his sandwich. "What do you want?"

"A friend of mine wanted me to speak to you." Seth picked up his fork and took a bite of the salad. Angela slipped her consciousness into Seth's mind to watch the conversation play out through his eyes. It was a lot easier than slipping into Dave's mind, and didn't take as much concentration as keeping the app going.

<I'm going to get you for this, Seth!>

<For helping you get the date you want so much you're having trouble concentrating?>

"About?"

"I'm tutoring Angela, not dating her. In fact, us dating would be a bad idea given the potential fireworks of a break up." He paused to take a drink. "As far as I know, and I speak to her frequently, she's not dating anyone. But does think you're adorably cute."

<You just had to throw that in?> she thought at Seth. At least Dave couldn't see her blush.

<I didn't need to, no. It's true, though, so what are you complaining about?> he replied.

"Fireworks? You're afraid of a public spectacle?"

<Want me telling Karen how much you like her?>

<You're planning to horrify her just to get back at me? I thought you two were friends.> "Between Angela and I? It has the potential to be a whole lot worse than that." Seth took another bite. He concentrated a bit, and Angela felt his power building. She bit her lip. *<Don't worry, he'll be fine…and find a different line of questions.>*

<I'm sure she won't take it too badly,> she returned. He mentally snorted in reply.

<You have heard her expressed opinion of me? I'm not hurting Dave, just… redirecting his curiosity from asking me these things. At some point he'll likely ask you, so you might want to be thinking about your answers.>

<I can work on that. And so can you. My opinion was similar before you saved me from a vampire!>

<Not exactly equal. You and Dave are interested in each other. While I'm interested in her she's not in return. And it wouldn't work. There aren't any more vampires nearby for me to save her from. Not unless I make a few, and she'd be furious if I made some just to save her from them.>

<Seth, for love of god, please, please tell me you're joking>.

"If you want to date Angela, I'm not in the way, Dave. Just go ahead and ask her." *<Joking? I know how to do it, Angela. You've sat in on the elf project discussions. Bridget makes unicorns. Jennifer's currently got a clutch of dragon eggs incubating. We've been discussing elves. Malcolm's figuring out mermaids. Why shouldn't I make vampires?>* "I'm not sure why she just doesn't ask you herself, but her moping about not getting your attention has been affecting her study habits."

<SETH! I was fed on by one of the damned things!>

<Oh, right. I can still make them, you know.>

<I figured as much after watching you make zombies. Just...>

<Johnson screwed up. He made himself that way, Angela. I know it's a sore spot with you, but let's go up the hill and examine what he did wrong and why it turned out so badly.>

<Do we have to, Teach?>

"Ok, Seth. Thanks," Dave said. "Any idea where she is?"

"I'm her tutor, not her father,' Seth replied. *<Johnson botched immortality, Angela. We think it can be done safely, but knowing how it was screwed up will be valuable information.>* She watched through Seth's eyes as Dave bunched his lunch remnants up and strode out of the room. Seth's gaze, though, didn't linger on Dave; he returned his attention to his peanut butter sandwich. She slid out of his mind and went back to her own lunch.

Angela was headed for the locker room after gym with Carmen when Dave caught up to her. "Angela!"

"Hey Dave," she said, curling a lock of hair around her fingers.

"What's up?" she asked innocently.

"Do you have a date for Fall Formal yet?" he asked.

"No. No, I don't." Carmen headed on to the locker room to change for history with a wink.

As she got further away, Angela turned back to Dave. "Why?"

"As it happens, I was hoping you'd go with me," he said with raised eyebrows. "If you've no other plans?"

She grinned broadly. Damn, Seth talking to him worked. "Sure, Dave, sounds great."

"Shall we meet up at 8 at the front door? Or can we pick you up?"

"Meeting would be fine." She didn't want to scare him off. "Here's my number. I gotta get changed before class, but call me!"

Angela walked into the grove on a high. Nothing could bring her down! Seth was waiting for her, and looked up from his pad. "Control, Angela, CONTROL."

"What, Teach?"

"You're a foot off the ground," he replied. "I take it Dave asked you to Fall Formal?"

She looked down and he was right. She let herself float down and land. "Yeah. Thanks. I thought you intervening would be a disaster."

"Just remember, control. Even if he pisses you off," he said. At her look, he continued, "we both know I don't know a damn thing about dating. But I do know about keeping control over my power."

Angela looked doubtfully at him, and he leaned towards her drawing a privacy bubble around them. "Angela, you wouldn't be going to the dance with Dave if I couldn't. I still remember who decided a urinal was where I wash my clothes. I nearly killed him twice." He sat back.

At that, Angela bit her lip. Seth went to football games to cheer on her and Alex, and he was now the waterboy, but most of the team couldn't be called his friends. She hadn't known Dave had been one of the ones harassing Seth, though.

"We have power, Angela. We have a lot of it. Any one of us could walk down the street as Destruction Incarnate. I can kill faster than anyone else, but fire or lightning or blunt force will kill just as dead as me terminating life. With our power comes a responsibility to decide when and where and how to use it. No one can make us use our power. It takes three of us to restrain a fourth, and even the restraints are only so good, because sooner or later we'll be free. The restraints last only as long as we're actively concentrating on them. We think it would take all of us acting together to strip someone of their power and leave them alive, although we haven't tested that. But if you're ready, we can get going."

He stood up straight and extended his hand. She took it, and he teleported them to a dusty, abandoned building with gaping holes in the walls and ceiling.

The police had taken away the fragments of Reverend Johnson and the other bodies that Seth had left behind him. But they hadn't gotten everything, and Seth wouldn't need much. But Angela's first reaction was to whip a layer of air molecules into a strong shield about an inch thick. The ceiling was still full of the holes Seth and the evil reverend blasted in it during their fight. "Whoa, Teach! You could have warned me we were coming straight here!"

"Yes." He glanced around. "Look more closely," he suggested.

She let her eyesight slip into the seeing the effects of magic, and noticed Seth's privacy sphere still around them. Then she saw what he was hinting at—it was already set up to keep things out. She shot him a dirty look. He smiled blandly back at her.

"Ok, that's one on me," she said.

"As long as you're using the enhanced sight, look around more closely. What do you see?"

"I see lingering residue of the fight. Yours are black, his are white. That's… the only power I'm seeing. Was this place ever consecrated?"

"Logical question. Have you ever applied the enhanced sight to a building you know was consecrated?"

"No."

"Call it homework, then," he said.

"You know, I get plenty of homework from the teachers at school. I don't really need more, and how am I supposed to go around finding consecrated buildings to check?"

"As I recall, you still go to church every Sunday. Take some dark glasses, enhance your vision, and look around. Consecration is normal procedure for building a church, isn't it?"

"Uh, yeah."

"Well, then, presumably they did the ritual properly. So look…"

"For common features between that church and this one?"

"Precisely."

"Would the denomination make a difference? Or religion?"

"Good questions. As far as we know, it doesn't. But you're a believer. The rest of us aren't. You might see something we don't."

"Isn't Solly Jewish?"

"Culturally. But he hasn't been in a synagogue since his bar mitzvah, and it's not like he keeps kosher. You may have noticed his fondness for sweet and sour pork whenever we get Chinese on game night?"

"This place was a battleground between a couple of wizards. What ever consecration it had may be gone."

He shrugged. "A point. Are you seeing anything else?"

She looked around. The struggle between them had left marks all over the place, blackened holes in the ceiling and wall, whitish holes, residue from where Seth and Reverend Johnson had their defensive spells. Drops and puddles of blood. "Sorry, Seth, I'm not seeing what you're hinting at."

"Check the area around that big cross."

"The one you pinned him to? Okay." She looked and found sickly white marks…the remnants of the vampire's body. She enhanced her vision even further, applying some detections Keisha had suggested to her once. She heard Seth quietly casting his own divinations behind her.

"He botched immortality. What he did was dependent on blood to keep him functioning."

"Why?"

"I'm not sure. I didn't get why when I was looking at it."

"Neither did I. I have a hypothesis."

"Seth, how could he be a vampire and walking around in daylight and..."

"Everything else vampires aren't supposed to be able to do?"

"Yeah"

"The stories and lore about such things are, as far as we can tell, exactly that—stories. Until we verify them, there's no reason to assume they're accurate in any particular. Certainly the cross didn't do anything to him. He wasn't afraid of it. He built a church following based on a fundamentalist reading of the Bible, or so Teddy tells me. His parents apparently loved his community access cable show."

"Getting back to his dependence on blood, do you have any idea?"

"I have a conjecture, but I'd like to hear your thoughts first. Can you conjecture, Angela?"

"No... wait. How much wine was found here?"

"A lot. All of it red."

"Seth... wine is used as the blood of Christ in communion. In the eastern churches, it has to be red, but Johnson wasn't of the eastern church."

"Aye,"

"Could he have been convinced that this was the immortality offered by faith in god? As long as he kept drinking sacramental wine..."

"And the blood of virgins. That's exactly what I think. Johnson's beliefs included requirements to maintain his immortality that weren't necessary." He incanted briefly, and sweated. He'd put up an illusion of Johnson's tissue and the spells on it. "Note these points," he said, making them glow brightly. "If you really want immortality, you need to bind your own cells to faithfully copy your DNA, in perpetuity, and actively repair any damage. Johnson didn't know what he was doing. He was basing what he thought he needed to do on pure mythology."

"So immortality's impossible."

"Sure it's possible. Bridget and I worked that out last summer."

"So, you're immortal now?"

He smiled at her. "Not yet. We're still working on how. But you will be too."

CHAPTER

21

She went with Seth out to the room at Fort Cronkhite again. They'd decided that an apprentice should come with her tutor. Of course, she was still the only apprentice, but this time Seth teleported them directly into the room, and they sat next to each other, dice and character sheets on the table.

"Hi guys," Jennifer said as she appeared. She was the last to arrive. "Reason I asked to see everyone before game is that Seth suggested we have a group name we can refer to so we can refer to it with no one being the wiser."

"Sounds like a good idea. We already use game night to do exactly that," Dawn said.

"I suggest "Bible Study," Teddy said. That appeared on the wall behind him.

"That'd work for your oldsters, Teddy, but no one would believe it of the rest of us," Keisha pointed out. "If the idea is to have a cover group, let's name it something we can all believably be in. Something to stop the questions."

"What about the Wizards of the Round Table? Just as a club, hide in plain sight."

"The Terraformers' Guild."

"LV Knights."

"The Brain Trust."

"The Curve Flatteners."

"The California Pantheon."

"The Resurrection Gang."

"I'd really rather not use that last one," Seth put in. "Resurrection men in the nineteenth century were grave robbers bringing cadavers to medical schools."

"Oh, right. How about the League Owners' Club."

"We can already use that as cover, and we're already fielding calls about new teams joining the league. Not to mention Angela's not an owner."

"The Z-Men."

"Do you really think of me as a *man*, Alex?" Bridget asked archly.

"No, we've all seen that you're not." She grinned at him.

"The Bear Knights."

"The Knights of the Hound."

"The Black Knights."

"Okay," Alex said, "I think we've got a bunch of options. Let's eliminate the ones that someone had an objection to. So not Bible Study, Z-Men, Resurrection Gang, or League Owner's Club."

"We've got enough knight variations that we probably won't be able to decide on one, but it seems popular. Similar connotations with Wizards of the Round Table, but it also emphasizes academic prowess. I like that one," Jennifer said.

"I'm a little concerned about calling us wizards though. My parents won't like that one, even though I do."

"I hear you, Teddy, but it's the best one for our purposes," Angela said. "If someone overhears, we can just say we were talking about the club."

"And you can tell them you were outvoted."

"Works for me. Tell us about your character, Angela."

CHAPTER

22

The Fall Formal was the last dance before the winter break. She met up with Dave at the door to the auditorium, her in a teal gown and him in what was probably his father's gray suit with a blue tie. He pinned a corsage of white flowers to her and they walked in just as Alex and Dani pulled up—in a Berkeley Avengers purple and gold limo.

The color scheme didn't end with the car, though. Dani's gown was gold with a purple sash and matching purple corsage. Alex was actually wearing an Avengers-purple tuxedo with gold cummerbund, and his gold studs glittered with amethysts. "Wow!" Angela said, looking at them matching head to toe.

"Dani, I am so glad you scooped up Alex. I'd never have been able to match that," Dave said.

"Well, here comes someone who can," Alex said, nodding at the orange and bronze limousine pulling up.

"Yeah," said Dani, "But Keisha's all Mike's, and I'm fine with that!" They grinned at each other as Mike handed Keisha from the orange limo. He was wearing his hair in a crew cut.

"Hey Mike. Feeling any better?" Dani asked. His suit was loose on him, and he looked a little pale.

"I am, thank you," he replied. He clutched tightly at Keisha's arm in her orange gown.

"We got to him in time," Keisha said.

"I think I should have sprung for a limo, too," Dave said. "Alex and Mike bringing their dates in limos, and it's' not even prom!"

Keisha smiled. "This one's mine, Dave. Alex and Keisha brought their dates in limousines. Shall we go in?"

"I can see getting a limo for prom," Dave said, "but what are the rates for renting one for an evening?"

Mike grinned at him. "You weren't listening. This is the owner's limo of the San Jose Sphinxes—and I have the honor, privilege, and delight of dating the owner." He pulled Keisha in a little tighter.

They walked in to the auditorium, and stopped in surprise. "Which of you sprung for the live band?" Angela asked.

"We all did," Keisha replied. "We put together a joint fund to help with things like this."

"Not without opposition," Alex grumbled.

"Let me guess—Seth the spoilsport didn't want to," Dani said sourly.

"Seth never comes to the dances. Why should he be paying for us to have fun, Dani?" Mike asked her.

"If he's not going to be here, what's he doing?" Dave asked. "Did he have a funeral to go to or something?"

"Watching his TV," Keisha said with a loaded glance at Alex and Angela. They both nodded, hearing the unspoken message. Seth was keeping an eye on them. "But, really, Alex, he accepted the vote and chipped in for the band. The least you could do is accept the win graciously."

"What were the totals?" Dani asked.

"Five to four. What's got him grumbling is that Mike's point was the one that the people opposed hung their vote on, that it was unfair to expect everyone to contribute when he wasn't coming," Keisha said. "And it was even closer than that, really. I know that a couple of people who voted to do it were waffling."

"OK, I can see that," Dani said. "Enough, though. C'mon, Alex, let's dance!" She led Alex out onto the floor.

"Can I get you a drink?" Dave asked her.

"Sure, water." He went over to the refreshments table, and Angela asked Keisha, "Who voted against it?"

"Bridget, Teddy, and Dawn. I was one of the wafflers."

"Well, Teddy's here with one of his groupies," she said, pointing him out in his blood red tuxedo.

"Now Angela," Bridget said coming up behind her with Chris Salerno. "The devout young women who hang on his every word as if he were a living god can hardly be called "groupies."" Bridget's gown was a deep forest green with silver accents, managing to suggest a pine forest in winter.

"What should we call them?" Malcolm asked as he arrived with Jasmine Alassad. "Priestesses?" Malcolm, like Alex, was wearing a tuxedo—in his case royal blue with pearl studs and silver cummerbund.

Dawn came in with Trevor Richards. Her gown was a brilliant sun yellow, with pink accents suggesting earliest morning. It was their first date, Dawn had said, but they were lab partners in chemistry. Trevor's suit was a standard dark gray, but Dawn had probably picked the tie; it matched her gown. "Hey Dawn, Trevor."

Shevaun came in with Benjamin Schmidt, and stopped, her eyes broad at seeing the Round Tablers' finery. "Damn," she said. Her gown was grey and red. "You guys make me feel underdressed."

"We're not trying to, really. We're just…"

"Next you'll be telling me you came in a horse drawn carriage," Karen said as she came up in a pink and blue gown.

"No, none of us did that," Keisha said as Mike came over to pull her up for a dance. Dave returned with drinks from the refreshment table. "But maybe next time."

"You didn't spike those, did you?" Bridget asked.

"Of course not! I don't even have any"

"See that you don't. You wouldn't like what we can do in revenge," Bridget said as she got up to dance with Chris.

<Things are going well, I trust?>

<Yes, Seth, thank you. Now if you don't mind, get out of my head and let me concentrate on my date!>

<No problem. Everything's clear; you guys should be fine.> "Where were you just now?"

"Hmm?"

"You seemed to drift off in a haze. Are you okay? Do you need some water?"

"I'm fine. Just thinking about a paper I have due on Monday," she lied. Damn. Dating while keeping all this secret was going to be interesting. They danced several dances before she bespoke Alex. *<Can I get a dance with you? I've got a question. When did you tell Dani about your magic?>*

He didn't respond, but he and Dani made their way over to them. "Hi Dave, Angela. I promised Angela a dance a couple weeks ago."

"Sure, no problem. Dani, will you dance with me?" Dave asked. "Of course."

"In answer to your question," Alex said as they got out onto the floor, "I didn't say anything until she already knew there was more going on. About the time she first got targeted."

"Oh. Damn. I was hoping for guidance on what to tell him," she replied.

"Keisha and I both had our hands forced, her by Mike's cancer and me by the attacks on Dani. I'm not sure when—or what—we would have said otherwise, and no one else has a steady significant other."

"Okay, thanks. I guess I'll figure it out as things go."

"One thing to be careful of is everyone else. However much you like Dave, Seth doesn't, and won't hesitate to adjust his mind—or have Teddy do it—if he feels it necessary to guard his secrets. He's warned me a few times about Dani knowing too much. Best I can suggest is to be open and honest with him that there are things you can't tell him."

"Thanks for the advice… and the dance."

"No problem."

"Thanks for coming with me, Angela."

"Thanks for asking me." Even if Seth did have to hit you with a cattle prod to get you to. "I had a wonderful time."

"Would you like to do dinner Saturday? Mexican?"

"Are you asking me on a second date?"

"Um, yeah. If you want."

"Sure. Junipero's?"

"Sounds great. Meet you there?"

"Works for me."

*J*unipero's was a little Mexican restaurant in a strip mall in Marinwood by 101. It served mostly a walk in clientele, so Angela went in and joined Dave at the table he grabbed. They ordered their burritos and rice and beans in Spanish.

"I really like this place. They put on plenty of chilis," she said.

"A little spicy for me, but still great," he replied. "Have you been here before?"

"A few times. Mom likes it. You?"

"One of my favorite places."

"Have you picked a book for lit yet?"

"No, not yet."

"Want to pick a book together?"

"Sure. Sounds like fun," he said. "You going anywhere for winter break?"

"No, I don't think so. Then again, I might get invited along somewhere at a moment's notice."

"Really? How?"

"I'm friends with the owners of the CWFL. They decide to invite me along to things, especially practices and games. They do have their own jets and stuff."

"Wow." He paused to take a few bites. "Think I could come some time?"

"I'll ask. It's not exactly up to me." Alex or Bridget might go for it, but she knew Seth wouldn't.

"You actually get to go to practices?"

"I even got to catch some passes last year up in Arcata, with the Unicorns."

"Cool. You going to play for one of the teams after school?"

"My parents want me to go to college. But I can probably play for one of them. You going for the NFL?"

"That'd be great. But it means I need to do really well on a college team."

"My mom keeps telling me to keep my grades up and not count on football. They're probably right, but it'd still be great to play professionally."

"Yeah." With their burritos finished, they got fried ice cream. "I know you're being tutored by Seth. What in?"

"Um, a bunch of things."

"Like what?"

"Do we really need to talk about my tutor? I spend enough time with him as is without talking about him."

"No, of course not. It's just that he sort of jumpstarted me to ask you out. I thought you were dating him."

"He mentioned that. But I'm not going to date my tutor, and while he's become a friend since school started, I'm really not interested in him." That was as close as she needed to get to the truth.

He nodded. She was tempted to read his mind, but resisted. Then his phone rang. He looked at it, turned it off, and put it away. "Sorry about that."

"Was it important?"

"Not really."

They sat there talking for what seemed like just a few minutes, until her phone rang. "Oh, damn. Mom wanting to know where I am."

"When are you supposed to be back?"

"An hour ago."

"Then maybe we should do this again and let you get home?"

"I'd like that."

95

CHAPTER

24

First weekend of winter break, and here she was back at school, because it was the most convenient place to meet Seth for a tutoring session. They were in the marble and granite of the Mausoleum a few seconds later, and then in the lighter gravity of the Temple. The yellow and black stones of the Venusian base on Ishtar Terra gleamed in the wizardly light. "How do you guys make the lights?"

"Jennifer fairly early on worked that out, plus the controls to shunt the heat elsewhere."

"Why are we on Venus?"

"Anxious to get back to your boyfriend?"

"He's not my boyfriend…"

"Yet. But to answer your question, I thought we'd go over some basic combat magic. And for that…"

"Even the Mausoleum is a bit too public. But why here and not the Castle?"

"The Temple is better shielded, in this case by the atmosphere. Mars has a number of satellites in orbit and robots on the surface, so even in the Castle there's more chance of something being noticed."

"Okay." They passed out of the arrival chamber, walking by the corridor leading to the apartments they'd established, heading towards the practice room when she noticed a new door. It was a teal door.

"Is that…?"

"For you, yes. Go on in if you like."

She put her hand on the door and it slid into the wall at her touch. The room was fairly large, with a couple of doors off it. There was a comfortable looking couch, a video screen, an easy chair, a desk, a small table, a computer. Looking through the other doors, she found a bathroom with a large tub and shower, vanity table, and toilet through one and a bedroom with a large bed, already made up, along with a wardrobe and dresser. She glanced beside her to look at Seth, only to find he wasn't there. Turning around, she saw he hadn't entered the room; he was still in the hallway.

"Does it all meet with your approval?" he asked.

"Yeah. I won't be able to use it until I can get myself up here, but definitely. Why are you still out there?"

"You didn't invite me in."

"And you can't come in without an invitation, or you're just being polite?"

"I'm being polite. You haven't been here long enough to put up wards," he replied.

"So the rest of you have?"

"I did. Alex put some up as a routine precaution. I'm not entirely sure about anyone else, but I think is smarter to presume they did."

"Okay. Come on in. What's with the apartments up here?"

"Sometimes it's easier to just sleep here than go all the way home. It was Teddy's idea at first, I know he expects a confrontation with his parents sooner or later and wants somewhere they absolutely can't reach. He suspects they'd be able to find Inferno and would be able to do something about it."

"Are there apartments on Mars, too."

"Of course. It's easier to sleep here, though, since the gravity's closer."

"I hadn't thought that would be a factor." He shrugged in response.

"Shall we?" he asked.

"Sure." They headed towards the spell-casting room used for practice. "What are we doing different?"

"We tend to reach for what's easiest for us when we're in a fight. Which means that you'll tend to manipulate matter. But that also means that someone who knows what we're doing can take direct steps to counter that. So…"

"Learn a different means.

"Precisely. Dawn's battle magic tends to be chemical in nature— electricity or fire, or outright energy manipulation. Alex animates nearby objects, kind of like Fantasia. Mine tends to be of the instant death variety. I suspect you'd prefer Dawn's or Alex's version."

"Um, yeah. No offense, but I…"

"Don't worry about it. I'm aware. Their techniques can leave people alive," he said. She thumped his shoulder. "But for either of us, using one of those techniques requires a bit more thought, a bit more conscious selection of what we're doing."

"What about those boards?"

"I tend to differentiate dead tissue from, say, stone or metal. It's harder for me to control granite or steel. Limestone isn't as hard."

"So what sort of targets are we using today?"

"Zombies." She looked at him. Sure enough, he was serious. Combat spells against animated corpses.

"They aren't going to react the same way as the living."

"No, but it would be wasteful to bring up living… OH. These are animal zombies, Angela. Once we're done using them as targets, they'll be part of the terraforming process."

"Well, that's a weight off my mind. I'm glad you're not using human corpses."

"Boars mostly, as part of Bridget's campaign against invasive species. And camels from Australia. But in terms of the animation…"

"There's no real difference. Yeah, I know. It's still there in my mind."

"Maybe we should have you do some animating of corpses. See it for yourself. Maybe some resurrections."

"I think I'd rather do resurrections."

He smiled at her. "I certainly do. Let's have Bridget available in case we need to bring you out of a coma, though. We'll also need to get our hands on some bodies. Animals are easy enough, but human bodies we'll probably need to get from a war zone somewhere."

"Seth, what do we do with people we bring back? If they're known to be dead we can't send them home."

"Yeah, I know. We can either keep them on Mars or Venus… or select people not known to be dead. Which is why we go to a war zone instead of a morgue. A disaster would work too."

"Okay, I understand. We can't have a bunch of people here or there."

"No. But we'll find something."

The casting chamber was large, with a scarred floor. That they had thrown everything in the room was obvious. On the floor were the bodies of twenty large dogs. She looked at him. "Euthanized fighting dogs," he responded. "We're not going to be bringing them back. I'm just going to animate them so you can blast them."

"Okay. Let's start."

Angela woke up Christmas morning with her usual happy thoughts. Not only was she going to be spending the morning opening presents, but Dave had invited her over to his place for Christmas dinner. She'd volunteered to bring rolls.

"Good morning, sweetie," her mother said. "That was on the doormat this morning, addressed to you." *That* was a large box, covered in decals from the women's football league. Well, that said whom it was from.

"I see my friends decided to play Santa Claus," she said. She found nine smaller boxes inside. She opened the smallest one first and found herself the owner of season tickets to the Santa Cruz Valkyries. "Wow." As she touched them, she realized Seth had enchanted them, for in her head she heard him tell her that she was naturally welcome to join him in the owner's box if she wished, but had needed to come up with something that wouldn't arouse suspicions.

"How's the job hunt been going?"

"Really, Mom? On Christmas morning?"

"What are those, Angie?" Dad asked.

"Season tickets. To the Valkyries. From Seth Dupree."

"I guess he's still feeling guilty," Dad said.

"Black tickets? From that boy? You should throw them away," Mom said.

"A-1 priority VIP tickets, Mom."

"It's an expensive gift. Season tickets don't come cheap, and the league's popularity is exploding. Even if she doesn't go herself—and I don't see heading all the way down to Santa Cruz for their home games, Angie—she could probably find people to take them."

"He's being nice, Mom. Least I can do is be civil. What if he was trying to help?"

They looked at each other. "Honey, I really don't like hearing you say that. You're making excuses for him doing what he did to you."

"I was unconscious and he's never taken a CPR class. He might have been trying to confirm what he didn't find at my neck." Why wasn't she just admitting what had happened? That she'd been dead, that Seth had brought her back? She'd told Karen. Why wasn't she telling her parents? She closed her eyes, concentrating, and didn't find any blocks in her mind. The only thing stopping her was... her.

"Has he still been bothering you?"

"No!" She grabbed the box and stormed off.

She sat stewing in her bedroom while she opened the other gifts. Bridget had given her a fossil opalized ammonite pendant. Keisha had given her an around the world culinary adventures cookbook. Dawn had given her a pocket sundial. Jennifer had given her a wand that lit up. Alex had given her a 49ers game ball. Malcolm had given her a choker of pearls. Teddy had given her a pair of expensive sunglasses. Solly had given her a bonsai kit.

Malcolm had given her a pearl choker that even had a spot for Bridget's ammonite gift. What? She let her gaze slip into the magic spectrum, and sure enough... everything she'd gotten in the box was enchanted. As she looked, she saw the hidden envelope. Pulling it out she recognized Seth's handwriting. Opening it, she saw a letter, on formal league stationary, welcoming her to a job as special assistant to the owners' committee. Seth had signed it as the current chairman of the committee. So had the head of the league's office of personnel.

Now she'd have to figure out what they did, but that could wait. She slowly made her way back out to the den and the fireplace that never got used due to pollution concerns. "Hi honey. I'm sorry for pushing at you."

"You know how you've been pressuring me to get a job?"

"I've got one. Special Assistant to the Owners' Committee of the California Women's Football League. And the pay is better than anything I could get flipping burgers or working retail."

"That's going to get in the way of school…"

"How? The owners' committee know exactly what my assignments are and I'm in study groups with all of them. From the letter, all my duties will be at the league office in San Rafael."

"And you won't have to travel?"

"If they want me to travel, I'll stay with Bridget or Jenny or Dawn or Keisha, even if someone else gets me there. These are, for the most part, friends of mine. I mentioned you guys pushing me to get an after-school job and they decided to give me one. Lets me work or study as needed."

Mom and Dad looked at each other. "I guess that will work." Mom and Dad didn't need to know it was a subterfuge to learn magic faster.

Dal's house was an older one up on a hill street. Single story, painted a blue gray, but the yard was very well kept There wasn't any grass, but that wasn't unusual; juniper bushes and gravel were the front yard. She was wearing a Christmas sweater and reindeer skirt. Dave answered the door when she rang the bell. "Angie! Thanks for coming!"

"Thanks for inviting me," she said.

"Well, don't leave her on the doorstep," called a woman's voice.

""Yes, Mom. Please come in," Dave said. A couple of younger kids dashed off giggling. The girl looked about thirteen, the boy a little younger. "Thanks," she said. The hall had dark paneling and a cement floor with a gravel inlay. The atrium was full of winter flowers and some small statues.

Dave's mother was about five six, in shape, with graying dark hair. She smiled warmly at her. "Finally my boy invites a girl over! I've been waiting for him to grow up." Angela blushed. "Pleased to meet you, young lady. I'm Eleanor."

"Angela. Angela Fujiwara."

"Let me introduce you to Kristin and Calvin," she said, referring to the younger children who had reappeared. "My husband William is somewhere around here. We're just waiting on the goose."

"Goose? I've never had goose."

"It's a Christmas tradition in my family. Rather than turkey or ham, it's always goose. Thank you for the rolls, Angela. Did you bake them yourself?"

"From scratch," she said with a smile.

"Well! Good for you."

"You must be Angela. Welcome," Dave's father appeared at the door. He was a blond man over six feet tall.

"Thank you, Mr. Cleburne."

"Well, why don't we let you kids be alone?" he said. "Kristin, Calvin, come set the table."

Dave showed her into the den, where the Christmas tree had been set up. There were no presents under the tree; they'd obviously cleaned up from earlier. Angela got the shark's tooth necklace from her purse and handed the box to Dave. "Thanks, sweetness!" He handed her a wrapped green package.

"Thank you, lovey," she said, opening the package. Inside was a silver chain with a cultured pearl pendant. She gathered up her hair so he could fasten it around her neck. "It's beautiful." She kissed him.

"Is your phone working?" he asked. "I keep trying it and I'm never sure if I'm going to get you."

"Some of my study sessions and activities are in places with really bad reception," she said, ducking the question. The Temple and the Castle, after all, were well out of range. "And I often turn the ringer off when I'm studying. I find it's better to do that until I'm finished."

"Oh, okay."

"Did you take his virginity?" Kristin asked.

"KRISTIN!" Angela blushed, and Dave was bright red.

"Oh, so not yet," Kristin said, munching on some almonds.

"Kristin, do you have any idea what I'm going to do to you?" Dave threatened.

"Nope. And you do anything to me you'll be grounded for life," she replied with a grin.

"Let it go, Dave," Angela said. "She's just giving us a hard time."

"Listen to your girlfriend, Dave. She's smarter than you."

"I have a better study group."

"Yeah."

"If her study group is better than those over-muscled idiots you hang around with, why don't you switch study groups?"

"The others don't want to add a new person," she explained. Well, that was true as far as it went.

"Any other person, or just him?"

"They're picky. But they took me in, so I have hopes for him."

"Really? Sounds good to me," he said in a suggestive voice.

"You've got some bridges to build first."

"What do you mean he's got bridges to build? Should I have gotten him a hammer?" Calvin asked.

"Kids, DINNER!!!!!"

"A hammer wouldn't help with these bridges," Angela said as they made their way to the dinner table, a large one set for six."

She sat next to Dave and across from Kristin. "I'm told you're on the football team, Angela," his father said.

"Yes, I'm a wide receiver."

"One of the stars of the team, actually," Dave said. "How many touchdowns this year?"

"Twenty-seven," she said with a shrug. "The goose is very tasty, Mrs. Cleburne."

"These rolls are really good, Angela," Kristin said. "You're a much better cook than Dave. Last year he burned the bread."

"Well, this year I made the ambrosia. Harder to screw up, and appropriate to feed Angela." She blushed.

"What does that mean?" Calvin asked.

"In Greek mythology, 'ambrosia' is the name of the food of the gods. Your brother just called Angela a goddess," Mrs. Cleburne answered. "Which is why she's blushing."

"Thank you."

"You do hang out with Ares, Artemis, Hades, Poseidon, Pan…"

She stared at him. That was getting uncomfortably close to their powers, even if it was just their interests. "Well, if you're going to call them gods, don't invite their wrath," Mr. Cleburne said laughingly. "The stories of the Olympians are fairly short on mercy."

"Wisdom," Angela said ominously before grinning.

"How are you doing in school, Angela? Dave says you don't study together much."

"I fell in with the Round Table last year when Bridget got assigned as my lab partner, so I'm doing really well. The guidance counselor is talking about more honors and AP classes for next year, and…" The conversation was smooth and easy. She really liked Eleanor Cleburne, and Kristin had all sorts of questions for her about the team. After dinner she joined them outside to toss a foam football around before Angela's parents arrived to pick her up for evening services. Kristin was pretty good at throwing catchable passes. Angela suggested she try out as a quarterback when she got to high school. Kristin even waved good-bye with Dave.

*F*our guys came into the diner, brandishing guns and declaring it was a stick up. They tied everyone up with plastic restraints at gunpoint. Angela went along, not wanting to show anything unusual.

Dave flexed a bit. "Good thing you're not here with Deadman Dupree. Give me a bit and I'll have us out of these."

Angela sighed, watching the gang. "Dave, do you trust me?" she asked. If she were here with Seth, he could've killed the gang anytime. Between them, they could have probably taken the gang peacefully. As it was, she'd have to get violent.

"What? Of course I do…"

"Can you keep a secret?" She asked.

"Sure. What's with the twenty questions?"

"Keep it no matter what, as if your life depended on it?"

"Angie, you're being kinda weird."

"Dave, this isn't my secret alone. They'll forgive me. But if they don't think you can, they'll ensure you can't betray their secret."

"Um, Angie…"

"Dave, I can get us out of this. That's not a problem. I'm not trying to figure out what to do. What's a problem is your reaction to how. I'm trying to figure out if it would be better for you to just sleep through this." She eyed him carefully.

He snorted. "Angie, I'm not tired, and even if I was I'm a little keyed up to sleep!"

"Not really problems. But ok."

<Thantoris, I beseech thine aid.>

<That's a formal way to do it. What's up Angela?>

<What secrecy strictures should I be aware of in dealing with armed robbers at the restaurant?>

<Are you or anyone with you in direct danger?>

<No, it looks more like they're taking hostages.>

<Which means the cops are outside, or at least on their way. I suggest doing nothing and letting the cops handle it. Concentrate on keeping the people in there with you safe.>

<That hardly sounds like you.>

<Your skills tend to be more visible than mine. Someone drops dead and no one's going to know why without an autopsy, but a plasma fire is fairly spectacular. If you're going to intervene, I suggest subtle.>

<Should I just kill them, then?>

<I don't recommend it. Not only for the consequences to you, but I estimate you'd have to get them one by one, which means they might panic and shoot someone. Subtle, Angela. Make it look like their plan's unraveling.>

<Great. You're suggesting subtle and Dave's feeling his machismo.>

<I can only suggest knocking him out to keep him from doing anything stupider than normal.>

<Nice to know you're so supportive.>

<Angela, you're a brilliant student, a star athlete, and a beautiful girl. Why you're with an idiot like Dave I haven't a clue.> She snorted.

<You wouldn't understand.>

<Probably not.>

"What was that?"

"Don't worry about it Dave." She whispered in Ainu and the sleeve of the thug over at the stove brushed hot grease and caught fire. As they put him out, she made a second gunman slip on a wet patch and hit his head on a table. She evacuated the air from another gunman's lungs. He doubled over gasping for breath and passed out, and his pistol accidentally shot the fourth guy in the leg—who hit his head on a cast iron pan.

"So the four stooges decide to rob a restaurant," Dave laughed. With all four of them unconscious, she and Dave bound wounds with the first aid kit and welcomed the cops when they charged in after hearing the shot. But Dave hadn't correlated her whispers in Ainu with any of the thugs falling over.

<It's handled, Teach. Neither Dave nor the cops suspect I had anything to do with it.>

<Excellent, Angela. You'll want to watch the Ainu around Dave now, though. He might figure something out.>

<I'll be careful. See you later.>

*L*ate in January was the school ski trip up to Squaw Valley. Again, a good disciplinary record and good grades were perquisites to go; Dave had managed to get himself in trouble last week, so he wasn't coming. Angela was sitting next to Shevaun for the trip up. She grimaced as the signs started coming up. "What's wrong?"

"How long before one of the idiots remembers I'm Lakota? I really like skiing, but I hate the resort name."

"I can see that. Best I can say is don't let it worry you. We're here and most of the real idiots are stuck back at school." *I hope Seth doesn't kill any of them while the rest of us are off skiing.*

"Oh, wow, I hadn't thought of it that way," Bridget said from just in front of them. "I was talking to Jennifer and Dawn, Ange, and we're going to be hitting the less popular slopes. Want to join us?"

"Sure," she said. She was getting an undertone from Bridget that said the wizards were deliberately isolating themselves. "What about Keisha?"

"I'll be surprised if she stirs from the lodge. She's more interested in doing some cuddling with Mike than skiing, so they'll probably wrap themselves around some mugs of cocoa and sit by a fire." Shevaun grinned at that.

"Mind if I join you, too?" she asked. "I've been wondering who I could join up with as a skiing buddy."

"Sure, Shevaun," Bridget said. "I hope you don't mind some tutoring while we're skiing. Seth may not have made the trip, but he asked Jennifer and I to keep Ange's nose to the grindstone for him."

Shevaun groaned. "Oh, come on, this is a chance to get away from school work."

Angela shrugged. It wasn't schoolwork, after all. "Might as well not let anything slide." They got up and made their way off the bus to collect their skis. Magic came in handy to identify them quickly.

"Ah, Squaw Valley. My favorite slopes," said Jim Edwards, the biggest ski fanatic in school. He'd been bragging all week about the carnage he'd wreak on the slopes. "And our school squaw," grinning at Shevaun.

She smiled sweetly at him. "Break a leg, Jim."

"Break both of them," Keisha added.

"In four or five places," Bridget suggested.

"On the first slope," Mike put in.

"Hey asshole. You have a problem with Native Americans?" Alex said. "'Cause my heritage is Mexica. Aztec."

Dawn said something in Tsalagi that had the senior wizards laughing at him—and Angela felt Dawn's power release—as Malcolm, Solly, Teddy, Julian, Dani, and Karen joined the circle.

"Disparaging any of God's children harms us all," Teddy said. "I think you owe the lady an apology." Other kids began joining the circle of the Round Tablers. Jim seemed intimidated as both Teddy's congregation and football players joined the circle. He looked around and no one seemed to be supporting him. "Now."

"Sorry, Shevaun," he mumbled. He stumbled away. With the spell Dawn had put on him, he'd be alone all trip. And maybe beyond.

"Thanks guys," Shevaun said.

"The Round Table supports you, Shevaun, even if you aren't one of us," Alex replied. The others nodded.

"Less popular" runs turned out to be an accurate assessment. Most of them were hard moderate runs. They kept letting Shevaun go down first, and giving Angela some practice with magic. Then Shevaun wanted to do a triple diamond run, one of the really hard ones. Dawn was a little less sure about it.

"What's wrong?"

"I'm not that good on skis," she replied in Tsalagi. "I'm going to have to cheat, and she shouldn't see that."

"What language was that?"

"Tsalagi. Cherokee."

"I didn't know you were part of the Cherokee nation!"

"I'm not. Japanese and Irish. I was just impressed when I read about Se-quo-yah creating a system of writing, so I wanted to learn."

"And you learned it. Damn, that's impressive."

Bridget smiled and said, "She's not the only one who speaks it here" in Tsalagi.

"Fuck. How many languages do you speak?"

"English, Gaelic, Tsalagi, Cornish, Coptic, Phoenician, Nahuatl, Cushitic, Hebrew, Aramaic, and I'm learning Ainu and Spanish," Bridget replied. "Jenny speaks a few more."

"Mandarin, Japanese, Arabic, Swahili, German, and Russian," Jenny added.

"Good morning, ladies," Julian said coming to a stop next to them. "Whadja stop for?"

"A little language discussion, Highness," Bridget said.

"I wish you'd just call me 'Julian'."

"Why do you call him that?" Shevaun asked.

"He's an actual prince, in line for the Hawai'ian throne," Jennifer said.

"Yeah, yeah. I have as much chance of actually taking that throne as I do of flying without a plane." The four wizards looked at each other with bemused expressions, but they didn't offer to let him fly. "Well, see you at the bottom," he said, taking off down the slope. They watched him go appreciatively.

"He's very pretty," Jennifer said.

"Yeah, but I'll race you to the bottom," Shevaun said.

"You're on," she replied. They took off, moving smoothly and gracefully down the slope.

"Ready, Dawn?"

"Not yet." She spoke several words in Tsalagi and tapped her skis. "Now I'm ready."

"What'd you do to them?"

"I'm having them enhance my skills, stay steadier, and float if I actually come away from the ground."

"How?" While Dawn explained what she'd done and Angela did the same to her own skis, Bridget kept other people away. A slight green glow escaped from behind her sunglasses.

"You guys done? Shevaun just wiped out."

"Let's go," Angela said, turning on her own enhanced vision. She led the three of them straight to Shevaun, whose leg was at an unnatural angle and bleeding into the suit. Her skis were broken and one of her poles bent. The root she'd hit was plainly visible now.

"Really did a number on yourself there, girlie," Dawn said.

"We can't wait for the ski patrol, guys, she's losing too much blood. We need to act before she becomes a problem for Seth."

"Hunh? Wha wazzat?"

"Okay, Angela, watch this," Bridget said. "Or do you want to?"

"I'll give it a shot; if I screw up…"

"I can fix it," Bridget assured her.

"Sleep, Shevaun," she said, releasing her from the pain. Then she concentrated, speaking in Ainu to straighten the bone, knit it back together, repair the muscles, tendons, blood vessels and skin. She was tired after doing all that, and could feel the sweat inside her coat.

"Just one more thing," Dawn said. "Blood."

"I think I'll do that," Bridget said. "Great job, Ange." She held out a chocolate covered chewy granola bar. "Replace some of those calories. We'll get down the mountain and be nauseated by Keisha and Mike for a bit."

"How many bugs are in it?"

"None, even though you could use the protein. If you want a scorpion pop, after the bar." The blood disappeared back into Shevaun. Angela dismissed the sleep compulsion.

"Ow. What happened?"

"You took a little spill."

"I remember that. I remember my leg hurting like a bitch. I remember bleeding. But I seem to be okay."

"Maybe you're not remembering right."

"No, it just happened, and you three came up."

"You look fine to me. Can you stand? Can you ski? Let's get you down the mountain and into some hot chocolate. Or did you want to wait for Snow Patrol's calendar boys?"

"I think I can make it. Help me get my skis back on, will you?"

"Sure," Dawn said. "They're right here. Maybe have them checked out at the bottom." The skis and poles were in perfect shapes, and the root was now deeper in the ground. Dawn and Bridget hadn't been idle.

"Yeah." They took it easy going down the rest of the way down. Jennifer met them at the lodge.

"Hey Shevaun, how are you doing?"

"Okay. I am going to chill for a bit and get checked out. Wait… how did you know? You have reception on the mountain?"

"We have reception everywhere."

"Well, thanks to Angela the witch doctor, I'm feeling fine."

"Hey, I'm not a witch! I'm Episcopalian, not Wiccan!" They shared a laugh. "Glad you're feeling better Shevaun."

"Back in a bit." She headed off to the medical station.

"That's enough excitement for today, I think," Angela said. "But what did you mean by case for Seth?"

"Just a shorthand, really, for bringing back the dead. Keeps people from knowing what we're talking about," Bridget replied in Gaelic. "I'd have done it here; I think it'd be better to have Seth overseeing your first time than me. It's easier for Seth, especially when all we have are fragments, but when there's a whole body, it's easier for me than anyone but Seth."

"In the meantime, Angela, what did you think of healing?"

"It was marvelous. Just… wonderful. I can't begin to describe it." The other girls smiled at her.

"We know what you mean. But all the same, I was watching you. That was somewhat strenuous for you."

"Wasn't that bad."

"Healing gives us a high. That doesn't mean it's not an energy intensive use of our power." Keisha and Mike came over with cocoas, a huge bag of fresh baked cookies, and box of bagels.

"Eat," Keisha said. "Long day on the slopes makes you hungry."

"Always does with me," Mike said, pulling a sesame seed bagel with cream cheese out of the box.

"That's going to ruin your diet," Carmen said.

"She'll burn it off easily enough," Bridget said. "Plenty of time on the slopes tomorrow."

"Not to mention a little magic," Bridget said in Ainu. Mike buried his nose in his cocoa and smirked. Karen choked a bit on her coffee, even though she couldn't understand. Angela knew she'd guessed.

*B*ack from the ski trip, Angela plunged into her studies with Seth. More and more of them took place in the Castle or Temple, and she turned her phone off for those since no one who could reach her—the rest of the Round Table—would interrupt a teaching session by phone; they'd just bespeak Seth telepathically. She got permission to stay the night with Bridget when she'd be studying on Mars or Venus. Seth surprised her one day in the Castle by suggesting it was time to craft her own lair.

"Where?"

"That's up to you. The Mausoleum's in a graveyard. Alex put the Citadel in an old, abandoned fort and cloaked it in enchantments. What appeals to you?"

"An undersea volcano. In the tropics." She gave him a look. "I'm tired of the chill of the grave."

"Okay." On the big computer screen he called up a spinning holographic Earth. "Which ocean?"

"Let's be simple. Pacific." Dots appeared in the ocean.

"Any of them particularly appeal?"

"Something with caverns. And not too deep. I want to be able to have sunlight coming down on me." As she spoke more and more of the dots disappeared. She picked the one closest to California. "How about this one?"

"It should do. Do you want to handle it yourself?"

"Do you think I can?"

"Of course. You're about where we were when we first established our lairs," he said.

"How much did you help each other?"

"Depended on what was needed and wanted. I didn't really need a lot of help with the Mausoleum. Whereas making Sunholme was a different matter. We all helped with that one."

"Sunholme being Dawn's?"

He nodded. "She's got a sunny rock in the desert, but it's a spectacular place. You should ask her to take you there."

"What did she have you do?"

"Sorry. Her privilege."

"Gotcha. But if I ask for help on it?"

"It's yours."

"What sort of things do the various lairs have?"

"A bedroom, a kitchen, fridge, food, bathroom, food, practice area, library. After that, pretty much individual. Teddy's is more elaborate, mostly because he's worried about needing to have a place to run to when his parents go off the deep end."

She sat at the computers in the Castle working on plans for her lair. Seth was around, ready to answer questions whenever she had them. Bridget, Teddy, and Malcolm popped in while she was working and answered questions that she put to them. Then they got into a discussion of magic and it's processes. After several hours, she suddenly remembered her movie date with Dave.

"Seth! I need to go back to Earth!"

"Okay. Do you need me to transport you?"

"No, I got it." She'd been getting steadily better at teleportation.

Angela met Dave at the theater, moving in a teal swirl to an out of the way spot where no one would notice her. She locked her bike and met him in the line for *The Beast of Kilmarnock*. It was supposed to be a good, scary movie. The others didn't go for scary movies. Something about Dawn incinerating a screen.

"Hey, Dave, sorry I'm a little late. Tutoring ran long, and I didn't notice the time." Easy to do on Mars, she thought.

"No problem. Show time's not for another five minutes. What were you studying so hard?"

"Chemistry." Well, alchemy. Regular study sessions were taking care of chemistry just fine, but getting alchemy right was another matter.

"Aren't you getting a A in chemistry?"

"The tutoring helps maintain that."

"Where were you today? I tried you four times."

"I can't say."

"Ange…"

"Dave. I can't say. I promised."

"Okay, okay. It's just…"

"I get it, Dave. I want to tell you, I do. But I can't."

"Can you tell me why?"

"Dave, I've got secrets. But by secrets I mean I'm not talking. I going to keep my promises."

"I understand." But he stayed grumpy through the whole movie.

CHAPTER

29

"*H*ey Ange. Ready to enchant your clothes?" Alex asked. "Sure." Alex said.

"Okay, what did you bring?"

"Shoes. Dress. Belt. Earrings, necklace."

"Socks? Underwear?"

"Do I need to enchant those?"

"We questioned it, too, when Solly suggested it. But there is something to be said for a layered defense. Which actually brings up a point. You don't have a horse or vehicle, so you're going to be flying. Do you still want to be in a dress?"

"Yeah."

"Okay. What we basically want to do is make it impenetrable. This," he rapped his knuckles on the breastplate he'd brought along, "is easy pickings for a modern weapon. But after I enchant it, it will turn aside a depleted uranium shell, laugh at armor piercing bullets, and keep out heat, radiation, electricity..."

"Does the material matter?"

"No, not really. Seth and Bridget prefer all natural materials, but that's their focuses in action. For the rest of us, it doesn't matter at all."

"But at the same time, I want to keep the feeling of it."

He nodded in understanding. "Of course. Unless we're going for a particular look, like this or Seth's skeleton in a robe, it's easier not to make that sort of elaborate change."

"Well, I'd like wings. Flaming wings."

"Do you want to do a full blown elemental get up?"

"Yeah, that works."

"Do you want the dress water or mist?"

"Let's go with water, with mist around my feet."

"What's with the jewelry?"

"Well, it's just a gold chain and earrings."

"Let's enhance with gemstones."

"Representations of fire, earth, water, and air?"

"Precisely."

"I want something that will let me breathe underwater."

"Let's go a bit beyond that—breathe anywhere, including in vacuum or poisonous gas. With your elemental focus, it should be fairly easy."

"Oh, right. Makes sense."

"So what other things do you want to build in?" They worked on it for several hours. At the end, her big disguise had teal plasma wings, a watery-looking dress that felt wet, with a misty base around her shoes and heavy gold jewelry studded with opals—white opals, fire opals, crystal opals, black opals. The jewelry would assume a different aspect without a word of command. The outfit would guard against as many forms of danger as they could think of, keeping her safe even on the surface of Venus. They were finishing up when she checked her phone.

"Oh, shit. Dave called five or six times."

"Does he know about you?"

"No."

"Dani learned about me fairly early on, so I can't give a whole lot of advice," he said.

"Do you think I should tell him?"

"No. He's too likely to draw the correct conclusion that Seth is teaching you magic, at which point Seth will consider him a threat and wipe his mind. And he wouldn't be gentle."

"He hasn't wiped Dani's."

"No, he hasn't. But he doesn't have the issues with Dani he does with Dave. What he'll tolerate from her, he won't from Dave." She grimaced, but nodded. "Dani irritates him. Dave pretty thoroughly managed to scorch the earth between them last year." This was going to be harder than she'd thought.

CHAPTER

30

"Hey, you wanna go over to Northgate after school Wednesday? Kaiser's Hof Brau?" Dave asked.

"Oh, Wednesday I have a tutoring session."

"Cancel."

"No can do. I let it slip over the break and they've been on my case about it." 'They' in this case was the rest of the nine, but it was vague enough to cover her parents.

"I'll join you, then, and we can go afterwards."

"No can do, I'm afraid. It's with Seth."

"So?"

"He doesn't like you. I can give you a call and meet you afterwards."

"We all have to put up with him at school, and we get over it. If he's helping you it can help me too. He'll get over this."

"No, he won't. He holds grudges, and I'm not going to piss off my tutor by insisting on your presence."

"C'mon, Angela."

"No, Dave. I'll meet you after the session."

"You're picking that weird twit over me?"

"This jealousy is really ugly, Dave. I owe Seth a lot, enough to keep his opinion of you in mind. I want to be with you, I have things

121

I need to learn from him, and looking at the situation between you through rose-colored glasses won't help. He's not going to tolerate you at a tutoring session."

"It's not that bad."

"Yes, it is. He doesn't wash his clothes in a urinal, Dave."

"What, he can't take a joke?"

"He's not laughing. He retaliated somehow. If you don't believe me, ask Alex. They've been friends for years."

"So that's how the dog shit got in my backpack. I'll…"

"Unless you want to take on the whole Round Table—including me—you'll accept it as account settled, payback delivered. I'm sure everyone else in your classes will thank you when the people who are already blowing the curve without trying very hard start trying to flatten it," she warned.

He looked at her, eyes wide in disbelief, starting to speak several times. Her steady gaze seemed to wilt something inside him, and finally he said, "Oh, alright. I won't go after him. But what did you mean about owing him?"

"He tried to save my life on that bus and I accused him of assault."

"Alex's phone."

"Hey, Julia, it's Angela. Where's Alex?"

"Making out with Dani," his little sister responded. "From the noises it sounds kinda gross."

She chuckled. "Would you mind knocking on his door and giving him his phone, please?"

"I don't think they want to be disturbed. But life is full of disappointments. Besides, you are in tier two now."

"Tier two?"

"Who to disturb Alex for. Tier one is Dani, and only Dani. Tier two is the you, Seth, Teddy, Keisha, Malcolm, Dawn, Bridget, Jennifer, and Solly. Tier three is Mom, me, and Dad. Tier four is the team and the other members of his study groups. Tier five are his other friends. Tier six is everyone else. But more importantly, tier two are the only people who we're ever to disturb him and Dani for. Not even Mom or Dad. So I get to enjoy disturbing him for one of the people I've been told to disturb them for. Granted, I don't know what got you promoted to that list, but it is an excuse." She heard a loud banging as Julia knocked on his door.

"Not a very nice thing to do to Dani."

"They've been at it for two hours."

"Julia, I am going to…"

"Angela's on the phone, ogre-face. She's on the list."

"Sorry," came through the phone, but it sounded like he was speaking to Dani. "What's up Angela?"

She responded in Nahuatl "Sorry for disturbing you two, but we're wondering where you are. The rest of us are at the Castle." Ordinary phones wouldn't reach interplanetary, but they didn't have normal phones, not any more.

Alex cursed. "I'll be there soon. Sorry, Dani. I forgot about an owners' meeting." He stopped talking to Angela but forgot to turn the phone off.

"With Angela?"

"She's working as a special assistant to the owners' committee, remember? So…"

"She gets jobs like calling to find out where you are. Can I come?"

"I haven't cleared it ahead of time, so not this time. I'll drop you at home."

"Let me fix my clothes…" Alex finally turned his phone off. She grinned as she hung up herself.

"He's on his way," she told the others.

"Finally," Teddy said. He checked his phone. "I should still be okay. Pass the milkshake?" Jennifer sent the pitcher over to him with a word in Cornish.

"Thanks." They waited a few more minutes, eating the burgers and fries Malcolm had conjured up, until Alex appeared in a purple swirl.

"Sorry, I was.."

"With Dani," they chorused.

Solly continued, "We know exactly who you were with. Even if all you were doing was history." They laughed at his expression.

"You're not quite as bad as Angela and Dave," Bridget put in. "But they're still at puppy lurve."

"Getting back to the point of the meeting," Seth said, "Keisha?"

"Right," she said. "We've been approached by groups wanting to start their own franchises in the league. They're in Bakersfield, Salt Lake, Oregon, Washington, Arizona, New Mexico, and Idaho. We're going to need to grow the league to attract more revenue."

"Does that suit our purposes though?"

"Not yet," Teddy said. "League owners' meetings are too useful, at least for me, to disguise what we're really doing."

"I agree. We're not ready to bring in real outsiders, who can't be trusted with the secrets," Dawn said.

"Good enough," Keisha said. "No expansion of the League this year."

"Was that it?"

"No, of course not. Where are we on the terraforming?"

"I think we've got the Martian plan pretty much set. We can't start it yet; for all our power we don't have the necessary endurance to work this sort of magic yet. Venus presents a different problem. We're still a lot further from being able to get Venus to where we need it," Bridget said.

"What about Luna?" Dawn wanted to know.

"No where close. The gravity's a big problem," Teddy said.

"How are we on Project Interstellar?" Alex asked. "Still looking," Seth said. "What about Our Bang?"

"Our Bang? What's that?"

"I was reading a book where it posited the artificial creation of a universe," Malcolm said. "A few weeks ago I brought up the idea that we should see if we can do that. You were busy. So, rather than find and alter worlds…"

"We create our own," Angela said. "I like that idea."

"Well, we're still distant from doing that," Malcolm said. "We're working on how still."

"Enough with the general. Let's get into the details," Alex said. "Bridget, Mars?" They spent hours on the details of each of the plans before they were finished. Bridget took Angela home again.

32

Mom dropped her at the bus pick up place for Muir Woods, and her ringtone came up quickly. She quickly spoke an Ainu phrase to let her spot Dave more easily and there he was. She smiled behind her sunglasses. At least they'd keep any telltale teal from Dave's eyes.

He greeted her with a kiss and they got on the bus. It wound through the hills of west Marin and down into the valley, finally reaching the entrance to the woods. The soaring redwoods rose around them, and they pulled their packs and water bottles off the bus. Heading for the trails, they soon made their way off the valley floor. Coastal redwoods towered above them, shading the valley and the ferns growing on the hillsides. Birds chirped in the branches. It was cool and fragrant down here.

They found one of the trails leading up onto the hills, where most of the tourists wouldn't go. "Looks like a good trail," he said.

"Works for me. Can you keep up?" she teased, setting a quick pace. She didn't enhance her speed, just moved quickly. Dave lengthened his stride to catch up, ad soon they were moving together again. They walked for a couple hours, looking at the plants, listening to the birds.

"I tried calling you yesterday afternoon. You didn't pick up."

"Do we have to do this again? I was out of range."

"Where were you? I got a better plan that should cover all California."

"I can't say."

"Can't or won't?"

"In this case, same thing."

"No, it's not."

"It is as far as I'm concerned. I'm not saying where I was. I'm not saying who I was with. I'm not saying what I was doing. I've told you before, I've got secrets that I'm am going to keep. And you wouldn't believe me if I told you."

He blew up. "Angela, I get that I you're your own person. But you won't return my calls. You're never available. You won't even tell me what the hell's going on with you. You're not a part of this couple. So I'm through playing whatever game this is."

CHAPTER

33

"Center, Angela! Center!" Seth called. He, Alex, and Dani stood at the foot of the biggest redwood.

"Shut up, Seth! You okay, Ange?" Dani asked.

"Dave just broke up with me, what do you think?" She paused and a thought occurred. "What are you doing here?"

"Oh, Ange," Dani said as she came forward with her arms open.

Seth and Alex glanced at each other.

Seth tapped his temple. "I felt a sudden surge of grief and rage from you. You're probably not okay. But someone needed to be here if you lost control," Seth replied in his cool, detached tones. "Short of killing you I alone couldn't stop you. You might exercise a little more restraint with Alex and Dani here."

"Oh, shut UP, Seth!" Dani said.

"Actually, he's right, Dani. And..." Alex was saying as Angela interrupted.

"And I devoutly hope that he never thinks I need to be stopped no matter the cost He might hesitate, but my sensei would do it."

"Danielle, do you smell something?" Seth asked.

"This isn't..."

"I'm serious. Do you smell something?"

"I smell it too," Alex said. "Where…? Ah."

"This is Muir Woods. There's all sorts of wet smells… and… is that smoke? Dani said questioningly.

Alex nodded, and summoned a small downpour to quench half a dozen smoldering spots. He returned to English from the Nahuatl. "Sorry if I got anyone."

Seth nodded, "Angela, losing control has consequences for anyone, but especially for us. What happens if I do?" He cocked an eyebrow at her.

"Seth, lay off!" Dani shouted at him.

"He's making a point, love. And a good one," Alex said. He breathed heavily. "We've never talked about what Seth is really good at, have we?"

"No, we talked about your skills, but not anyone else's. You never confirmed he had any until today. Besides being a creep, what does it matter?" *God above, Dani, quit picking a fight with Seth!*

"It matters because what Seth is good at is necromancy," Angela answered for him. Dani looked confused. "Death magic, Dani. If any of us can kill when and where—and who—he wants to, it's Thantoris. You've been picking a fight all year with the single deadliest person on the planet. I died on that bus, and Seth brought me back." Dani stared at her, and flashed a glance at Alex, who nodded grimly. Seth gave a slight half smile at her expression of dismay. "You remember when we asked the team to leave him alone? If he'd lost it the people harassing him would be dead. Giving everyone the flu was a mild, calculated retaliation for Seth." She paused. "One of the lessons he's been trying to impress on me is that any of us are capable of walking down the halls destroying anything or any one in sight, but with Seth… the death toll would be one hell of a lot higher. Seth took on Johnson's people alone."

"What? You were there! And I know Alex brought the team!"

"I had to be saved, and Alex didn't get there until after the fight was over. I didn't know how to DO anything yet. Even calling out to Seth was a wild I-hope-this-works."

"And it normally wouldn't have." Alex shook his head. "Without that bond that came from him restoring her life, it wouldn't have worked, love."

"Calling to Seth was an act of desperation," she said. Dani gave her a look of incredulity. "No, really. Johnson was an honest to evilness vampire and he was biting my neck, I couldn't move in his grasp, and my tries at calling out produced zilch. Even if he heard me, he could have left me." She looked at Seth. "After the way I talked about him last year, Dani, he easily could have let me twist. He didn't. He's one of the good guys."

They stood there for a few minutes while Angela let some of her emotions out, with Dani comforting her while Seth and Alex kept others away—and her from burning down the woods. Somehow chocolate appeared, rich and dark. She almost laughed when half of it was made up of Halloween skulls. "Thanks. I needed that."

"Not a problem. Yours is the first breakup we've had to deal with, but we've been trying to anticipate. Older siblings are useful for some things," Alex said.

Karen joined her on the bus, squeezing her hand as she sat down. "How are you?"

"Better than I was Saturday," she replied. "I could have reduced Dave to a cinder! My first boyfriend, and my first breakup."

"I hear ya. He's a jerk."

"I can understand part of it. There are things I wasn't telling him. The sort of things," she glowered at Karen, "you figured out that I never told you."

"Hey, that's what you get for falling for an idiot," Karen said playfully, smiling softly at her to lessen the blow.

"First boyfriend, first breakup—and a lecture on control."

"A lecture? I hate it when my parents do that! I just had my heart broken by Chris and here they are with a "teachable moment" that just makes me feel worse about the whole situation and picking better guys..."

"From Seth and Alex," she corrected, and cocked an eyebrow at her friend.

"Seth and Alex?" she asked blankly, then got it. "OH. That kind of control." *What did you do?!!* she mouthed. Some subjects were secret.

Angela took her hand, muttered in Ainu, and *<Telepathy's easier with contact. Just think at me. But I was sparking smoldering fires in Muir Woods.>*

"Shit." *<What were they doing there, anyway?>*

<Seth brought Alex and Dani along to help keep me from doing anything unfixable.>

<This is cool! I get Alex, they're old friends. Why'd he bring Dani? I thought they didn't like each other.>

<They don't. I got good at this from magic tutoring; my sensei sometimes finds it easier to just put the info in my mind. But Alex and Dani were together when he went to get Alex, so he just brought her along, I guess. From what they said, getting to me and making sure I didn't burn down the woods or something was more important than keeping the secret from Dani.>

"Ah." Her phone suddenly tolled.

She looked at it. The text message would seem innocuous, but it was enchanted. Anyone but her saw only the "Sry 2 ear U + D. How r u?" Her eyes saw Seth's true message—and it was in written in hieroglyphics. She groaned.

"Are you getting messages with some sort of secret priority or something?"

"Why?"

"You've been staring at the screen. And I've seen you do that a few times, but it doesn't look like a long message, and you're not texting back."

"I've got a tutor concerned about me. Unfortunately, he expresses that concern by trying to distract me from my troubles with extra work, the first part of which is to translate the text message."

"Translate? Secret code? Or just a foreign language?"

"Hieroglyphics. I think it's in Coptic, too, but I haven't gotten through the hieroglyphics yet."

"Seems like an asinine way to tutor you."

"He does know about Dave. I think he's trying to distract me. Oh, damn. Really, Teach?"

"What?"

<He's handed me three necromantic procedures to practice, and told the other seven of my problem. He's asked everyone to give me some sort of task or practice.>

"Wow. Can I see?"

"One sec." She called up the spell that would let someone else see through her eyes, then gripped Karen's hand a bit tighter. *<You're looking at it through my eyes now. Can you see the hieroglyphics?>*

<Uh-huh. Wow. I didn't even know there was an app that could do that.>

<Half app, half enchantment.>

<Oh, I see.>

<No you don't. But don't worry about it. Close your eyes to eliminate the extra feedback.>

"Hey thanks." The bus stopped; they were at school. "If you want to talk more I'll be around."

"Thanks."

Angela was eating lunch—turkey on rye—in the courtyard when Dani sat down next to her and squeezed her shoulder. "How are you doing?" she asked.

"Okay, I guess," she answered dully. "I've had a lot of extra homework piled on me distracting me." She gave Dani a weak smile.

"How did you come to be a wizard?" Angela's eyes snapped open and she spoke a few words in Ainu to draw a privacy bubble around them.

"Don't get up until I drop the privacy screen," she warned Dani, who shot a question at her. "I'm not sure what Alex's is like, but I've got the air molecules moving at such intense speeds that they'll cut you if you try to cross them… but they're also interdicting the sound we're making so no one else will hear the conversation."

"You know you're talking like a brainiac and not our star receiver?"

She shrugged. "I've been associating with them for most of the past year and a half. After the bus crash, I was marked for murder. If the Round Table hadn't decided to step up and protect me—on their own initiative, without even telling me about it—I'd be dead.

"But that's really why I decided I wanted to learn magic. I'm grateful to them for what they did, but I don't want to depend on someone else to protect me."

"Gotcha. And Seth? You two really were not friends last year."

"It took me most of the year to figure out what had happened," she replied. "Because Reverend Johnson was targeting me, I knew who the people defending me were by the end of the year. But on the back of a killer whale they told me Seth was the one warning them."

"You know who they all are? Alex won't confirm anyone," Dani interrupted.

"We're free to tell anyone we want our own secrets, but not anyone else's, is the reason he won't. Alex took protecting you into his own hands, from what they told me. The others could keep a low profile around you; just step in subtly if they were needed. But Reverend Johnson wasn't targeting you with anything like the intensity he targeted me. I think he was certain he'd killed me, but I was still alive. And when his minions ran into Alex…" she paused to take a sip of lemonade, and cocked an eyebrow at Dani. "Has Alex ever cut loose in front of you? Drawn on his power with no restraint? Do or die?"

Dani considered for a moment. "When I was directly attacked was the first time he openly called up his power in front of me, but it was quick, over and done with, and same with the other times." She shook her head. "So, no, he's never done that. He's never needed to, I don't think. Why?"

"At White Hill's church last year, I watched Seth cut loose with everything he had." She shuddered at the memory, a memory that chilled her even now. "He killed Reverend Johnson's minions and sent their corpses back into the fight. He animated the *wooden boards of the church* to his command. Zombie apocalypse, except half of what he was having the zombies do was drag kids out of the fight. It was really fucking scary to watch. The boy is deadly as anything, Dani. I figured if I knew how to do that, I wouldn't need to worry about… well, anybody. So when I decided I wanted to be able to do that, I asked him to teach me at the beginning of the year.

"I had no idea how much extra work would be involved, though. Novels, textbooks, practice. I've even been learning languages. Grandma had me learning Japanese since I was a baby, and a few years ago I thought it would be cool to know Ainu too, but… Coptic, Nahuatl, Aramaic, Tsalagi, Gaelic! I've gotten to know the creepy Goth over the last few months, and he's not that bad, really. Scary rather than creepy, given what he's capable of doing." Her brief smile was wry.

"Wow. I had no idea," Dani straightened on the bench. "What's it like? The magic?"

"Weird as hell, but so… right at the same time. 'Impossible' seems a word to get around. Turns out my talents are in elemental manipulation. Not like earth, air, fire and water—actual chemical elements. Excite atoms from solid to plasma. That's why I was accidentally starting fires in the woods. I was so angry! I'm glad they were there to keep a disaster from happening." She took a chip. "What did we interrupt?"

"A picnic out at Point Reyes. Alex has this favorite spot, and he has to get us there. Just the two of us, no one else in sight. One minute we were laughing and talking about nothing and the next Seth had appeared. I don't know where he came from, but he said we had to get to you *now*." She reached out to grip Angela's shoulder. "Well, I think he would have left me behind, but Alex insisted."

"He travels by teleporting fairly often. Those were some of the early lessons. I guess Alex has been seriously practicing, though. He couldn't take someone with him last spring."

"Last… oh, that turkey," she giggled. "I shouldn't, I know, but when I heard that story… Did Alex really make you a pair of lightsabers?"

"Almost. Mine was black, thanks to my connection with Seth. It's teal now."

"Can I see it?"

"Sure," she said pulling it out of her book bag. Dani manipulated the switches on it, and seemed disappointed when all it created was a teal light. Angela grinned at her antics. "We modified it. I have to incant to actually turn it into a weapon. As is, I'm just carrying a flashlight replica."

"Smart. That's all just about anyone would think it is anyway. Think Alex would make me one?"

"I don't know. You could ask him." She looked at Dani for a moment. "How much combat training do you have?"

"Until last year, none, but Alex has been teaching me. Sword, pistol, rifle, club, martial arts. I was really tempted to whack Seth one in the woods."

"Bad idea."

"Yeah, I get that. When he dropped me off at home, Alex told me he'd cramp my muscles himself to keep me from giving Seth the idea I was a threat. He's just so…"

"Powerful? Lethal?"

"Morbid? Creepy?"

"I thought so too, before I got to know him. But for god's sake, Dani, quit picking a fight with him! I don't think he'd actually do anything to you, but you're twisting my stomach in knots every time you start in on him, and I don't even want to think about what sort worry you're giving poor Alex! I know any of us can be scary, all of us are dangerous in a way almost no one would believe, but most of us would still leave someone alive. He needs to actively pull back to do that."

"Really? Alex doesn't."

"Really. As he says, death is his domain. In a fury, we reach for what's easiest for us. For Alex, that's weather and enchanting. For me, it's matter manipulation. For Seth, it's death. His giving the team the flu was being merciful."

"We had to forfeit that game," Dani grumbled. She just looked at Dani, who sighed. "But them bullying him was stupid. Seth's predilection for vengeance is well known. And if he's really that dangerous…"

"It is, and he's probably even more dangerous than you think." Angela paused to clean up her lunch trash. "You might want to think about making your own peace with him. I'm not suggesting you become BFFs. Just… polite and civil."

"I'll do that."

$\mathcal{S}$he was sitting in the courtyard, reading a novel Dawn had recommended, when Karen dropped herself next to her. "Morning, lass."

"Good morning," she said. "What's up?"

"I need a favor."

"Name it."

"Stacey broke up with Owen over Christmas. He's being possessive, and it's causing problems for the squad. Can you do something about that?"

"Stacey?"

"Stacey O'Brien. She's a freshman."

"I think so. It won't be immediate. I need to observe them and figure out what to do. I'd rather not have the others step in and reverse it."

"That wouldn't be good."

"Why not have her join us for lunch? I'll get a better idea of what's happening."

"How?"

"I'll probe her mind a little. It won't hurt her, and I'll put a ward on that small corner table."

"Reserved seating. I like it. See you at lunch."

"Thanks for asking me. It's a big confidence boost." She smiled wickedly. "Especially when you could have asked…"

"There's the bell."

Lunch was the usual sandwich, but Stacey's problem was obvious. She pretty much just let Stacey talk while she scanned her mind. What to do about the blonde girl's problem was another question. Owen had been a jealous boyfriend and wasn't willing to admit it was over. And, fuck, here he comes now.

Owen Standish was a big guy, a dark haired senior over six feet. He'd transferred in after getting kicked out of a private school for fighting. He towered over all three girls. "Stacey, we were supposed to have lunch."

"No we weren't. There is no 'us'. There hasn't been for a month. Leave me alone."

"We have lunch every day."

"She said no, Owen. Go away," Karen said.

"She broke up with you, Owen. Accept it and move on," Angela said. She notices movement out of the corner of her eye. Dawn and Jennifer had brought their trays over to a nearby table, and they were speaking in Cornish. Her Cornish wasn't really up to following the conversation yet, but she did hear her name mentioned.

"Who the hell are you?"

"I'm Angela Fujiwara."

"Stay out of it, Angela or I'll…"

"I've got the Lord of Vengeance as a tutor, Owen, and he's been teaching me all sorts of things." Karen and Stacey barely held in guffaws. "Wanna bet I can make your life a living hell if I put my mind to it?" she asked, smiling sweetly. Dawn and Jenny had swallowed their most recent bites and were paying close attention. "Should we discuss your stalking activities with Ms. Zuccaro at the DA's office?" Angela asked. "I got to know her last year, and you're eighteen now. It all gets written down. Or am I going to need my karate training?"

Owen finally seemed to notice the unfriendly looks he was getting from the next table and backed away. Witnesses weren't something he wanted. "Thank you," Stacey said.

<Direct confrontation in public won't do it, will it?> Angela asked Jennifer and Dawn with her mind.

<It probably won't,> Dawn responded. *<He'll probably wait until he can get her alone, and then act.>*

<Then I think I should look into altering his mind. Maybe give him an overriding interest in sports or something.>

<Should do it,> Jennifer responded. *<Want help?>*

<Advice, so I don't screw anything up too badly. Tomorrow?>

<You got it.>

<Do it today,> Dawn said. *<Karen was part of the confrontation, and if he raises his hand against her his life will end as soon as Seth finds out about it.>*

As they finished lunch, Stacey and Karen both turned to her with knowing looks on their faces. "What?" she asked

"Angela, just what…" Karen began in a teasing voice.

"…has Seth been teaching you?" Stacey finished with an arched eyebrow. She initially glared at them, then flashed her eyebrows and smiled. It wasn't like she could tell them.

She modified Owen's mind to a baseball fixation that afternoon. She had to make several attempts, but Jennifer let her do it all. She was proud of her accomplishment. Owen wasn't much of a baseball player. He'd never get beyond the minor leagues.

CHAPTER

36

$\mathcal{A}$ngela broke away from her hurried conversation with Rick to join Seth and Bridget at the study hall table. Their joint privacy bubble was something special; even knowing it was there, what it was, and how to counter it; she still felt the desire to avoid Seth and the uncomfortable feeling in her guts that she needed to hit the girls' room ASAP. Then her countermeasures worked and she felt fine. Seth and Bridget were having an animated discussion on the chemistry assignment; the bubble was more to keep their voices contained than anything else. Bridget looked up at her arrival, while Seth didn't bother; he'd known she was there.

"You and Rick, huh?" Bridget asked as the discussion dwindled. Seth had buried his nose back in a text, muttering to himself. Not the one they were using for class, either. She'd gotten used to that. All of the Nine routinely checked other texts and sources against what their school books said. She'd started doing the same, and she'd found some amazing discrepancies. "Glad to see you're bouncing back quickly from Dave."

"Just the Valentine's Ball. You going with Chris?" Well everyone called it that, but it was official named the Winter Formal.

"No... We broke up last week."

"I'm sorry, I didn't know."

140

"It was mutual. We just weren't really having fun together anymore."

"Still. Sucks. What about you, Seth?"

"It's in here somewhere, I know I read it last week. Give me another minute or two…" Angela blinked and exchanged a look with Bridget, who was shaking slightly with her lips quivering.

"Who are you going to the Valentine's Ball with, Seth?" Angela asked directly.

"I'm not." He turned another page of the chemistry text. "Here it is!" He put the book on the table and pointed at the passage. To Angela, it looked like the words were raised above the page. "There's our problem, Bridget. We're not binding the sulfur into a form that can resist reacting at those temperatures and pressures." Oh. They hadn't been talking about chemistry class at all. They were discussing the terraforming of Venus.

"Oh, damn," she said, She sat back, concentrated, and muttered something. The book's pages started flipping on their own. Bridget looked at it every time it stopped, then set it flipping again. "I guess we're going to have to bind it into more complex rock minerals. We need to save some of it for the biosphere, and those deep sea bacteria would make excellent agents."

"Why aren't you going to the dances, Seth? The prohibition against being close to me is gone. And it's not like there's someone gunning for us anymore, so we don't really need anyone on supernatural watch."

"There are more comfortable places to sit and read a book than those chairs, and more comfortable clothes to wear while doing so than a suit," he replied as he pulled out his tablet. "And being paranoid enough to have someone on supernatural watch is a good idea."

Angela blinked. "Um, you do know it's a dance? Get up, move around? Do something with a pretty girl?"

"I do things with pretty girls quite often. Even now, as a matter of fact. But I've actually been to a dance before, and there's nothing to do at one. So I'll read something at home and monitor things."

"Oh, come on, Seth, there's plenty to do at a dance, even if you're not out on the floor. It's called "socializing"!"

"I can communicate telepathically with almost anyone I want to talk to. In fact, I have to communicate that way, because sooner or later we start drifting into subjects that need to stay secret. And since I'm not going anyway, I might as well provide security."

"You know, Seth, for someone who actually CAN read minds, you can be remarkably obtuse," Bridget broke in as Angela drew back in surprise.

"What do you mean?" Angela asked her.

"His problem is that he thinks no one's going to go with him. He hasn't asked anyone. He probably hasn't even scanned anyone. He's convinced himself that it's a waste of time. And if he went stag, no one would dance with him anyway."

"What? That's nuts."

"It was bad enough as the creepy Goth kid. Now I'm the creepy Goth sexual predator. And I might point out that absolutely no one has demonstrated the slightest interest in me, so why bother?" He spoke mildly and without rancor, but Angela felt blood rushing to her face.

"Wow, Angela. That blush is as spectacular as one of mine!" Bridget said with a laugh.

"I said I was sorry, Seth. And I correct anyone I come across spouting that…"

He shrugged "You essentially believed what we wanted you to believe. Yes, the lingering effects are somewhat annoying, but we could do something about that if it was really that important."

"Not important?" Angela replied. "It means you're not coming to dances, asking no one out. How is this not important, Teach?"

"Seth's one of the people who keeps voting against taking that sort of action, Ange." At Angela's glance, "Yeah, we can fix that. Alex and Teddy have already worked out how."

"Well, I caused it. I'm going to fix it. Want me to see if Karen will go with you?"

"She won't. There's really no point in even asking. And, yes, I'm sure about that. She's going with Steven Meyers, I saw him ask her."

"OK, so maybe she won't go to this one. Seth, get your butt to the dance. My turn to teach you something."

"I'm fine, Angela." He took on a bit of a dreamy look and sound as he said, "Besides, they sold out."

"Oh, you're not getting out of it that easily, Seth. You're coming with me. No excuses. If you're sick I'll cure you. Even if I didn't already have an extra ticket we could make one easily enough. Snowflake and I will meet you and Orcinus. And, yes, I will make sure no one thinks he's anything but a horse," Bridget said. "The school was wowed at Alex and Keisha using limos. Now they'll see real romance is on horseback!"

"And if I simply don't want to go?" he asked. His voice was mild, but his eyes were a flat black.

Bridget sighed. "Well, if you don't want to go, I won't actually make you. You're right about that. But I want to go. I want to go with some one. So let me put it another way. Will you do me the favor as a friend and come with me? We can discuss secret matters in Gaelic and Coptic if you want and drive the rest of the school nuts."

CHAPTER

37

In environmental news, it appears that the Steller's Sea Cow was not hunted to extinction shortly after discovery in the eighteenth century. A relict population has been discovered by Russian scientists in and around Bering Island.

In a swirl of bubbles Malcolm brought them to… a cave half filled with water, a couple of tables, and a bookshelf. It smelled of the sea. "Welcome to the Grotto," he said.

"Almost as chilly here as the Mausoleum. Glad I brought the sweater."

"I'd have preferred you left it behind, since we're practicing summoning things to you." She shrugged. He smiled.

"We sort of have two options when we need something. Easiest is to summon the specific item we need directly to us. The hard method is to make it on the spot. You might have an easier time than the rest of us, if your matter manipulation lets you directly convert energy to matter. Otherwise we need to draw the atoms from somewhere."

"We're stealing?"

"If we need a pencil and know where one is, it's easiest to summon that pencil, rather than some random pencil."

"Familiarity helps. Okay, makes sense. But most mass produced stuff is kind of the same."

Malcolm let out a sonar click of agreement. "Which is why knowing where something is helps. But if we don't know, or don't have one…

yeah, we just sort of take. Keisha and Teddy figured out a spell that lets us pay for it from a private account if we need to."

"How private?"

"Very, since we put magical security in place over and above the toughest encryption we could come up with. Jennifer will need to add you to the spell so you can access it, too."

"Cool. Okay. How does this work?"

"Envision the item you're wanting in your grasp. If you know where it is, you can get the picture better."

"Okay." They spent time practicing, from summoning things from her room or locker to creating things on the spot. Even in the chill of the Grotto, she was sweating. Then she smelled something delicious.

"What is that?"

"Seafood stew. Mostly shellfish—clams, mussels, oysters. Kelp. I thought we should probably do lunch here and some more work this afternoon."

"I like that idea," she replied, smiling at him. The changing light patterns of the Grotto made for a very strange atmosphere. Crabs crawled up out of the water, picking away at the rocks.

"What's your name, Malcolm?"

"Cuan. I remember Seth challenging you to find out, but I'm not sure why."

"I'm trying to figure out who wants to wipe my mind or let me die."

"No one now. Being cautious about threats is smart in our situation."

"I'm threat?"

"Not now that you're one of us. Remember when Bridget and I opened the door to let you in?"

"Yeah. How is that whale?"

"He's fine. But the reason I brought it up was to make the point that at that point, you had enough knowledge to be a threat to us. You weren't one of us. But you are now. We can and do trust you to keep the secrets. Ready to practice some more?"

"Yeah, I am. Let's get back to it."

Liz and Joy met her at the park by the library to work on their book reports. Liz and Joy were reading the same book. She'd read it back in November on Jennifer's recommendation.

"You didn't go out for volleyball this year," Joy said.

"I've got too much else on my plate," she replied. "My tutor gave me some stuff to practice after I get done here."

"Oh."

"Did you get the math homework?"

"Yeah, with a little help from Shevaun and Karen."

"Could you explain it to me?" Liz asked

"Sure," she said, pulling the sheet towards her. They went through the algebra problems together, and by the end Liz and Joy both were getting the assignment they'd gotten. Neither was in Angela's class for math.

"How'd you get so good at math?"

"Study and hard work. You know that group? Jenny, Dawn, Bridget, Keisha, Karen, Shevaun. They work their tails off and make anyone hanging out with them do it too. I've learned a lot, more than from some of the teachers."

"Makes sense. What'd you think of this book?"

"Not that great. I thought it was pretty boring, but Jenny thought it was important enough to be on the syllabus, so we read it. Teachers sure pick boring books."

"Oh, great. Do you remember enough for the report?"

"Yeah, I do." Jenny had had her practicing data storage spells when she read the book.

"Well, let's get to it…"

"Morning, Dawn. We're working on invocations today, right? Battle magics?" Angela wore her jacket and jeans, while Dawn appeared ready for basketball other than a coat.

"Manipulation of energy, which has a lot more application than fights. But it is very useful in combat," she replied. "Since you manipulate states of matter, this out to be fairly easy for you."

"What I'm more worried about is that I'm more likely to raise something to plasma when a rapid oxidation would do fine."

"Fire isn't quite as hot and destructive as plasma. But it also has other applications. Bridget mentioned you making plasma to provide heat and light when you were reviving the sea cow. A small spark would have worked better, with less danger if you lost control."

"True. So what you do is basically…"

"It doesn't neatly fit any scientific explanation, but applied chemistry would work if you needed one. But first, let's get to Sunholme." With that, Dawn transported them to a hot, shaded room high up on a mountain. Sunlight streamed in, and they tossed their coats on the couch.

"Okay," Dawn said. "Let's start with the easy—fire." She promptly unleashed a bolt at the target Dawn had set up.

"No, that was plasma."

"Whoops!"

"Try again, just… flame." They worked at that for a while. Fortunately Seth wasn't bad at it, and he'd passed on what he knew. Soon she was blasting away only a beat or two behind Dawn. They worked at all sorts of energy and chemical manipulations before Dawn called a halt.

"Thanks," she said. "I didn't want to ask for one."

"Angela, what we're doing here is stressful. If you need a break, tell me. Seth told me not to overtax you, even though this seems fairly easy for you." She smiled. "You're already more precise than we were. But we need to build your stamina, not wear it down. The better prepared you are the sooner you'll graduate to full member."

"Is that when I find out your name?"

"I'm Grianne," she said. "I know Seth challenged you to find out, but… I'm not that secretive."

That Monday was the start of swim practice. A couple of hours in the afternoon, getting out of the pool into chilly temperatures. Malcolm caught up with her on the way to the Aquatic Center. "Go ahead and win, Ange. Just not by much."

"Still concealing it?"

"Yeah. You and Dawn are both on the team and competing, but she already knows this. You'll need to modulate." She waved to Karen, Joy, Carmen, and Liz. Her friends had been on the team the previous year. So had Malcolm--the clear star of the team--and Julian Kanekawa. Dawn hadn't been, but having her there wasn't going to be a problem.

Everyone was wearing purple speedos and most wore yellow caps. Dawn proved to not be quite as fast as she was. Or…

"Why didn't you go out for the team last year?"

"I'm not that good at hiding." She gestured at the sun, low on the horizon. "I tend to shine at what I do. But we need to conceal just what we're capable of doing. So I just didn't go out for a sport where I'd shine in individual performance. Soccer and basketball are more my thing."

"So that's why you pass so much. I remember watching your games. You never play forward and always pass the ball to someone else. Your points scored per game are low."

"Oui. I'm a good teammate, though. I feed the ball to the scorers." She paused and toweled off her hair. She used a cloth cap, not a rubber one. "Have you been practicing the magic we worked on?"

"Yeah. I need to practice it. I'm too prone to shifting elements instead of adjusting chemical bonds."

"You do just fine when you remember to do it that way. Words of power are the key. Are you being picked up?"

"Yeah, Mom's going to be here in another couple minutes."

"I officially rode my bike, so I'll ride off. See you tomorrow."

CHAPTER

40

"Angela, good morning. Do you know what we're doing today?"

"Divination magics, finding things out."

"Precisely. Fortunately, this isn't big or flashy. We don't really need to go anywhere."

"No crystal balls?"

"Nor magic mirrors, or even television sets," Keisha replied. At Angela's raised eyebrow, she said, "When Seth enchanted his TV and remote, most of us thought that was a really good idea and enchanted our own. Bridget went whole hog and enchanted her parents' movie screen, too."

"She hasn't mentioned that."

"If all you're doing with divination at her place is watching the guys' shower, I'm not surprised. Her parents disapprove. And while they know about her, she has a pretty good relationship with them. She doesn't like disappointing them."

She blushed. "Does the device make a difference?"

"For learning things, not really. The only real benefit to a crystal ball or something like that is a three-dimensional image. A big screen is actually somewhat better, as it lets you see details you otherwise couldn't."

"Seth told me that sometimes people can pick up that they're being watched."

"They can, and it's actually fairly easy for us to do. It's one of the reasons we use foci in the showers. One time I was curious about where Malcolm was diving in the Mediterranean and I scryed him. I almost immediately got a telepathic question from him asking me what was up."

"I see."

"It's also possible for people without our abilities to realize it's happening. Seth was watching Karen several times and mentioned she'd picked up on it. Mike's noticed when I'm watching him."

"You sure about that?"

"Positive. Mike's even said hi."

"How'd you know about…?" she asked.

"It's over. No real need to get into it." She paused. "I'm not trying to squelch your curiosity, Ange, but it's sort of sensitive. You can ask Seth sometime, although he may not answer."

"Oh, gotcha. Kara."

"Process of elimination?"

"Yeah. I knew Bridget and Jennifer, and Dawn just told me. Which left one girl—you."

"Not bad. But back to divination. Visual methods are only part of it, as are other sensory enhancement techniques. A lot of the spells I use—such as for working the financial angles—are more about rapidly collating data to predict how things will go, since there aren't any angels or demons or faeries or anything like that to ask."

"How do you get the information?"

"I'm not entirely sure. It comes in, and it's accurate. Our theories are fairly involved; I'll email them to you."

"Thanks. I'm not entirely sure when I'll have time to get caught up. What should we focus on first?"

"Let's focus on someone we know. Try to find Rick."

She concentrated, watching the TV, and then Rick appeared. He was at baseball practice, judging by the bat in his hand.

"Good job. Can you hold the image?"

"I'm okay. Why hold the image? He's just doing batting practice."

"Veritas. But it's more about you than how interesting what you're seeing is. I thought Rick would be interesting to you."

"It was a good evening. But I'm not that into him."

"Well, then, let's pick someone else. How about Ms. Kravitz?"

"The biology teacher? Okay. I think she's going to be just as boring as Rick."

"But you got an A-plus in her class, so it's not like you've got an issue with her."

"True." They spent their time peeking in on various people. Mrs. Kravitz was grading papers. When the moved on to the Round Table, they were picked up almost immediately…and challenged. Fortunately, Dawn and Jennifer were inclined to say hello.

CHAPTER

41

"So where's this secret study place you're dragging me off to have the oh-so-secret conversations?"

"Dead volcanic seamount in the middle of the Pacific."

"Oookaaay, if you don't wanna tell me…" Karen paused, looking at her face. "No, that's not it. You just told me where it was and I wasn't believing you."

"Building it took some effort, and it's not done yet. But most importantly, it's private, as in no one is getting in without me knowing it."

"Angela," Seth said as he passed them in the hall. "Study session after school." He smiled briefly. "Be ready for dirty work. Hello, Karen."

"Got it. Muddy?"

"Graveyard." Oh, ugh. Necromancy.

"What's with the face?"

"Never mind."

"Just who are they, anyway? You haven't said," Karen asked as he walked on.

"As a lawyer might say, I'm not going to confirm or deny any one is or isn't one of the group." She shrugged. "That's not MY secret. Speaking of which…" Once Seth was around the corner and no one else was in sight, she shifted them to her hidey-hole.

The great one-way window onto the sea clearly impressed Karen.

"Wow," she said, gazing out at the shark swimming by.

The wheels were still turning in Karen's head, though, despite the distraction. "Okay. I'm ready to name them even if you aren't. Last year you were actively avoiding Seth and you weren't hanging out with Keisha Johnson or Teddy Pope or Solomon Levison or Dawn Takugawa. I'd be shocked if they weren't in the coven, or whatever you guys call it. And I already knew about Alex Menendez, you let that slip when Dave dumped you. Which means Bridget Sullivan, Jennifer O'Neill, Danielle Serafini, and Malcolm Muir are the others in the group." She paused and cocked her own head. "I got one wrong didn't I? Dani's Alex's girlfriend, your teammate, but she doesn't really hang with the others. There are only ten of you, and I just named them all."

"Assuming you're right… everyone else would be more powerful and experienced than I am." But she could tell that Karen wasn't buying the non-confirming act.

"But why is Seth doing it? Penance? Why *not* Bridget? I mean if I'm right about her being one of them, I'd have thought she'd be perfectly happy to teach you."

"Karen, if you're right, and I'm not saying you are, it might be because I never wanted to need someone else's protection ever again, and the boy I'd watched kill with a word and rip a vampire to shreds made for a damn impressive display of 'don't even think about fucking with me.' He would be the single most dangerous member of a very dangerous group." She shrugged. "If I did see that, I might have asked him to teach me, and persisted when he tried to suggest someone not as dark and gloomy. And in the process learned he's the person who brought me back from death, saved my life, alerted the others to the threats to me and came to rescue me when I begged his help. And," she continued, "I might have learned that what I thought happened was how he brought me back, so was kind of a wash."

"Okay, that makes sense. So he did the same to me? Creep put his hand…"

"On you there was a bullet hole he poked a finger through to establish the contact."

"There's no hole in my shirt!"

"Not anymore. He's the necromancer. He's very good at controlling dead tissue, so he repaired your cotton shirt. I watched it stitch itself back together. I'm not sure why he left the blood for me to clean up," she explained.

"Okay. But you didn't bring me here to have this talk just to show off or to praise him, so what's with the oh-so-secret? It's not like I forgot you had that lecture from him when Dave dumped you."

She gave her friend a crooked smile. "Well, there aren't a lot of people I can trust enough to show off too, you know. I wanted to impress on you the need for silence. We're not ready to come into the open yet. Some of the things we're planning are big enough that they will get noticed, but we want to be the ones who decide when and how to let the world know what we can do. The possibility of pitchforks and torches worries us more about the collateral damage than actually threatening us. We've all got different focuses… Foci? I can't remember."

"For example?" She asked with an arched brow.

"I do states of matter and elements. Not like earth, air, fire and water. The periodic table. Solid to plasma. Yeah." She turned to the plates of sushi she'd sent earlier, handing one to Karen. "If you want to talk, I'm more than happy to. But we haven't made a decision on you yet, and I'm still an apprentice; I don't get a vote. I haven't even mentioned that you've put t together. Please don't talk with anyone else, though. If anything is likely to provoke a bad response, that is."

"What could they do?"

"What *couldn't* they do. No, really. This group… we can modify memories. You've seen the news reports about there being Stellar's sea cows off Alaska? I watched three of them resurrect the sea cows. I've ridden a unicorn, spoken with the memories of my dead grandmother given form, been fed on by a vampire, lived through a zombie apocalypse, walked on Mars, swum on Venus. We're having active discussions on how to terraform them, plus the moon. Karen, I teleported us here, remember? One second in in the hall at school, the next here?"

"Whoa, okay, okay…"

She leaned in to give her point added emphasis, brushing aside Karen's placating gestures. "Karen, sometimes it scares me what I'm learning how to do. It sure as hell scares me what the others are capable of doing when they put their minds to it, and they don't think small. I mean, the ten of us, all by ourselves, making Mars, Venus, and the moon habitable? Tell you what, one Christmas I'll take you to Olympus Mons or Ishtar Terra or the flag they left on the moon. Your choice."

"Really? Cool. Can I bring my camera?"

"No problem. I brought mine when I got taken along."

"When can we go?"

Angela smiled at her eagerness. "Not yet. I don't have enough control or endurance to keep us both alive, not outside the Castle or the Temple—a couple of caves they made sealed tight with air—and we don't have a secure spot on the moon yet. For that matter, we usually take two of us as a team and a third monitoring us back on Earth, ready and able to teleport us home. Unless you want to admit to Seth you know it was him…"

"No, no, that's ok, lass. I think I'm happier with him pining for me from a distance."

"Is that right?" she said as they finished off the sushi. A quick spell cleaned everything up. As Angela scryed the hall to make sure the hall was clear for them to get them back, Karen gave her a long look.

"He can do that too, right?"

"I learned how from him."

"So he could be watching me any time he wants to?"

"Don't be so paranoid."

C H A P T E R

42

"Good morning, Mother Elaine," she greeted her church's pastor on a chill Saturday morning.

"Good morning, Angela. Were you waiting for me?"

"If you have a moment," Angela said.

"Of course. Let's go in to the adjunct, that's where the office is. The work on the Church itself should be taken care of by the end of next month." They walked over to the white building next to St. George's, amiably talking about school and her parents. They sat down in a pair of battered armchairs that were still very comfortable. Mother Elaine had a painting of the Crucifixion on one white wall, a large bookcase, and photos of herself from around the world at Anglican churches.

"So what did you want to see me about?" She busied herself with the pot. "Coffee?"

"Thank you. This goes no further than us?" she asked.

"Of course Angela."

"I've been keeping something from my parents. I've been keeping it from almost everybody."

"What's wrong?"

Angela didn't say anything. Exposing this much was hard, and she knew most of the others would find saying something to a member of the clergy foolish.

"Are you pregnant?"

"Oh, no, nothing like that. I'm not even seeing anyone now."

"Well, that means you're not dating someone they'd disapprove of. What about your grades?"

"Straight A's," she said with a smile.

"Then?"

"I'm a wizard. There's not a lot of other people I can discuss it with. Most of the others who know are my fellow wizards… the people who've been teaching me."

"Oh? Angela, I know you started playing that game…"

"Fiat lux." She gave Mother Elaine a tight smile as the source-less teal light came into being and the pastor sat bolt upright. "No, Mother Elaine, I'm not delusional enough to believe those spells work. But this usually ends an argument. I could levitate you to the ceiling, if you like."

"Alright. Okay. Um… I think I need a drink."

"The other thing that light does is leave no trace. Your bottle appears almost empty, though. Allow me." A few words in Ainu refilled the bottle.

"Wow. Thank you, Angela. So who are these teachers of yours?" She shrugged. "No one I'm going to name or confirm without their permission. And I don't think they'd give it in your case."

"What do you mean? Why not?"

She got up and paced a bit. "We decide who knows about us, and not all of us have told our families. Others have families that know perfectly well, and take advantage of what my colleagues can do. It's easier to take risks if you know there's someone along that can teleport you to safety.

"But, they don't know you. They aren't going to trust you. To the point of wiping your memory."

"You can do that?"

"Yes." She crossed her arms over her chest and leaned against the wall. Then she told Mother Elaine about her year. "I hope you don't mind, but I'm sort of using you as a warm up for letting my parents in."

"Well, from what you've told me, you seem to have fallen in with a remarkable group. Not just in terms of the magic they're capable of, but they're out to save the world."

"It bothers me how ruthless they can be. Up at White Hill," she shuddered.

"Your rescuer was alone, with the exception of you. He was facing a vampire and a bunch of people loyal to it. Yet he still managed to remove the innocents from the fight. And you didn't say so, but I think, from your story, that he's the same person who restored you and your friend Karen to life?"

"Yeah, he is."

"Then I'll add your colleagues to my prayers, but they sound like good people trying to do the right thing and use their power wisely."

"They're more impressed by Spider-man than the parable of talents."

"Wisdom can come from many places," Elaine said with a smile As Angela pulled her sweater back on, she asked, "Did you forget a hat and gloves?"

"I don't need them anymore, really. The sweater was fine on Bering Island in November. It's enchanted." She smiled and waved on her way out the door. She almost skipped down the hall. Talking to Mother Elaine had been a real help.

43

"Jennifer, what do we do if someone figures out who we are, what we can do?" she asked in their study session. Well, it was supposed to be her and Bridget, but Bridget was running late and had asked Jennifer to fill in.

"It depends," Jennifer replied. "On you, on what they do. Do you trust them to keep the secret? If she's not a threat, if she understands the need to keep quiet about it all, no need to do anything. If not, we can modify her memories. It's a little harder than if we'd told them—we need to go in after the clues that led them to the truth in the first place and fudge those, too, or they'll figure it out again."

Jennifer demonstrated the gestures she was trying to learn, ones that helped with transformative spells. "Good, Angela. I felt the power there. Were you just curious for future reference, or is there a potential problem? You're instinctively good with states of matter, and I know you've been doing some transforming of inanimate objects. So let's try transforming yourself. A gorilla would be easiest."

"Gorilla? Why a gorilla?"

"Thanks to the evolutionary closeness between humans and gorillas, the body plan is similar and they're close in size. You're not needing to grow a tail, shrink down, or change arms to wings. But getting back to your question, is there a potential problem the rest of us need to be aware of?"

Lying to one of the nine was a bad idea. Jennifer was clearly alert and probing. "A friend of mine was noting that I was hanging out with a different group of people from last year," she said. "I'm not getting the extra curricular activities she was expecting me to. And my grades have drastically improved, I'm studying all the time. I mean, I'm hanging out with Seth, and I accused him of sexual assault last year!"

"True," she said, pondering for a moment. "You told Karen about yourself and she slotted everything else in place?" She smiled at Angela's thunderstruck expression. "I've never said there was anything wrong with Karen's brain, even though she's a cheerleader, and you're bringing this to me instead of to Seth, who's your primary tutor for learning how to use your power. Which means there's a reason you aren't asking him. He's had a crush on her for years now. Even asked her out once. That didn't go so well."

"She's never mentioned that. Neither has he," she said in amazement that Seth had ever actually asked someone out.

"I don't know her that well, but Seth...I'm not surprised he's never mentioned it. Not if he doesn't have a reason to."

"Okay, I can see that. But what do I do about it? I don't really want to do something like that to her, Felarie. We've been friends since second grade. Well, here goes on the transformation."

"I hear you. I hear you," she said considering. She raised her gingery brows as Angela concentrated, spoke a few words in Ainu, and felt her form slip into a gorilla... in uncomfortably tight clothes.

"Sometimes it's better to be naked."

"I'm so sorry I'm late!" Bridget burst out as she appeared in a swirl of green. "Dad really needed me at the launch of that cruise liner in Florida, and I missed the time change." She looked at Angela in the extremely tight clothing and exploded with laughter. "Wow, Angela. That's a new look for you!"

Her waistband was digging in to her. Her arms had split her shirtsleeves; her thighs had done the same thing to her shorts; and her tennis shoes had burst open. Jennifer summoned up a mirror, and she saw herself—a gorilla in the tattered remnants of her clothes. She put her hand over her eyes, and the other girls started laughing harder.

When Bridget had recovered, she said, "Changing yourself in clothes doesn't work very well. The proportions are all wrong. Trying to change *back* can be even more complicated, especially if you've taken a shape that doesn't have the same limbs. Go back to normal."

The painful tightness eased, but her clothes were still ruined. She looked down at herself in despair. "Don't worry about the clothes," Jennifer said, "fixing them can be part of the lesson."

"When it comes to the clothes, you can either ditch them or enchant them. Alex can enchant them on the fly pretty easily; the rest of us take a little longer, so ditching them is easier. Unless it's something we really like and want to go through the whole process of enchanting them. I know Malcolm's enchanted a speedo so he can shift at the beach without a spectacle."

CHAPTER

44

The Valentine's Ball was as spectacular as she could have wished to get her mind off Dave. For one thing, Alex's and Keisha's arrivals in limousines were eclipsed by Bridget and Seth arriving on horseback… but Bridget had actually found an old side-saddle to not interfere with her deep forest green gown. Seth, of course, was in a black and white tuxedo with bone studs. As he handed her down, there were a number of sighs and exclamations. They provided feed bags and went in to join the Round Table. Angela noticed that Bridget almost had a smirk on her face.

Shevaun spun into a chair at their table and fanned herself. She was wearing a silver-gray silk gown that really showed off her hourglass figure. "Whoosh!" she said. "Six in a row! I need a break."

"Oh, that gown is gorgeous, Shevaun," Bridget said. "That silvery gray really works for you!"

"Thanks! Did you really come by horse?"

"In the saddle. Snowflake's outside. He's getting buddy-buddy with Orcinus for the evening and munching on corn." Keisha's lips quivered a bit at the non-correction.

"Those stallions are awesome. I don't get to ride much."

"I thought you had a horse," Angela said. "I've seen your Personal page, that's a great pinto."

"I do. Dad adopted her off the set, but we don't have a lot of room, so she's back at Standing Rock with my aunt and cousins."

"Standing Rock? Really? You have family there?"

"Yeah, it's where my parents are from. Why?"

"During Spring Break, Dad has a meeting he's supposed to be at there. He's got meetings in Nairobi and Sydney the same week, though. He's worked it out so he can make all of them, just barely, but I was wondering if I might be able to sub in for him at Standing Rock. I've been wanting to see the bison herd and was planning to accompany him anyway, but if I could fully sub in for him I'd appreciate it. He's getting seriously jetlagged, and the week after that he's supposed to be in Monaco and Singapore."

"I have no idea. What's the meeting about?"

"I'm not sure, I think it's just a formality, that everything's already worked out. I don't think I'd be making any decisions."

"Bison steaks?" Angela asked.

Bridget shrugged. "One of the biggest sellers in the restaurants, but it may be with some craftsmen for the gift shops. He thinks authentic handicrafts are better than mass-produced crap."

"What's he do?" Rick asked.

"You know the Wildlife Casinos?" Seth answered.

"Yeah, never serve beef, chicken or lamb. Why? He's an executive for them? Cool."

"Not exactly," Angela said. "He's the owner."

"Which is why Bridget might be able to sub in for him if the meetings are ceremonial formalities," Shevaun said. "I'll ask my aunt."

"Thanks."

"It's not like she's on the council or anything, though."

"But she still might have a better idea of who to ask than Bridget," Julian said. "Even I get the occasional call asking me to talk to someone back in Hawai'i, and there's a cultural thing at UC Santa Cruz I've been invited to."

"If it doesn't work out, no big deal, I'm just trying to ease the travel burden."

"Sure. Like I said, I'll ask."

The current dance finished, and she and Rick made their way back to a side table for a brief rest. Across the room, she saw the Round Table had claimed a pair of tables of their own, and Seth was in animated conversation with Bridget, their pads on the table in front of them, plus a high end laptop, and even a couple of really thick reference books. They'd left a couple of seats open for her if she wanted to join them, but she and Rick were over by Carmen and Karen. As they came back from dancing the other full members would make their own contributions to the discussion, and Bridget got up to dance fairly often. Shevaun, Karen, and Julian frequently stopped by the Round Table, but didn't sit down, unable to comprehend the discussion.

"What a pair of…" Rick said, glancing over at them.

"Geniuses," Angela filled in. He looked at her. "Rick, pay attention. What are they speaking?"

"Gibberish."

"I didn't ask what they were saying, Rick. I asked what they were speaking, and no, it's not gibberish. They're speaking two different languages, and understanding each other perfectly well."

"Oh, come on, Angie…"

"No, really. She's speaking Gaelic. He's speaking Coptic. And judging by the tablets, they're having a discussion simultaneously on Martian planetology and arctic ecology." Actually, she suspected they were discussing terraforming Mars—her Gaelic and Coptic weren't up to following their rapid conversation yet—but that was one of the secret projects. She shook her head. "Rick, really. Leave Seth alone. I got to know his friends last year, and I get what he was trying to do." She looked directly at him. "He threatened Alex once with replacing our Sportyade with a laxative. He's kicking ass in chem. He's creative and knows how to get himself a little payback."

Rick said, "I should be worried about a stupid little creep like Seth?"

Angela looked at him. "Rick, do you trust me?"

"Of course, Ange. Why do you ask?"

"Then believe me when I tell you that the boy known as the God of Death doesn't like you, is fully capable of sending you to the hospital—or the morgue—and will do it without the slightest hesitation if you give him cause." She looked into his eyes. "Even if it weren't just a really dickish move to harass him, and the rest of the Round Table will back him up, me included. Mess with one of us, you mess with all of us." She cocked her head as the music started. "Ah, the song I requested. Please excuse me, Rick."

"Wait, if you requested it, why aren't we dancing it?"

"Because there's someone I owe a big, splashy, and public apology to, and this is it."

She walked away from Rick, her teal gown rustling as she moved. She concentrated and muttered in Ainu so that a silence fell over everyone. As she got to her target, she dropped into a low curtsey as the girl stopped talking and poked the boy who hadn't seen her. "Seth, may I have this dance?" her quiet question carried to the entire room.

He slowly stood, blinking. Bridget grinned broadly at them. The rest of the Nine poked and winked at each other. Dani seemed astonished that Angela would have approached Seth.

"Of course, Angela," he said quietly, his voice carrying to the whole table. Just for her ears, he said, "I've been shown the steps but fair warning that I suck."

He did suck. He kneed her, stepped on her feet, dropped the lead, held her too tightly, held her too loose, indicated a spin and didn't catch her. He barely seemed to know what he was doing. If Seth hadn't quietly speaking healing spells, she would have been limping and bruised when the dance ended and she got go back to her seat. As it was, her feet were even feeling better than they should for spending the night in heels. But when it was over, he bowed low.

"Thank you, Angela."

"Good job, Angela. Now, if you'll allow me, I forgot to teach him to dance," Keisha said. She and Mike pulled Seth off into a corner of the room and began showing him how.

"That looked really painful," Rick said.

"I feel better than before I asked," she replied. "Let's dance!"

CHAPTER

45

The day after the dance, Keisha cornered her in the study hall. "Let me guess, you haven't learned how to make shoes comfortable as well as great looking?"

"No," she replied.

"One of those things your tutor might simply not think about," she said. "He doesn't wear heels. We've got a practice session down in San Jose this weekend, and I'm evaluating the team. Why don't you join us?"

"Ok, sure. Sounds great."

She caught a ride with Keisha in the Sphinxes' limo down to the practice facility. "Where's Mike?" she asked.

"He's got a treatment this weekend. Once it's knocked down some more, I'm going to use some of Bridget's DNA techniques to make sure it doesn't happen again. That should be in June, right before I leave for southern Africa."

"Oh? What are you doing?"

"Archeology in Great Zimbabwe and Tanzania."

"Cool."

"Did you bring your shoes?"

"Yeah. What do we need to do?"

"We're not actually transforming them to something comfortable. I don't think that can actually be done, and still have heels. This is an actual enchantment."

"Cool. Alex told me that in an enchantment, everything needs to go in."

"He's the expert, so pay attention to him. I think the last time he enchanted shoes, though, it was to give his hiking boots wings, like Hermes. Something about a Doom Turkey." They grinned at each other. "Basically it's the same as anything else, just a difference in what you want them to do."

"And the more things I want them to do, the more complex it is."

"Correct." She took a drink from one of the microbrew sodas she favored. This one happened to be cherry. "I'd suggest just making them comfortable, maybe automatically resize. Once you've got that down, you can do the same with your other shoes."

"What about changing shape?"

"That's doable. It's considerably more complicated."

"Yeah, but if I've got a pair I can switch to anything I never have to buy shoes again, do I?"

Keisha's smile was brilliant. "Not unless you lose these or want to."

"Cool."

$\mathcal{D}$ad dropped her off at Wild Dog Ranch—Bridget's place. "I got a text from her to head for the barn, so I'll see you later, Dad."

"Have a fun party!" Bridget's sixteenth. But she hadn't gotten a text, just a telepathic communication. She trotted around the flagstone path to where the barn was, but didn't see Bridget. Then something huge moved through the redwoods. "Wow, Bridget. Jungle girl you are!"

"Not quite. Gomph here isn't an elephant. Gomph, say hello to Angela. She's a friend." The trunk came up between the massively curving tusks and sniffed her all over as she stood still.

"He sure looks like one! A little furrier, but…"

"He's my birthday present."

"An elephant?"

"From Seth."

"From Seth? Then no, not an elephant. A *mammoth*."

"Yeppers! A California native Columbian mammoth. Dad's already got the permit paperwork filed, and it's going to go through, though we are listing him as *Elephas*. Private zoo involved in endangered species breeding."

"Ah. In that case," she concentrated and spoke a few words in Ainu, causing a Satsuma orange to appear in her hand, "pleased to meet you,

Gomph." She held out the orange. The mammoth took it with his trunk and ate it, then wrapped his trunk around her for a playful squeeze. The strength and power of that trunk were amazing.

Bridget grinned. Gomph let her go, and raised his trunk to lower Bridget to the ground. "Okay, Gomph, thank you. There are some more treats for you in the barn; can you stay in there, please?" The huge head nodded, gave Bridget a hug with the trunk, and Gomph walked into the massive barn.

They headed up to the house. "With the exception of Seth, you're the first arrival, and I wanted to show Gomph off to someone. I've got enough people coming who don't know the truth that I need to keep most of the critters out of the way. Gomph might get mistaken for an elephant, but I don't want to rely on that."

"And so the unicorns…"

"Are safely away. Thanks for coming a little early."

"Not a problem. Thanks for introducing me to Gomph."

"He'll meet all the Round Table sooner or later."

"You know, how you deal with animals is really uncanny. You just ask them to do something and they do it. I know you're careful, but…"

She nodded. "Sooner or later I'll slip up and do it where the uninitiated can see me do it. I know. But it's hard not to do, y'know? Animals like me. Solly has a lot of the same problem."

"Yeah, but even plants obey you!"

"I know. Still, it's hard, a lot of the time not to do it. We don't exactly have natural environments on Mars and Venus that produce plants and animals."

"Mind a suggestion?"

"Shoot."

"Let's put a few new caverns in as bio caverns. Something approximating a day-night cycle, plants and animals to be released onto the surface, when there's enough atmosphere."

"Thanks, Angela. Great minds and all that. We've been preparing to do it already."

"Can I help?"

"You'll be a big help. Matter manipulation would be enormously useful. The only reason you're not already onboard is that we didn't want to disrupt your training. But soon you'll be working on projects."

"Cool. Any idea when?"

"I'm not your tutor," she replied. "I have only a general idea of where you're at, outside of the sessions with me. You'll have to ask him. And there he is." Seth was sitting on the porch in his usual black.

"Ask me what?"

"When's graduation?"

"Two Junes from now," he replied. "But if you mean when you're ready to join the rest of us…I'm not sure. We've only taught ourselves before you, so there's no real measuring stick for it. By August, at least. Maybe sooner."

"That fast? Less than a year?"

"That fast. You're advancing rapidly." He smiled at the confusion. "There's no point in keeping you at the apprentice level any longer than necessary."

"I…uh, thanks, Seth. I won't let you down."

"Good to know. I'm sure you won't. Party should be almost ready to start, right, Bridget?"

"Yeppers! And no bugging out early this year, Seth."

"Aye-aye, ma'am."

"Bug out early? How often does that happen?"

"Depends. When it's just us, it doesn't. Add outsiders, and he flees."

Seth may not have left the party early, but he didn't really seem to be there, either. Angela thoroughly enjoyed it; Bridget's Dad had set up a casino atmosphere for her, complete with games and prizes for the winners. She was surprised when Bridget's friend Kaitlin won the poker tournament and the prize. None of the Round Tablers had used their magic to win.

CHAPTER

47

Angela was at the Sphinxes-Valkyries game as Keisha's guest, but she left five minutes into the first quarter to give Keisha and Mike some privacy. Fortunately, Seth was by himself in his box when she knocked. The door swung open on its own. "Come in, Angela," he said without bothering to look through the door. As she expected, his box had a big couch, a table, some chairs, a mini fridge, sink, bathroom, and a couple of reclining chairs. Seth had chosen one of the latter.

"Thanks. They want to be alone."

"When don't they?" he asked rhetorically. He nodded at the field. "I hope Fiona Kendrick is up for this, after Natalie Buoanano got hurt last week," he said as Kendrick took her first snap of the game.

"Your receivers have been doing a lot better this year," she commented as Beth Jones caught the pass for a first down. "Damn, I can't wait until I can try out to play professionally."

He cocked an eyebrow, looking at her intently. "You have family in Nevada, right?"

"Yeah," she said absently, her eyes on the field. "Oh, good catch! My Aunt Marilyn is an executive chef at one of the Vegas casinos. Why?"

"We voted to expand the league on Friday."

"Cool! What city?"

"That's up to you." He picked his root beer back up.

Angela sat watching the Valkyries score, when the implications caught up to her and she dropped her glass. "ME?!"

He smiled. "You. This is something we can do without more training."

"Um, Seth, I have no where near the sort of money it would take! I don't even know where to begin." She quickly spoke a spell to repair the glass and send the root beer and ice to the sink.

"Keisha set up an account we can use to loan it to you. Among other things, we use league meetings as a smokescreen for getting together for one of the secret projects." He smiled briefly. "Friday's meeting was at the Temple."

"Fuck." She sat still for a minute. "I never thought that I'd be in this situation, Seth."

"Why not?"

"I thought I'd need to get my hands on my college money for Keisha to work her financial witchery on, and..."

"The only way you can think of to do that involves controlling your parents' minds?"

"Actually, that possibility hadn't even crossed my mind," she told him.

"It didn't cross ours, either, until Teddy had problems and solved them that way." He paused to take a drink and watch the Valkyries recover an onside kick. "But like I said, we'll loan it to you."

"I was expecting to play for one of you one day, not own my own team!"

"I expect Dani will end up on a team. The Avengers, unless there's a break up there."

"The rest of you guys don't think she's good enough?"

"The rest of us don't think the inevitable fight with Alex is worth it. Putting the girlfriend of one of the other owners on the team?"

She smiled. "Yeah, I can see that. Should I be thinking of a team name?"

"Do you want to do this? We're not going to make you, of course, but you're so rapidly catching up with the rest of us in terms of what you can do, we thought having an additional cover story would be a good idea. I doubt you'll need tutoring in Junior Year, but "league owners' meetings" make good cover."

"You know, I hadn't even thought it would happen, but yeah, I do. I'll have a group to practice with."

"Well, that's one way to look at it." She raised her glass in salute, and he returned it. Remarkable how comfortable she'd gotten with him, she thought.

Once the game was over, she and Seth made their way to the other side of the stadium to meet Keisha and Mike at the stadium's restaurant. The stadium was undergoing some retrofitting to meet new earthquake standards, scaffolding and ropes all over the place. They saw Keisha drop back from Mike to talk to a team of reporters. Seth moved ahead of Angela to go join Keisha for the impromptu press conference. Mike smiled and waved to them, moving forward to stand in front of some scaffolding when there was a horrid tearing sound.

The scaffolding ripped away and smashed into him, a rope cutting through his neck as the rest of it crushed him. "MIIIIKE!" Keisha screamed. Angela and Seth were with her in seconds, holding her back from heading towards the wreckage.

Keisha looked at Seth. "Do something!" she demanded, almost pleaded.

Seth shook his head slowly, and the compassion in his voice was something she almost never heard from him. "Oh, Keisha. I'm so sorry, but no."

"Seth, it's Mike…" Angela said, the tears coming down her face as well.

"I know."

"You brought Angela back," Keisha said fiercely.

"In a creek bed, where there was no one to know and no one to see. If you want this, we need the others."

Keisha glared at him, but held his eyes and nodded, and led the way into her box.

"Seth, can't she do it herself?" Angela asked sotto voce.

"Of course she can," Seth replied in the same way as they followed her. "Unless I actively oppose her."

"You have a problem with bringing Mike back?"

"No. That it's Mike isn't the problem. That he died on national television is the problem. If she does this, or more precisely, if I do at her request, since she'd be barely functional for a week if she did it herself, we're out in the open, and we long since decided that THAT is a decision for all of us."

She considered that. "Even if you did it in the middle of the night, in an empty morgue, with no one around and you departing immediately, it would still be an impossibility. The cameras would never stop. Mike might not know what happened, or how, or why. And much as I like Mike, he's really not cut out to be the object of veneration, was he?"

They shared a sad smile. "No. And if I stayed…"

"Karen and I can keep the secret in part because no one knows to ask either of us the question. I didn't have a concussion, but I was bleeding from my head. I cleaned Karen up, so there's not even a hole in her shirt. Sooner or later Mike would tell someone, because they wouldn't leave him alone."

"Precisely. But I think she's going to need to hear it from people besides me." *<And I've never mentioned reviving Karen to them.>*

As they entered Keisha's box, they saw the others already gathered. "Seth," Alex said without preamble. "Why are you opposing raising Mike?"

Seth looked at each of them. "Have we changed our agreement? No one informed me."

Teddy raised his hand, and glared at Alex. "No. We have not. Keisha burst out the problem while you were still instructing Angela." He looked around. The others nodded. "Please, Seth. State your case."

"Mike Wu is dead. He was killed in an accident on national television, decapitating him and crushing his body. The question is not whether or not Mike should be raised. By itself, I don't care one way or the other. The question is whether or not we come out in the open. Mike cannot be revived without it being an obvious impossibility." They looked at each other, and a couple of them actually glared at Keisha.

"I know I don't have a vote. May I speak?" Angela asked. Bridget nodded, glancing at the others. No one said anything.

"I've known Mike since I was ten. I've been his friend for five years. The very idea of never seeing him again fills me with pain.

"But. I don't think he would handle being revived well. I didn't, and I didn't even know what had happened. I do not believe that he would be able to keep the secret if you asked him to. Nor would he be able to deal with the religious adoration that might come with being resurrected. I'm sorry Keisha. But we need to remember Mike. Not raise him." Now that she had said what she had to say, she let the tears run freely.

Jennifer turned to Keisha. Her tears hadn't abated in the slightest. Jennifer's voice was caring but insistent. "Keisha, is what they say accurate? Did Mike indeed die on camera?"

"Yes, but he is trustworthy. He will keep the secret!"

"Angela," Dawn asked, "why do you believe Mike will not do so? You have."

Angela wiped her eyes. "This isn't about what sort of person Mike was. I am sure he would try. But it's not the same. I was revived in a ravine. Only Thantoris and Toranos were present, and they already knew. I did not know I had been dead. Had I not been marked for death, I may never have known.

"If revived, consider what Mike will face. He was dead. Everyone will know it. He will be asked how he came to be alive again. The questions will not stop. For me, they never started. Only ten people knew what happened, and we are all in this room. It would be considered a miracle. Would he let that stand or tell them he knows it wasn't one?" The seven others nodded and turned to each other. The discussion took place telepathically, and Angela, Keisha, and Seth were excluded. Then they turned back.

Teddy spoke. "Keisha. I am sorry. I must support Seth. For one, I don't like the support we'd be giving to religion. For another, we are not ready to come out of the shadows yet."

Dawn said, "We agreed that a public death would not be revived. We all liked Mike, Keisha, but our agreement stands."

"I'd rather have Mike back, personally. I think it may be time to come out in the open." Alex's tone was almost defiant.

"I think we're being too cautious," Solly said. "Let Mike be revived and draw anyone else with these abilities into the open."

"Mike's death is a tragedy. Thantoris, however, is correct," Bridget said. "Solly's suggestion of a lure may have future merit, but we're not prepared for it now. Until we're all agreed that it's time to go public, we should not publically do the impossible." She raised a hand. "Kara, I know. It was remotely possible small populations survived unknown. You'll notice no large flocks of passenger pigeons."

"I'm already out to my folks," Malcolm said with a shrug. "I'm fine with reviving anyone. Speaking of which, Thantoris, about the Antarctic cetacean project...?"

"I really hate being put in this position again as the deciding vote," Jennifer said. "I agree we're not ready to come into the open. But there's another possibility. We could provide a fake corpse and revive him elsewhere. Keisha, would Mike be able to accept being confined to the Castle or the Temple? Never speaking to, never interacting with, his family—just us, and those few we brought with us? When we don't know how long that will be?"

"Damn, Felarie, you don't make it easy. I'd be willing to support that, Thantoris," Bridget said. "We could use someone on permanent assignment to either, but I'm not so sure Mike would accept it."

"You're talking about replacing death with indefinite imprisonment." Solly said. "I'm not in favor of that, not unless he was on board with it."

"Keisha, do we have any sort of advance directive from Mike? A lot of the people at the hospice have them, so we know their wishes," asked Seth.

"That's an idea. Can't you ask him now?" Angela asked.

"No," Seth replied with a dreadful finality. "Kara never asked for or prepared a memory vessel," he lifted his little flashlight, "and if the question was never put to him, the answer isn't in his memories, so I can't extract it."

"But you built my grandmother a ghost from memories…"

"The difference is that I had the benefit of a number of long talks with your grandmother and was able to use my abilities to help her remember more, which I was able to store. That let me use my power to give her form and voice," he said. "I never had that sort of interaction with Mike."

"I want him back, Seth."

"I know, Kara. I wish I could spare you this pain. Should we bring him back elsewhere?"

"Oy." Solly closed his eyes and bent his head. "I know we're talking about Mike. I know, Keisha, that you are in deep pain. But I can't justify imprisoning Mike just to spare your pain. He will resent it. Are you willing, Keisha, to keep your lover imprisoned? Adjust his mind to keep him happy?"

"There is no equivalency in power between us and a boyfriend or girlfriend," Jennifer said. "This should really be Mike's decision, not ours."

"Only one way to give it to him now," Teddy said. "His resurrection would need to come with an immediate suicide option."

"That's not much of an option."

"I know."

"Welcome back, Mike."

"Did anyone ever tell you your hands are really, really cold, Seth?"

"Angela, when I did the same to her."

"Welcome to Venus, Mike," Angela said with a worried smile.

"We're where? And why do you guys look like you raided Seth's closet for clothes? And why am I naked? And…" Keisha stopped the questions with a passionate kiss. Alex cleared his throat.

"Mike," Alex said, "this isn't going to be easy. You are now officially dead on Earth. We just came from your funeral. You died on camera before a nation-wide audience. Seth, as it turns out, is capable of reversing death. In resurrecting you, we modified your memory a bit to take the memory of the moment of death from you. We're happy to have you back—Keisha most of all—but bringing you back comes at a cost, and we don't know if it's one you're willing to pay."

"You're naked because we transferred your ruined and bloody clothes to the dead clone we left in your place," Bridget said. "Getting back to where we are, yes, we're at our secret, concealed base on the planet Venus. You'll probably notice the lighter gravity. Be careful when you get up."

"What was that about a price?"

"We're not ready to go public with what we can do back home. We don't have a plan or timetable. Which means that you need to stay here—or at our base on Mars."

"What?"

"No communication with anyone other than us. No internet. No phone. And you can't go home."

"Whoa, guys, I don't know about that. I mean, it's cool that we're on Venus and that I'm alive, but I don't like these restrictions. How can you…"

"Mike. I hate to put it like this, but this isn't a negotiation," Malcolm said bluntly.

Seth pulled a pyramidal black vial from his pack. "If you prefer, you can drink this. It will be painless, I assure you."

"Be a prisoner or a suicide?"

"Mike, don't think of it like that…" Keisha said, crushed.

"Keisha." Malcolm was reproving, and she subsided.

"We don't like it either, Mike," Dawn put in

Seth pursed his lips and said, "We're not the only ones who can do what we do. We've destroyed at least two others, far older than us. We'd rather not have our families and friends targeted. But if we went public, what then? How ugly would it get when I refused to bring back the dead?"

"And if I don't want to stay? I don't, you know."

"We were worried about that. Jennifer?" Teddy asked.

She shook her head regretfully. "He doesn't have it." The indigo glow faded from her eyes.

"Forgive me, Mike. I wanted to be sure of that before I answered you. The truth here is harsh. We think it better that you understand clearly. You physically can't leave without one of us deliberately taking you. Even if you grabbed hold when we teleport away, you wouldn't come along unless we chose to bring you. This is Venus, and there's no way out of this set of rooms to the surface or back to Earth. The atmosphere is lethal, crushing pressure, acid for rain, immense heat," Teddy said. "Or there's Seth's vial."

"Mike, please, stay with me… us. Maybe we'll figure something else out." Keisha said, pleading.

"Keish, darling…. I'm not ready to die. Again. I hate the restrictions, though. You guys are worse than my parents. Oh, god, they don't know!"

"No, they don't. And for the time being, they're not going to." He considered that for several moments then turned to Jennifer. "I don't have what?"

"Angela died in that bus crash at the beginning of last year. Since they were in a ravine with only Seth and Alex present, Seth resurrected her, and they didn't tell her. At the beginning of this year, she asked to learn how to access power. It turns out she has just as much potential for it as the rest of us. We hadn't picked that up in her before so we wondered if the act of resurrection triggers it. It doesn't, or you'd have the same potential now."

"The key problem you represented was that the accident killed you in public, on camera, and in obvious fashion. If you'd choked to death in Keisha's box, I'd have revived you there and no one would know the difference. If there was a chance you could have survived, we'd have revived you right there, and you'd be hurt but alive. But that wasn't an option."

"Guys, I get it. Thank you."

"Let me show you around," Keisha said.

"I'm still not wearing anything." Keisha's eyes glowed orange and she spoke in Cushitic. Shirt, pants, boxers, socks, even shoes appeared. Mike's eyes went wide.

"Yeah. That's the sort of thing we can do if we don't worry about exposure. We'll leave you two to it," Teddy said. "I need to get back."

"I know you told me you were a sorceress, but…" Teddy gave him a crooked grin before he spoke in Aramaic and vanished. "Where'd he go?"

"Inferno, I expect." At Mike's expression, "We all have a little hidey-hole. Teddy's is called Inferno. Mine's the Grove," said Bridget. "It lets us disguise what we're talking about."

"So yours would be the Opera?" he asked Keisha.

She smiled. "Yes. This is the Temple. The Castle's on Mars. We don't have a name for our proposed base on the Moon yet."

"It's kind of small here still. We don't really use the place for more than sleeping and occasionally eating. Malcolm's made what's essentially a magic version of a Star Trek replicator, and we've loaded it with a bunch of the foods we like. We'll come up more often to keep you company, and we should be able to let you visit Mars, too," Alex said.

"Is there anything I can do?"

"Yes, actually. We've prepared simulations as detailed as we can think of for the terraforming projects. Could you run them and take notes? You can fiddle with some of the parameters. We're looking towards the best way to do this."

"Sure."

"Since you'll have a lot more space once the atmosphere is breathable and the temperature is tolerable," Bridget grinned. Mike grinned back. Angela went with Bridget when they left Keisha and Mike to explore.

"I just had an idea. What about concealed trips back to Earth? Not necessarily home, I get that. But could Keish and I go to, say, Disneyland in disguise? I know you guys can take animal forms. Could you transform *me*?"

They looked at each other. "We could probably give it a shot," Solly said.

CHAPTER

49

<Fawedea, I beseech thine aid. Angela, can you hear me?> She jumped at Seth's voice in her head. He sounded distant, and weak—not at all like his usual self. Fortunately Karen was out of the room at the moment.

<Yes, I can hear you>

<I'm barely getting an awareness of contact. Can you speak aloud?>

"*<Someone will hear,>*" she said, projecting mentally as well as speaking aloud.

<I can't move a muscle. Something's blocking the connection. I can't feel myself at all. I'm willing to risk it if you are.>

"*<Not exactly time to be doing that, Teach,>*" she said, giggling.

"What's funny?" Karen asked as she came back in with a bowl of caramel corn. Angela held up a hand and brought her cell phone to her with a few quick words in Ainu. She didn't bother turning it on as she brought it to her ear. "Hi Seth. Kind of creepy you calling, with me here. Were you spying on me? Didja have it on vibrate?" Then her mouth fell open in an "oh" of understanding as what she'd witnessed caught up with her.

<*Can you help me?*> His weak voice was sounding desperate now. "<I don't know, Teach. I'll try. I don't know how much I can do from here, though, and I can't get away. I do have someone listening in.>"

"Something's wrong, isn't it? What's happening?" Karen asked. Angela nodded at the first, then shook her head.

"<Teach, can you give me an idea of what I need to do? Should I call Morgan le Fay?>" Karen mouthed /Morgan le Fay?/ at her, but Angela shook her head. Calling Jennifer 'Morgan le Fay' was the best she could do, along with projecting a picture of her to Seth. Angela returned her focus to him.

<*I may need her,*> came the grim reply.

"<Is it just your mind, or what? 'Cause you are reaching me. That may just be due to our bond.>" Karen tapped her own temple and waggled her hand.

<*I've tried to access my power several times, Angela. I don't know if I succeeded.*>

"<Oh, fuck.>"

"What?" Karen asked.

"<Let me give her a call. I'll be right back to you.>" she said to Seth. "Karen, he's in real trouble and I need to get someone out to him. Could you go run interference? Let no one come down here? I'm going to need to tighten the security bubble."

"What do you mean, real trouble?"

"He's been lashing out blindly with necromancy to kill whoever is holding him, and he doesn't even know who or what he's killed doing it. Which means I need to speak a name you don't have permission to hear."

"Oh, fuck is right. Be back soon. We need some Cokes." She closed the door tightly as she left.

"Felarie, hear me. I beseech thine aid." <*Ugh. What's up Fawedea?*>

"Thantoris is being held against his will, he doesn't know if he has control of his power, and he's lashing out."

<*Fuck.*> She could sense Jennifer calling up her power and going looking. <*I'm not picking anything up. Fuck. See if you can help him. We're going to need Kara at least.*>

<Need me for what?> Keisha asked. *<C'mon, guys. I told I was going to be on Venus today.>*

"Finding where Thantoris is being held." Angela said grimly. "He's lashing out blindly and can barely communicate with me."

<That's not good.>

"You have a gift for understatement."

<Angela, get back to Seth. If that means teleporting to him, do it and send up a flare. We'll get him back don't worry. We'll modify any minds near you if we have to, but the Goth of Death is a loose nuke. We've gotta get him back.>

"Understood."

"Hey, Ange, how's he doing?" Karen knocked and came back in. "Don't know yet, but the others have been alerted. I may need to teleport away."

"*<Seth, I've gotten in touch with the Round Table and they're searching for you now, but they weren't picking up you just now.>*"

<Thanks. I think I hear someone coming.> He was trying to put on a brave front, but she could pick up the fear from his mind.

"*<Can you give me any teleportation landmarks? Anything that will let me get to you?>*"

<I wish I could. I haven't been able to open my eyes.> "*<Seth will you let me in?>*"

<What? Like give you control of my body? For all I know you'll be trapped in here with me.>

"*<I get you. But I might be able to defend you and give the others a beacon to find your body so she can purge you of whatever is blocking your conscious control of your power.>*"

<You've still got someone listening in, don't you? Okay, I'll do what I can to get you in here.>

"*<Yeah, I do. But here goes, Teach.>*" She lay down on her bed, closed her eyes, and stretched out her mind along the link she shared with Seth. "Don't disturb me unless someone teleports in here, and then let them do it," she told Karen, putting her ear buds in. Karen's agreement was barely audible. Angela concentrated completely on the link to Seth.

She found her way to Seth's mind. He seemed to be in full defense, for he'd erected slick shields to prevent any access, shields that to her perception gleamed black. Shit, she thought. No way in.

Well, maybe there was. A secret way, maybe? She tried rapping on the shields. That didn't do anything but make her hand ache. Hand? She'd envisioned herself floating in front of a vast wall. She breathed deeply and tried something else. "Thantoris! I am Fawedea! I am here to help you! Let me in!" It seemed to get colder, almost as if a blizzard was brewing up.

"Seth! I can't help from out here!" The icy cold increased again, and this time she used her magic to enhance her senses and focus on her link with Seth. There! That shield…she got closer and closer, but it seemed farther away than ever. She remembered this from some of the novels Seth had passed her. She closed her eyes and went straight at it, letting her link to Seth guide her. When she no longer felt the cold, she opened her eyes.

She was standing, not floating any more, on the other side. She stood before a massive black pyramid, but unlike any she'd seen in pictures. There were cylindrical towers at the corners. There was a gatehouse built into the base, a balcony overhanging it, and the surface looked even slicker than those shields. She looked at the formidable defenses at the gate, and flew up to the balcony without a second thought.

The balcony went nowhere. It was a trap; she recognized the multitude of lethal defenses Seth had erected. Fortunately, she'd seen many of them before, when she took a look to get ideas for her own defenses, so she didn't approach any closer. No other choice; in through the front door. Fuck. Well, maybe this is like "Lord of the Rings". She spoke the words for friend in twelve languages, starting with Tolkien's dwarvish and elvish, moved on to Coptic, and then through all other languages of the Round Table. None of them worked.

"Thantoris Master of Death, I come in peace! I am Fawedea, Mistress of the Elements! In Karen's name, open and admit me, your friend!" She didn't know why she added that last bit. But it worked. A bone bridge extended itself out from below the gatehouse.

She floated across, and found herself surrounded by skeletal knights. The symbols on their armor she recognized from game night descriptions and pictures—kingfishers, stags, crowns, harps, chalices, and roses. It took her a moment to recognize that what she wasn't seeing. Not a single cross, crescent, or star of David. Not even an ankh. Well, Seth could set up his mental guardians as he wished. The dead knights formed up around her and she walked into the pyramid fortress of Seth's mind.

She looked at the walls as she did so, and realized, on the long trek, that she was seeing images from Seth's memory. Karen featured prominently in them, and so did the rest of the Round Table. She even recognized scenes between herself and Seth, and saw last year through his eyes. She recognized naked images of Bridget, Dawn, Keisha, and Jennifer, obviously from that episode in the woods. There were other naked images of the four girls, obviously in preparation for transforming themselves, glamour nudes downloaded from the internet. Being a boy was weird. Oddly enough, the images of her and Karen were always clothed…

She felt herself falling down a slide, and landed in a torture chamber. A large figure was bound with spiked cuffs to a metal table, his head completely covered, another leather band across his—the figure was naked—chest with a third over his stomach. Blood seeped from his wrists, legs, head, chest, and it seemed a dozen other places. Seth!

She dashed over to him and removed the mask covering his face, to find it had also prevented him from speaking with an ugly, ridged mouthpiece. She started to undo the straps to find metal—bent spikes— holding him down still. "Don't," he said.

"Seth, it's metal, I'll have it off in no time."

"It's not metal."

"Oh, it's just how you're envisioning it? God damn it."

"Such language, invoking a deity here."

"You know, I never considered it from that angle. Keisha's come back from her Venusian booty call and Jennifer's heading the search."

"I don't think we should refer to it that way around Mike."

She grinned. "Ok, probably not. Karen's running interference with my parents, so let's see about getting you back in control of yourself."

"Do you think you're up to it?"

"One way to find out, and it can give Keisha a position fix"

She reached out with her own mind and power, trying to discover what was holding him back. She ran into a figurative wall, and bounced. "Ow. Maybe that should wait for Bridget and Jenny. I think, though, that I can take control of your body. It seems to be fine."

She muttered in Ainu and expanded her mind, then opened her eyes. This wasn't her room. It was still a bedroom, she was laying on a bed. She was bound hand and foot by steel cuffs, and a few quiet words in Ainu melted them away. It sounded strange, much deeper… she was using Seth's throat. She raised her head and looked around. The hot metal had burned through the blanket. She swung herself out of the bed… and stumbled. Seth was several inches taller that she was, and she wasn't used to it. His feet were bare… well, so was the rest of him. She looked down and twitched his hips. Interesting. She reached down.

<Do you mind?>

<Sorry.> The room had no windows, just white painted walls. Cement. Either it was a precaution against a breakout, or they knew not to put dead tissue around Seth. But solid concrete was no real barrier to her, and she drew on her power to melt the concrete away. She was rewarded with a man's scream, and put up a defensive shield.

As the melted mass flowed away, she saw a burning couch and a rough-looking man frantically putting out the fire on another one. Her version of lava melted the guns, and she levitated Seth, moving forward. The guard took a look at him, pulled out a pistol—an automatic—and fired desperately. The bullets harmlessly bounced off her shield. Angela melted the gun; he screamed at the liquid steel running over his hand.

<Gotcha!> Keisha said in her mind. *<Jenny, Bridget, and Dawn are on their way.>*

<Why them?> she wanted to know.

<Jenny's the most powerful of us, Dawn's the battle magic specialist, and Bridget's the person best suited to purging me.> Seth said. *<I'd probably be with them if we needed to get someone else.>*

<Angela, since you're tapped into Seth's mind, can you let me into yours?> Bridget asked.

<Sure. Can you do something through me?>

<I'm not sure.> Suddenly, though, she felt Bridget's presence.

<Okay, now…> Bridget mused as a woman walked in holding a gun. Angela melted that one too. The woman screamed at the molten metal hitting her hand. She floated Seth's body out through the wall, and a barrier of pure force. Suddenly Bridget, Dawn, and Jennifer were standing beside Seth. Seth screamed as Bridget and Jennifer swept their joint power through him. She felt the barriers within him fall away, as if he was rising from a table, and quickly ceded control back to him, just as a group of men burst in through the door.

She stayed behind in Seth's mind to make sure he got out, but she could easily tell the difference between his power and hers. The hint of decision, the sense of finality, the dreadful certainty of something that could not be resisted that characterized Seth's power wasn't at all like hers. The might and power of the Goth of Death coursed by her and she felt it snuff out his assailant's life like a candle, turning his brainstem into so much jelly. Even knowing why, and how, she felt like weeping as Seth's implacable gaze swung around the room even as he stood still. The other girls barely had to do anything as Seth exterminated the opposition, although Dawn sent a blast of electricity through the wires to short everything out.

With that, Angela withdrew back to her own mind. Her face was wet. "What's wrong?" Karen asked. "Is Seth okay?"

"He's fine. Using my power let the others find him, and three of them are there now. They'll make sure he gets out and home." She gulped air, wiped her face, and composed herself.

"Then WHAT, lass?"

"I was still in his mind when he took control back, and I… tasted the edges of his power." She shuddered and felt the tears come again.

"When I first asked him to teach me, he warned me his power had to do with darkness and death. I knew that. I've felt it as he worked with me. I never suspected just how much he was shielding me from it, keeping me from sharing the burden. It's one of the reasons he helps so much with Gaia's projects. That's what lets him experience the joy of bringing life back to the world, not taking it."

"Damn. I... I... had no idea. You sound admiring and horrified all at the same time."

"Fairly accurate description." She shook her head, then gave Karen a quirky smile, and teased, "No shame in dating him, you know. Even if you die on a date, he'll make sure you're home safe."

Karen groaned and threw a pillow at her. "You first."

"If I don't have a boyfriend by the next dance, I might just do that. We've been teaching him, and he's not as much of a disaster as he used to be."

CHAPTER

50

It was a week later that she met up with Solly for defensive instruction.

"Hey, Ange," Solly said. "Your protection spells have been pretty good, from what I've seen."

"Thanks."

"Don't mention it, Ange. But it looks like most of your defenses are of the stop everything variety. Which isn't surprising, as it's the approach Seth favors. What we're going to work on is stopping specific things and letting others through. Put up a privacy sphere."

She did. "Okay. Pretty good. You're still whipping air molecules to enormous speeds, I see. It's effective, but it just a little limited. There are going to be times when you want to let someone through without bloodying them or dropping the protection of the sphere."

"I see that. What do you suggest?"

"Image what you want to specifically block is one method. A second is to image what you don't want to block, and block everything else." He paused, then "I know you've seen Seth's privacy screen. He uses the fact that a lot of people don't want to talk to him. His screen induces fear, nausea, disgust, even horror. He can set it to kill someone trying to come through. Well, we can all do that. Malcolm wants to keep people getting in, their lungs start filling with water. But Seth's more common method is a powerful force effect that lets only light, oxygen and carbon dioxide in and out."

"That's important?"

"It is. You can block everything if you want. But sooner or later you'll run out of air, and too much carbon dioxide will make your lungs burn. As for light…"

"Okay, gotcha."

"They practiced for several hours, building a new privacy screen. The new one—once she'd practiced more—would build on her elemental mastery, chilling or heating anyone coming near, much more of a layered defense. She could also follow Alex's example of winds picking up speed until it reached her current level. When the session ended, she had far more ideas on how to defend herself.

"Thank you, Solly."

"No problem. We all need to learn defenses."

"May I know your name, so I can bespeak you?"

"I am Bestarion. I am known as "the Fertile One"." He shrugged. "My parents are fertility doctors. You're rapidly approaching our levels of power. I think you won't be an apprentice much longer. Have you picked a team name yet?"

"Well, that tells me who the last one is. Thank you, Bestarion. I think it'll be the Las Vegas Gorgons, teal and copper. Medusa's head on the helmet.

"Mazel tov."

Wednesday she finally got back to the Sunset Dojo for her karate training. She hadn't been entirely letting it lapse, but Alex as a sparring partner wasn't much more knowledgeable than she was. The real difficult was the enhancements she'd been applying to herself. The Round Tablers were faster and stronger than normal people. She'd beat Seth or Dawn hands down; they weren't trained. But they'd still move faster than anyone she trained against, and once they got a grip they could break bones with their bare hands. If they bothered; either of them had far more deadly options available to them.

Sunset Dojo had several mats, dummies, and weight bags people were working out on. Next door was a weight room with several exercise machines. Angela waved to her friend Merelan Choy as she sparred with Tom Guganov.

"Hey, Ange. Long time." Larissa Ito was one of the instructors. She was shorter than Angela by half a foot and probably fifty pounds lighter.

"I'm sorry, Sensei. My time has been eaten up and I'm not very good at extending it yet."

"Well, let's see where you're at at the moment. Work out on the bag while I evaluate." She spent half an hour on kicks and punches on the bag when Larissa called a halt. "Okay, you still know the basics. Obviously you need tougher opposition. You aren't even sweating or breathing hard. Work out with Wendy." Wendy Mosaddegh was a little older than she was.

Wendy had been well trained. That was clear; she pushed the pace. She came at Angela high, low, and everywhere in between. Angela unconsciously increased her speed and strength to compensate. She ended up launching Wendy into the wall.

"Oh, I'm so sorry, Wendy! Are you okay?" She was by her side quickly, using some of the healing techniques she'd learned from Seth and Bridget. They wouldn't cure everything. She'd still be injured, just not as badly as she might have been.

"Oof. I think I'm okay."

"Angela, come next door for a few minutes," Sensei Larissa said. "I want to get a feel for something. Get on the bench press."

She lay down and gripped the bar. She moved it easily. After a few moments, Sensei Larissa fiddled with the controls again. It wasn't any harder to move now. A few more adjustments and it was as easy as ever.

"Okay, Angela, you can stop."

"Well?"

She shook her head. "If I hadn't seen it, I wouldn't have believed it. Look down." She did. She'd set the resistance to maximum. "You weren't straining. You weren't even breathing hard. What happened to you?"

"I can't discuss it."

"I'm afraid I have to insist."

"The secrets involved are not mine alone. Some of those involved have rather drastic ideas on how to preserve them from any outsider. So I'm not going to tell. I like you too much."

Larissa gave her a sad smile. "Thank you for that, but you aren't aware of your own strength. Until you are, I can't risk you injuring another student. You tossed Wendy like a paper dummy. You're welcome to work out on the dummies, but not other students."

She digested that. There was another option--Alex. He was just as strong as she was, and they could treat each other's injuries. She'd just have to work out with him on Venus or Mars.

"I understand, Sensei, and will comply."

CHAPTER
51

Angela found Teddy in the library, and she stood there regarding him. She concentrated, spoke quietly in Ainu, and the privacy bubble formed. No one else needed to hear this conversation.

"Problem, Angela?" Teddy asked, flipping somewhat idly through the Royal Journal of Genetics. As he came to an article that interested him he made a bit of red ribbon and marked his place.

"You're Angoral."

He gave her a crooked grin. "You're right."

"What did I do to you?"

"Nothing as far as I'm aware. Why?" He turned his attention back to the journal.

She looked at him in stunned amazement. "You wanted me dead! You wanted my mind altered!"

He looked up blinking. "You're misunderstanding me and my motives. Sit, please." He waited until she did so. "You aren't the question, Angela. You never were. To put it another way, it wasn't about you. No more than Mike was. Resurrection—any resurrection—carries risk. So do our names. So does almost anything we do, but what Seth calls "obvious impossibilities" are even worse. If we are to maintain our secrets, and as a result our freedom to do what we need or wish to, we have to be a lot more ruthless about who knows and who doesn't.

"Your resurrection was carried out without even consulting the rest of us. I see why they considered it safe, with only him and Alex knowing you'd died in the crash. Considering Seth's specialty, it would have been hard to actually stop him." He snorted. "Hard? Next to impossible."

"He's that good at it?"

"To stop one of us from exercising our specialty isn't easy, even for something like my illusions. It's hard enough even when it's an interest, like Alex and storms. As long as your body was reasonably intact, it would have required more than one of us acting, deliberately and in concert, to stop him from exercising his specialty. Remember when Dani got roofied? And if one of us had wavered, or stopped paying attention? He'd have accomplished it, even if he temporarily gave up and did it later. You've seen him resurrect the sea cows. Working with what, nearly fossil remains? The truth of his power is that if Seth wants to resurrect something, sooner or later he'll be able to do it. If Seth wants to kill something, sooner or later he'll be able to do that—and even faster. The only real ways to stop him would have been to destroy your body—down to discarded hairs—or to have made your death public and gotten him to stop himself.

"But at the same time… it had consequences. It led to you learning about us. It led to a battle with Reverend Johnson, and before we were ready for it. Don't get me wrong. I'm glad Seth won. I'm glad the body count was as low as it was. I'm glad you're alive. But when Seth goes into battle, the dead pile up. He's our most terrible… option. And he knows it. If it had happened on our time table, when we were ready, Johnson the vampire might have been the only fatality, or even survived." He paused. "We have enormous power. We have the responsibility to use that power as wisely and carefully as we can. Any of us can kill by an act of will, and only how really differs. Seth's focus on death makes it more certain that his attack is lethal, but I know you've seen Alex's electrical discharges, and just because Seth's method is to snuff out a life like a candle doesn't mean the rest of us can't do exactly the same thing. It's just more tiring for us, and doesn't come as quickly to us. Consider what you're capable of, in dealing with that guy in Golden Gate Park, and you're the newest at this. We need to use it as wisely as we can. We're too capable of too much damage if we don't.

"So, I play devil's advocate. I try to think of the worst consequences. The more people who know, the bigger the chance of exposure. Imagine what might happen if reversing death were seen as blasphemous by some groups. How many more would Seth have to kill to defend himself? And it's not like the rest of us would sit on the sidelines, not this time. He excoriated us for doing that last year, and he was right. So far the rest of us haven't killed anyone, but that can change.

"As for the name thing. You've heard the phrase "speak of the devil and he appears"? We're not really that bad about it, but as you know, we're still attuned to them. And it's ANYONE speaking them, doesn't matter who. I don't particularly care for the idea that I need to stop and pay attention when just anyone says it." He paused, cocked his head, and smiled. "Speaking of which, are you just going to use Fawedea from game?"

"Thanks for telling me where you were coming from. It makes more sense now, and I'm glad I don't actually need to worry about you."

"No problem."

CHAPTER

52

"Ange! I'm taking the boat out to the Farallons this weekend. Want to come?" Bridget asked. "We can go diving."

"I need to ask…"

"Yes, there will be adults with us," she said, but that wink was definitely there. "My mom's a field biologist, remember? She wants some samples and such."

Angela switched to Gaelic. "Who's actually going?"

"You, me, Jennifer, maybe some others from the Round Table. Mom's already out there; this is a supply run in a lot of ways," Bridget replied in the same language. "She's got a research permit that lets her and some assistants dive out there."

"Aren't there a lot of sharks…" she started, then felt a little silly when Bridget arched an eyebrow. "But you'll be there, so that's not a real concern, is it?"

"No, not really. Have you told your mom about your abilities?" She shook her head. "That would involve telling them who I was learning it from…"

"It's your choice. We'll keep your secret. If you want to bring my name into it, OK."

"I sort of have to bring you into it, or it wouldn't make sense."

"Well, if they raise concerns about sharks, Mom's dive master. They've got cages, the works out there. No need to worry. And if necessary, I've never seen a shark flash-broiled in the water before."

A dolphin leaped out of the water directly towards the stern of the boat. As she watched, it sprouted legs, the flippers became arms and hands, and Bridget landed lightly. Her landing set the whole boat rocking, but Seth kept his balance as he handed her a towel. She thanked him and unselfconsciously began drying herself off. As she raised the towel to her hair, she caught Angela's expression. "What's wrong, Ange?"

"Don't you mind that Seth is right there?" she asked.

"Mind? Why would I mind?" Seth had turned back to examining a dead shark they'd pulled out of the water.

"The only thing you're wearing is the towel he handed you?"

Bridget shrugged with the towel over her hair. "It's just natural me. Nothing he hasn't seen before." At Angela's widened eyes, Bridget continued, "Oh, right, you weren't with us yet last summer when Dawn botched invisibility." She laughed in rueful memory.

"What happened?"

"She turned our clothes invisible," Seth interjected. "It took about three hours for us to figure out what exactly she'd done and how to reverse it."

"Those poor hikers!" Bridget laughed. "After half an hour of not looking at each other, Keisha got frustrated and suggested we just get on with it. We were perfectly normal and everything."

"And then those hikers found us. We wiped their memories, but nothing worked to get us covered up. Not even illusions. As soon as the clothes came near the illusion it dissipated. New clothes went invisible as soon as we put them on. Keisha finally said we were being ridiculous trying not to look at each other; we'd worn almost as little swimming and we'd known each other for years. So we basically went about reversing the spell—we couldn't go HOME like that—and paying not much attention to each other's bodies. It worked fairly well, I think," Seth interjected. "Okay, we've seen each other naked."

"We're normal, healthy, and capable of altering our appearance if we really want to. Funny as hell when Solly grew out all his hair follicles as his attempt at a 'modest' outfit that wouldn't vanish," Bridget continued. "It might have worked if it didn't send us all into laughing fits. I thought Malcolm was going to have a seizure, he laughed so hard." She shook her head. "So it's your choice, really. We're not going to turn your clothes invisible or rot them off you, but we're also not going to pay much attention to it if you happen to see us without them or choose to take yours off. Well, Seth's a little shy," she said, grinning at him.

"No one wants to see me," he replied. Jennifer pulled herself up out of he water; unlike Bridget she was in a wetsuit. "Hey guys. Beautiful down there. I saw you swimming, Bridget. Are you ready to go down, Angela?"

"Um, sure."

"Let me make it easier," Seth said, stripping off his trunks. He dove naked into the sea, and a large amount of water welled up from where went in. Then a massive black fin broke the surface, and Seth the killer whale breathed at the surface, filling his lungs before diving deep.

"Now that he's down deep, let's practice some transformations," Bridget said.

"I hope he won't wreck the boat coming back aboard."

"Never has," Bridget replied and got into the sweats she was wearing aboard. Jennifer pulled the wetsuit off and jumped back in the water, bobbing to the surface, transforming herself into a sea lion. "Seth's going to provide us security out in the water. Sea lions are a bit easier than seals or dolphins, since you're using all your limbs."

"Okay." She concentrated and turned herself into a sea lion. It felt very weird to have flippers in place of hands and feet.

"You know you just turned yourself into a bull?"

<I turned myself into a male?!?> she twisted around to look down at herself, and sure enough she was a lot bigger than Jennifer.

"Yeppers!"

<No wonder I feel so strange. Seth really doesn't need to know about this, does he?>

"Well, I suspect you'll let it slip at some point yourself, and it's not like there's anything wrong with taking a male shape. We've all taken the other gender form at one point or another. We just usually retain our own gender. I remember Seth turning himself into a cow once."

<Give me a sec.> She concentrated, and felt herself shrinking down to a female sea lion shape. She looked back at herself. *<That's better! Why a cow?>*

"It was a game of hide and seek, practicing our detection spells. Seth got the bright idea to hide in plain sight as a cow in a field."

<Think he'd take a female form some other time?>

<Hard to say,> Jennifer responded. *<It's probably how they stick the scrying foci in the showers—I know some of us take male forms to stick our foci in theirs—but we've never found one of Seth's.>*

<Can he use dead tissue as a focus? Like, say, hair?> Jennifer and Bridget looked at each other in chagrin.

"I think he could," Bridget said. "It's a question to put to Keisha. But for now, go swimming! I want you to take four other forms out in the water, and one of them should be a fish!" She barked back at her and dove in.

Swimming as a sea lion was a lot different than swimming on the team. She slid through the water fairly easily, got herself to the surface to breathe, then dove back down. Jennifer was right there with her, and Seth's massive form came back to keep an eye on them. A lot of real sea lions were out here too, hunting for fish. There were some smaller sharks, too, but no great whites. Bridget seemed to be keeping them away.

They spent about an hour as sea lions when Bridget called to her, *<Okay. Take a different form.>*

A massive form swam past them. The whale was enormous, but paid no attention to the sea lions cavorting around it. She didn't want to go that big, but she shifted to a dolphin. The motions for swimming as a dolphin were a lot different from the sea lion, all in the spine. This was going to hurt later, but for now, it was great fun swimming around the massive whale as it swallowed up schools of anchovies. Echolocation took some getting used to, but Jennifer and Bridget were able to give her some pointers. Then it was time to select another form.

She turned herself into a great white shark. That should satisfy the fish requirement Bridget had tossed at her. What she wasn't expecting was the change in sound coming from Seth. His killer whale form was speeding back towards them… no wait, towards HER. In an unmistakably hostile way. *<Seth! Stop! I'm the shark! I'm the shark!>*

She felt his sonar and mind wash over her as her gills pulsed rapidly, but he slowed and didn't actually attack. *<Warn the guard when you're switching to the form he's watching for, would you?>*

<Sorry, Seth. I thought you were paying closer attention to us.>

<If you want to surprise Bridget, try a cormorant. She's got several visiting her boat at any given time.>

<Why not a penguin?>

<We're talking about the goddess of nature. She'd immediately think a penguin off the Farallons was you, Jennifer, or me.>

<Why do you guys refer to each other as gods?>

<As a joke. It started with me and "Goth of death" getting misheard by Alex's little sister, so Julia started calling me 'god of death. It grew from there. We're out here with the goddesses of nature and magic.>

<I'll try to give your holinesses the respect you're due.>

He snorted. *<Don't worry about it, o goddess of the elements!>*

She hung motionless in the water for several moments, drifting down, then shook herself and started swimming again. *<WHAT did you just call me?>*

The killer whale swam around her, getting a firm sonar picture, but didn't answer. He flicked his flukes at her and powered off to challenge a real shark. Jennifer swam up to her as a mermaid.

<How do you get that to work together?> she asked.

<It's tricky. Just about any unreal creature is tricky. Want to give it a try?>

<Maybe some other time. I'd kind of like to be back aboard soon, even though it's fairly easy to breathe as a shark. Seth gave me an idea.>

<Okay. I'll go find him. We're having dinner with Bridget's mom on the island.>

Angela took Seth's idea of a cormorant and joined several others on the boat. Bridget had put on a jacket over the sweats when a black fin split the water, coming fast straight at them. The real cormorants scattered as the killer whale jumped straight at the boat… turning into Seth. Bridget handed him a towel. He thanked her, got his own sweats on, and sat chatting with Bridget as Jennifer pulled herself back aboard. Bridget handed her a towel too.

"Since we're all back aboard, let's head to the island," she said. She turned to Angela. "Did you want to stay a cormorant for the ride in, or do you want to return to normal?"

She let out a squawk. Seth went below chuckling. Angela returned to normal. "How'd you know?"

"You were the only one not to react to an orca coming straight at you."

"The cormorant was his idea."

"He played you, Angela. Get him back next time." She toweled off and got back into her own sweats.

"By the way, Mom's research team isn't clued in, and we don't really know what languages they speak."

"So keep quiet about the transformations?"

"Yeppers."

Dinner was at the research camp. They'd brought the supplies over in a zodiac. While they enhanced their strength to unload them, and made sure of calm waters, they did things the normal way so Dr. Sullivan's team didn't notice.

"How was the dive?"

"Great! There was a blue out there today. Seeing her was awesome."

"See many great whites?"

"Just one, and she didn't stick around long," Seth said.

"So how did you wind up on the trip with the girls, Seth?" a young woman in a wool cap and glasses asked.

"Bridget made a general invite to the study group." Dr. Sullivan cocked an eyebrow at Bridget, who quietly tapped the circular table. Dr. Sullivan nodded her understanding of that.

"Well, thanks for coming out. We can really use the supplies you kids brought. But you should probably be on your way back while there's still light," said the senior researcher, a Dr. Lewis, with graying black hair and mostly gray beard.

"We'll be fine, but we should get Angela back to the pier in time."

"We'll make it in time," Jennifer said.

"Can you take some samples back and drop them at the lab?"

"Sure. I'll call Dad and let him know we need to make the stop." They got the samples out to the boat and sailed back. They were making remarkably good time.

"You're cheating, aren't you?"

"Yeppers! No reason not to."

"I'll teleport straight home unless you need me for something," Seth said.

"Let's get a little farther from the islands," Bridget said. "No need for you to suddenly disappear if someone's watching."

"Okay."

"Something you need to do, Teach?"

"Avoid a pointless confrontation with your ride?"

"Ah."

"When are you going to tell them, Ange? You don't have the same problems Teddy does. My parents love to gossip, so they don't know. Keisha's parents run a popular business blog, so they don't know. And Alex's mom is a reporter, so he told his dad but not her. Your parents are what, a developer and a realtor? Not as much danger of exposure there," said Jennifer.

"I don't know. I've been trying to figure out why I haven't told them since Christmas, and it's just never seemed like the right time."

CHAPTER

53

The team hike this year promised to be a lot less… interesting than last year's. Alex actually missed it; the Avengers were playing the Unicorns, in Arcata. Dani's parents had put their feet down about her going with them, so she and Angela partnered. "At least if something weird happens, you can handle it," Dani said.

"Shouldn't be anything weird. I'm not scheduled for a test today."

"Do they always announce the tests?"

"Day of, if it's something dangerous. But more to the point, I asked Seth and he told me there wasn't anything. Since he's my primary tutor…"

"He'd know."

"Got it in one. But the Valkyries are facing the Sirens in the City, so he's just a shout away if we need backup."

"That's a relief."

"I've noticed you've stopped picking fights with him."

"I thought about what you told me, about not wanting to ever need protection again. And I thought that I don't really need protection, but I was antagonizing someone for no real reason—and the only reason I didn't get the flu with the rest of the team was him not wanting to piss off my boyfriend. I don't want to hide behind Alex. I can at least be civil."

"Glad you came round."

"Thanks. I may just be a dumb linebacker, but I'm not that dumb."

"Oh, come on! You're not dumb!"

"It's all Alex can do to keep my grades up to keep me on the team. We spend half our dates with him tutoring me."

"Really? Maybe you should start studying with us. It's made a ginormous difference for me."

"Will they let me? I mean, I know there are already ten of you. And with my GPA I think I'd be getting behind quickly."

"Do you speak Nahuatl?"

"Alex has taught me a little."

"Well, we can drop into another language if we don't want you knowing about something. But we've got a few other people studying with us—Shevaun, Julian, Karen, Trevor. You'd fit right in."

"With MENSA? I don't think so.""

"We're not in MENSA. But I'm remembering a conversation we had back in fall."

"We did?"

"It was about them expanding the league, with Seth thinking you'd have the votes if you had the money. So I don't think they'd have a problem with you studying with us."

"Oh, right. Was Alex telling me right that they're loaning you the money?"

"Yeah, mostly because they like to use League meetings to disguise what they're up to. The last time I was at one we spent five minutes on approving the Las Vegas Gorgons in teal and copper—and spent five hours discussing Martian terraforming."

"Oh, gotcha, chica."

"Alex doesn't need to know I told you that, by the way."

"Oh, of course not!" they grinned at each other.

"You did just tell me who else is in the group, you know. Process of elimination and all that."

"You'd already guessed. Karen figured it out months ago. As long as you keep your mouth shut, you should be fine."

"How'd Karen find out? Seth put a love spell on her?"

"Not a bad guess. He brought her back from the dead when she got shot," she said, "and I told her about me trying to explain what had happened. Everything came together for her then."

"Ah… hey, what's that?" It was a large building, with peeling red paint on the boards and what looked like the remnants of a painted sign on one wall.

"Looks like an abandoned barn. Let's check it out," she said, pulling out her light.

"You brought a flashlight… oh, that's your lightsaber."

"Yeah. It wouldn't make sense to have a flashlight swinging from my belt. Stick close to me, I'll raise shields. At least you already know I can do this," she said leading the way.

"Raising shields and pulling out your lightsaber? You expecting a fight?"

"Looking at all the holes in the roof."

"Oh, right," she said, looking up. There was still more ceiling than holes, but it didn't look stable at all. Inside they could see the hay loft and a number of horse stalls, along with quite a bit of junk. Dani went forward in the light to check one of the piles out. After a moment, looking around to make sure there was no one else around and even speaking a spell to make sure of it, she made a source less light and put the lightsaber away. She brought the light with her, then made one for Dani and went to check out her own pile.

It was junk, mostly. Long since rusted or rotted into uselessness, no doubt why it was abandoned here. But there was always the possibility something interesting had been abandoned. Angela incanted to move things out of the way and sift through the pile, while Dani used her hands. "You want a pair of gloves, Dani? I'm seeing some black widows." Perfectly normal to see the spiders in something like this, but "normal" didn't make their venom any less dangerous.

"You brought gloves?"

"No, but you know I'm a wizard. So…" she took some of the abandoned leather and turned it into a pair of gloves for Dani. She floated them through the air over to Dani.

"Thanks!" she slid them on. "Are these going to be tough enough? They're so soft."

"Of course they will. I made sure of that. They're not quite as impenetrable as Alex's combat garb, but…"

"For work they're fine. Hey, look at this!" She stepped over to the stall and the floor collapsed. She summoned her power on the way down and arrested her fall in mid air, but her lightsaber kept falling. A heavy beam fell on top of it, and she heard an audible crack.

"Whoah, you okay?"

"Yeah I'm fine. But I think the light saber is toast." She was still hovering in mid air.

"That sucks."

"I'll talk to Alex. Having a lightsaber was cool, but I'd kind of like something more thematically consistent. When decked out for combat, Seth carries a scythe."

"A what?"

She put up an illusion of Seth. "Image of Death."

"So that's a scythe. Seth as Grim Reaper." She shuddered. "I wouldn't like that thing coming at me."

"Well," Angela said as she drifted over to a firm floor section, "I don't want to leave it lying around." She used more magic to lift the beam and the debris. Then she levitated the remnants up. "Yeah, making it look like a flashlight wasn't the best idea. Looks like I actually turned into plastic. Next time I'll have to make it sturdier."

"Glad you're not too bummed out about it."

"Alex made it on the fly to deal with that frankenturkey Seth sent as a test," she shrugged. "I never really planned to make it my primary tool. This just accelerates my replacing it, really."

"Well, this place is shot as a cool place to hang. Where should we go?"

"Top of the hill?"

"Let's go. I'd offer to race you, but you're a little too fast for me." Angela grinned at Dani's remark, and they set out up the hill. The panorama from the top was marvelous, and they just sat there for a while, enjoying the view. Angela found herself tempted to take off and join the birds.

"Oh, look at the time," Dani said. "We're need to get back, they're leaving in five."

"I'll teleport us there." She put her hand on Dani's shoulder and took them back to their starting point. "Good enough?"

"Oh, yeah. Sounds like the Avengers are winning." She hadn't taken out her phone.

"Update from Alex?"

"Si." They boarded the bus and relaxed until it was time to actually go home.

*B*eing a future team owner meant getting to go to owners' meetings, rather than using the meetings as time to study and practice magic. Which meant that she wasn't surprised when Seth knocked on the Owner's Box door for the Avengers at the Avengers-Valkyries game.

"Come on in, Seth," Alex called, tossing him a Coke. Seth closed the door before it reached him, and he popped the top while it was still in mid air.

"Thanks," he said.

"Looks like you guys need to talk about secret stuff, so I'll go to the bathroom," Dani said.

"No need to leave, Danielle. I am here to discuss the secrets… but in this case, you need to be part of the conversation. Last night Alex asked that you be admitted to knowledge."

"Thank you, sweetie!"

"Don't get too gushy. You already know about me. So I get the job of determining whether or not it's a good idea." Dani blanched.

"Sweetie…"

"Sorry, love. Someone else needs to make the determination, and no one else was willing to reveal themselves when you already knew about Seth."

Her look of chagrin was almost comical, but she took a deep breath, squared her shoulders, and sat down opposite him. Angela bit her lip. She wanted to warn Dani that being able to get along with Seth for a civil conversation was part of the test, but she couldn't. She and Alex exchanged a sympathetic look.

"I know about Angela. What about…"

"I'm still learning, so I don't get a vote, and I think telling you would be a good idea. Good luck," she said.

"Okay. Makes sense. Alright, Seth. What do I need to do?"

"Convince me." No embellishment. He cocked his head at her. "How? You hate me!"

"Do I? Have you read my mind?"

"You know I can't do that." Then she seemed to catch a look from Alex. "But you can."

"True."

She seemed to steel herself. "Then do it. Pluck it out of my brain."

"Why?"

"So you can make your determination."

"Why do you want to know? Why should we let you in? I'm not the gentlest person in a living mind, Danielle. If I were to enter your mind, it would not be a pleasant experience. So why?"

That surprised her. "I love Alex. I know he's powerful, and so are you. All of you. While Alex hasn't confirmed anyone other than you and Angela, I'm pretty sure who the others are. I know you've faced powerful enemies. If I know what's going on, maybe I can help."

"If you don't know what's going on, you can't reveal anything."

"I want to help, Seth. I can't release a bolt of lightning or just kill someone. I'm not on the first team. But I can be the water girl. I've kept Alex's secrets."

"And demonstrated a lack of concern about others." At her expression, he continued, "You didn't even start to care about mine until Angela nearly burned down Muir Woods."

"May I say something?" Angela said.

"Sure," Dani said. Angela waited for Seth's response.

He made it in Ainu. "What did you want to say?"

"Let her know that she needs a unanimous vote," she replied in the same language.

"We agreed no coaching," Seth replied. "If she asks the question on her own, I'll answer it." He returned to English to resume his interrogation. "Pardon us. Where were we?"

"You were about ready to decide I shouldn't know."

"I never said that, Danielle. I did say you needed to convince me. You have yet to do that."

"How? I've said go ahead and probe my mind."

"Probing your mind could lead to serious embarrassment, even pain or damage. If you can't convince me, there's no reason to probe your mind in the first place. So I won't subject you to it."

"Can you at least tell me how many votes I need to change?"

"Two."

"Can I ask another question?"

"You can ask me any question you wish. I will not reveal other people's secrets."

"How many are in the group?"

"Full members, nine. One apprentice."

"So the vote was six opposed to three supporting?"

"No."

A shadow passed over her features. "It was seven in favor to two opposed. And to get let in, I need a unanimous vote."

"Correct."

"Which means I need yours."

"True."

"Only one of the rest of you is pretending to be something he's not. Which makes him paranoid about being revealed. So I need Teddy's vote."

"You need one vote besides mine. Who's it is… is their secret. This person does, however, trust me to make the determination."

"Alex won't tell me who else is one of you. But while I may not be flattening the curve like you guys are, I can guess that the Wizards of the Round Table is you guys hiding in plain sight. That membership lines up precisely with the owners of the League. I've kept that secret, Seth. I may not like you, but I get what you're capable of doing. I do not, ever, want you to have the idea that I'm a threat to you. From what I've seen from the sidelines, your response to a threat is to kill it, and it's really, really, really easy for you to do that."

"Are you afraid of me, Danielle?"

"Damn straight I'm afraid of you, Seth. You're the fucking God of Death in human form, and I know I've pissed you off, and I don't want to die. Happy now?"

"No. Fear isn't something that can be counted on, Danielle. Fear prompts desperate attempts to strike back. I don't want you afraid of me."

"Then what do you want?" she sounded almost desperate.

"Seth, please…" Alex said.

"No Alex. Either she has the strength of character to do this on her own, or she doesn't."

"Seth. I'm sorry for how I've treated you in the past. I've been changing ever since Muir Woods. I may not particularly like you, but that's no excuse. Please accept my apology so we can move past this. I want to be with Alex. If the cost of that is keeping these secrets, then that is something I want to do. If it costs me my life, this is something I want to do."

"Very well, Danielle. Take my hand, and I will do the probe"

She took it and he stared into her eyes. Angela saw Dani wince, sweat, and tremble. But then Seth dropped her hand. He sat with his head bowed for several minutes. Then Teddy appeared in a flash of blood red light. "Welcome to knowledge, Dani. There's someone at the Temple who'd like to say hello."

"The Temple? I thought that was part of your D&D game. Where's…"

"Ishtar Terra. Venus. I'll have to take you," Alex said. "But yeah, he'll be happy to see you."

"At least that disguise worked."

"Who will be happy to see me?"

"That part's a surprise," Angela said with a grin.

"Spill!"

"Nope. I've been entrusted with secrets, too. Although I do kinda hope I'm up there to see it. Teach?"

"He should be awake after the game. Angela, would you mind letting the others know?"

"Sure, but I'm supposed to head home after the game."

"No problem," Seth said. "My car can drop you off. Or do you want to call and say you're having dinner with Alex and Dani before heading home?"

"Which would also neatly explain why it was your car, since you could catch a ride back with them after dinner."

"Aye."

Angela got her phone out. "Hi Dad. Dani and Alex are getting dinner here and they invited me to join them."

"Is it healthy?" Dad asked

"Maybe not for you, but it's fine for healthy, active athletes." Seth and Teddy snorted.

"Okay. What time do you think you'll be home?"

"Maybe around ten or eleven, Dani wants to go over the history homework."

"Oh, if you're going to be studying, too, that's fine. When do we need to pick you up?"

"Oh, I can catch a ride from Alex. He's got the Avengers limo here."

"And he and Dani won't mind a third wheel?"

"Someone needs to chaperone them," she replied with a smile. "Okay. See you when you get home."

"You may still end up riding with Seth, you know."

"I need the illusion practice, anyway," she said. "I can make the Valkyries limo look like the Avengers' limo, at least through a window at night." All four of them grinned.

"Well, then, I'll see you for the after party," Seth said, heading for the door.

"As will I, but I need to get back to Hollywood before I'm missed." Teddy vanished.

"You two want to be alone?"

"Thanks, Angela, but stay and watch the game with us. Maybe you'll tell me why all the secrecy."

"Nope." She smiled at her friend. "For that matter, I might just go on ahead and get things started."

"Gee, thanks. *He's* not going to tell me, any more than he told me anything about you."

She grinned and teleported herself to the Temple.

Mike wasn't asleep; he was in his apartment watching the Sphinxes-Amazons game and talking to Keisha. She didn't bother him, but turned on the four games in the kitchen area. Avengers and Valkyries, Starlets and Furies, Amazons and Sphinxes, Witches and Sirens. Enchantments let her receive them in real time. Bridget showed up a few minutes later, as the Unicorns weren't playing this week.

"So Dani passed the test, I hear."

"Yeah. It took her awhile to get Seth to probe her mind."

"Really? I was expecting her to offer that up first thing."

"She did. He insisted on being convinced."

"Oh, that must have been fun to watch."

"Kind of hard, really. I kept wanting to step in and help her. Ever since they talked me down in January, Seth has intimidated the shit out of her."

"Not that surprising."

They lapsed into a companionable silence while they worked on their homework, occasionally asking each other questions, then emailing it to the other to check. After an hour Mike came in. "Hey, Bridget, Angela. What's up?"

"Seth and Teddy finally let Dani in on the secrets. Everyone'll be here for dinner."

"Cool beans. It'll be good to see her again. I mean, you guys are great, but I miss people."

"Yeah, we get it."

"I mean, I'd really like to see some of the guys from the team, even if they think it's a dream. I know, I know, don't hold my breath."

Angela felt her lips quirk. "I hear you. But the people you really have to convince are Teddy and Seth."

"Oh, fuck."

"Yeah," Bridget said. "You saw them at the discussion of bringing Dani up to speed. She already knew about Alex. She knew about Seth. She knew about Angela. She'd guessed the rest of us."

"Which meant a lot of the danger in bringing her fully inside was there anyway," he said, drinking a grape soda. He looked at it. "But Teddy doesn't want to bring in anyone, and the team has generally been such assholes to Seth that he's doesn't trust them."

He looked at the magic replicator. "Any chance you guys could modify that thing to make beer?"

"We'll upgrade the library and provide an ag cavern where you can grow the stuff and make your own," Bridget said. "Another project for you. But over all we're not really drinkers, so we don't have any beer. Keisha might."

"I'll ask her."

"Speaking of Keisha…"

"Formal dinner party?"

"Excellent idea. Let's do it." The two of them conjured up a multi-course dinner and a chair for Dani. The chairs were color-coded; Mike's was orange and bronze, while Dani's was purple and gold. The table was big enough for all of them and a few more besides. The silver domed dishes gleamed against the dark wood. "Well, that'll keep everything warm. Oh… piece of cake."

"That is one monster cake," Mike said. "Looks almost like a wedding cake."

"Dani likes marzipan and fondant," Angela shrugged. A word in Gaelic from Bridget locked the cover.

"How is everyone on the team, Ange?"

"Pretty good. Felix broke up the Olivia, so he's pretty bummed…" they talked about people they knew with Mike to help his homesickness. The rest of the Round Table started showing up in pairs from the games. Finally Seth, Alex, and Dani appeared.

"Mike? Mike Wu? My god… I thought you were dead! How…?" She hugged him.

"Not unless your god is named 'Seth'," Jennifer said with a grin. "He was dead. Keisha didn't want to accept that. We grabbed his body, left a fake, repaired it, and Seth worked his magic."

"Well this is an awesome surprise. It's great to see you alive again, Mike."

"I'm really glad they decided to let you up here," he said. "Even if they won't let you say anything about me."

She glanced at Alex for confirmation. He nodded. "That seems cruel, especially to his family," she said.

"They don't know," Mike replied. "Everyone who knows I'm alive is at this table." He passed the bread to Dawn

"Oh," Dani said. "You weren't kidding about secrets. How do you guys not weigh three hundred pounds?" She was staring at all the dishes. Meat, fish, bread, vegetables, salad, lasagna…

"Magic," Keisha said. Dani rolled her eyes. "No really. It takes a lot out of us."

"Being on the field most of the game is less tiring than the same amount of time working magic," Angela said. "At least for me." Alex nodded agreement.

"On the subject of secrets, Dani," Malcolm began.

"Check with Alex first," she finished for him. He let out a sonar click of agreement.

"How do you do that?"

"I spend a lot of time in cetacean form. It just sort of carries over," he told her, shrugging as he took a bite of the steak.

"No wonder you're such a good swimmer."

"That has little to do with it. I'm not developing the same muscles when I dive as a dolphin as I use in the pool." He spoke a couple of words in Phoenician and images of Malcolm and a dolphin appeared. The muscles each used while swimming flashed blue. Dani's eyes bulged at the casual use of magic while Malcolm launched into a technical explanation.

"Malcolm, you've lost her," Dawn said.

"Sorry. I was getting the lecture. It's just that I'm not used to someone whipping out magic at the dinner table."

"Date night isn't really the time for it, love."

Mike said. "They're away from cameras and satellites and the only witnesses are you and I, whom they trust. And it's impossible to get here without getting through lethal defenses. So here they relax."

"Lethal?"

Solly nodded. "Lethal. We all worked on it, but even the defenses Seth didn't put in place are designed to be as dangerous as possible."

"Teddy, um, how to say this…"

"You're surprised I didn't say grace."

"Um, yeah."

"I do illusions. The one I've been maintaining the longest is being religious." He smiled at her sudden blinking. "Here, just among friends, I can be me." From there they started telling Dani what had really been going on. It took a long time, past dinner, past cake. She and Seth teleported to his limo, and she put on the illusion that it was Alex's.

CHAPTER

55

Late in May, the school sponsored a day trip out to Stinson Beach. It had originally been a field trip, and there was still a writing assignment linked to it, but it was mostly a day off for a good year right before finals. The school buses wound their way out to the beach full of happy kids. Some of the seniors and juniors had permission to drive themselves, ad they'd done that with surfboards on their roof racks. Even those seniors who didn't surf would rent out space on their racks.

Those who didn't surf looked forward to beach volleyball, or little nature hikes, or just sitting and talking with friends. Seth, as usual brought a heavy looking pack—that wasn't that stuffed. Much like her bag, it was enchanted to hold more than it should and look a certain way. Her bag looked like next to nothing was in it. Seth's looked like it was stuffed to capacity. She asked him what all he was bringing, and he replied in Cushitic.

"Not much. It's linked to the Mausoleum, actually. Anyone who doesn't know what they're doing will find a bunch of thick books. Mummification, *Dracula* and a bunch of similar things."

"Someone else would find something to confirm their own prejudices about what you're bringing."

"Precisely."

"Kind of a sad way to live, Teach."

He shrugged. "There's no reason to do otherwise. Besides, I'm not going to spend much time with people today. Macaria's going to be flying over the area, so I'll join her."

"What are you guys talking about?" Karen asked. Angela confidently expected Seth to ignore the question… but this was Karen.

"Angela wanted to know what I'm bringing to the beach."

"So you answered in a language no one else understands? I don't even know what language that was!"

"It was a private conversation. And I can think of at least eight other people who would have understood it."

"That wasn't the obscure language you normally use," Rachel Strauss said in a small voice.

"No, but I know Coptic well and I needed the practice in Cushitic. I don't use it much," he replied. Karen rolled her eyes and Rachel subsided into her usual withdrawn quiet self.

"What you're bringing to the beach is a conversation so private you switched languages?" Karen challenged him. "In what universe?"

"Had I wished others to know, I would have used English."

"I worry about you sometimes, Teach. You could have told her. I don't think she'd gossip about it."

"She might not. But replying in a language she'd understand would also mean replying in a language the rest of the bus could understand."

"Karen, you want to hit the volleyball courts or just hang out on the beach?"

"Volleyball sounds like too much effort. I just want to relax on the beach, catch some rays, maybe go for a swim."

"You do know the California Current comes down the coast from Alaska?"

"No. Is that why the water's cold? When did you?"

"Aye. Some study session or other with Malcolm and Bridget."

"And you remembered that snippet of info?"

"I guess."

"Mind some hang out company? I don't really have any plans either."

"Welcome. Just a warning, I'm going to be hanging out with the squad most of the day, and I know you're not friends."

"I don't have a real problem with them either." They were just turning into the parking lot when the bus behind theirs ran into them… and it was part of a chain reaction of other busses.

The accident of the busses meant there was no easy way back. Angela stood with the Round Table while they quickly came to an agreement…good lord, they were *each* speaking a different language! They sent Seth over to the principal, and she tagged along. "Excuse me, Ms. Nguyen," Seth said.

"Not now, Seth, I need to find some busses out here and call some parents," she said.

"That's what I want to talk about. We want to help. And we've already put some calls out. The team busses for the Santa Cruz Valkyries, San Jose Sphinxes, Berkeley Avengers, San Francisco Sirens, Sacramento Amazons, and Fresno Furies are enroute. Bridget, Dawn, and Jennifer are figuring out where the busses for the San Diego Witches, Hollywood Starlets, and Arcata Unicorns are, and if they're in reasonable range we'll get them here, too. We've also called for the cars at the league offices. With the busses remaining from the school, we calculate we'll be able to get everyone back." He paused. "Teachers included."

She stood there blinking at him. "Thank you, Seth, but there are some legal issues, you don't have a license…"

"I can get where I'm going faster than someone with one, but I won't be driving. Our drivers are fully licensed to carry large numbers of people."

"How? I know you guys have a lot of pull with those teams, but getting them to send their team busses and the limos all the way out here to pick up some high school kids…"

"We do have a lot of pull with the teams. The team owners usually do. The busses and cars will be here by three. Good enough?" She sort of stared at him, barely breathing. "Ms. Nguyen? Are you all right?"

"Um, yes, fine. Team owners?"

"We don't make a lot of noise about it, and our ownership interests are held in trust until we're eighteen, but yes. We own the teams."

"I think we need to talk some more later, if you guys are willing to do some stuff with the teams and the school, but that can happen later. Will you excuse me, Seth? I still need to get the busses sorted out."

"Of course, Ms. Nguyen."

Hanging with the cheerleaders was fun for a while, but she'd been getting more used to being with the Round Table. She'd been studying magic—and schoolwork— so hard that she'd only barely been aware of a lot of the recent shows and music that they were discussing, so she went for a walk a little after lunch.

Angela was coming up the sand to where the native grasses had recently replaced the ice plant Seth had killed for Bridget when she saw two girls in a passionate embrace. Whatever. Then she did a double take. Carmen? She didn't realize she'd blurted it out loud, but their reaction was obvious. The girls broke apart suddenly and Bridget recognized Grace Minh. "Hi Angela."

"Hi guys. Sorry for interrupting you. I'll just be on my way and let you get back to it."

"You're not surprised?"

"I don't randomly read my friends' minds, so I am surprised, but you want who you want. I learned *that* lesson from Alex and Dani. Glad you found someone. See you around, Carmen, Grace."

"Later."

Angela headed over to where she could see Bridget and Solly. "What's the project?"

"We're doing some restoration of the natural vegetation," Solly said. "Were you expecting us to join Malcolm out in the water? He's probably already shifted form; I didn't see him at lunch."

"I did. He's surfing with Jasmine."

"Didn't know what you'd be up to. I guess I was expecting more relaxing."

"That's what Teddy and Dawn are doing. Seth's up there with Macaria and her mate," Bridget said, pointing to the three condors over head. "I think Alex and Dani snuck off somewhere to be alone, and Keisha left for the Temple as soon as she could shake everyone. I know she fudged Ms. Nguyen's memory about being around for lunch."

"I'm not surprised. A whole day at the Temple? They're even worse than Alex and Dani." The three of them chuckled.

"Keisha tells me they're going to pay us back for every remark when we get SO's."

"I look forward to it," Solly said. "Not that it's stopped anyone from calling me "The Fertile One", you know."

"What's the unofficial tally, Solomon? No baby splitting for you."

"What makes everyone think those babies are my kids?"

Bridget arched a brow at him. "It doesn't exactly take Keisha to divine the answer to that. You can tell at a glance. It's almost as easy for me, you know."

"As far as anyone has been able or tried to prove, none of them is mine."

"So three. So far." Solly didn't answer.

Bridget smirked at him and changed the subject. "From what Seth told us, you're really coming along. Next test is supposed to be endurance?"

"That's what he told me, too." She shrugged doubtfully. "We'll see how well I do."

"Confidence is important, Ange," Solly said.

"You guys have plenty of that."

"We need it," Bridget said. "But you're right about where we were when Seth rescued you at White Hill."

She felt her jaw drop. "Really?"

"Only thing you haven't done is something that would be very difficult for everyone else, but we all progress at slightly different rates," Solly said. "Seth and Jennifer have been a bit precocious."

"I think I know something. But it would be just slightly noticeable. Even at the Temple or Castle."

"What?"

"I need to talk to Seth before doing a demonstration."

"Ok. Want to give us a hand here?"

"Sure. What do you need?" She mostly provided a look out for them. They already had a shield in place—one of Bridget's that made someone suddenly need to head for the nearest bathroom—so she didn't need to do that. She reconstituted some of the sand to be more useable by the grasses they were putting in. Almost before she knew it, it was time to get back. Seth sought her out telepathically and offered her a ride. She asked him to save some seats for her friends, and he agreed, since unlike the others his wasn't full.

"Hey, Karen, Carmen, Stacey, you want to ride in a limo?" Angela asked them where they were lining up for the busses.

"I thought they were full up," Karen said, puzzled.

"All but one, and I do think he'd do anything for you, Karen," she smiled. "C'mon, I asked Seth to save us seats."

"Oh, um thank Seth for me, but I'll ride back on the bus," Carmen said. She looked at Karen. Grace had already boarded a different bus.

"I'll go with you. But do thank Seth for the offer," Karen said.

"I didn't think I'd get to ride in a limo until prom! I'm there!" Stacey said enthusiastically.

"Suit yourselves." *<Karen and Carmen decided to ride back on the bus, Seth.>*

<Not really surprising, you know.>

She and Stacey joined Shevaun, Julian, Seth, Rachel Strauss, and Erik Montoya in the limo. The inside of the Valkyries' limo was again black and white, but other than that it had a very Nordic theme. She'd been expecting more skulls and bones.

So had Erik, who went ahead and asked Seth about it. "Nordic decorations seemed more appropriate for the team car," he replied.

"This is really comfy, Seth. Wow. A mini bar!" Julian said.

"I keep root beer in it, but you're welcome to have some," he said.

"Not real beer? Ah, man!" Erik said.

"I don't drink. It would be a very bad thing for my inhibitions to be lowered, Erik."

"Thanks for the root beer, Seth," Julian said. "Your team's doing well this year." He looked again at the bottle. "Never heard of these guys, but damn good root beer."

"Thanks. The micro brews are better than most of the big cola makers, I think."

"Are the Valkyries going to get to the Magic Bowl this year?"

"I hope so. The Unicorns are still pretty tough, and they won it last year."

"How'd you guys ever get the money?"

"Keisha's investor abilities border on the supernatural. We got our hands on our college money—not without some parental opposition—and let her invest it. She bet right on the markets. And, so, we put the college money back in our accounts and had plenty for her to keep playing with, and that gave us more than enough," he replied.

"I should see what she can do with mine," Shevaun said. "Couldn't hurt."

"Hey Julian, we're going to Hawai'i this summer. Any highlights you'd suggest, my prince?" asked Angela.

The long, lazy, curving trip back to school was dominated by vacation plans. Julian did have a lot of good suggestions for each island for Angela, and mentioned he'd be in the islands himself if she wanted to meet up away from the tourist traps. Seth was going to New Orleans and the Caribbean, and was talking about meeting up with Bridget. Angela quirked a smile. If he was hooking up with Bridget, something else was coming back from extinction. Erik was going to Europe with his parents, France and Germany and Italy. Shevaun was going to be spending time at Standing Rock and with her Dad on location in New Zealand. Stacey was talking about touring the East Coast schools she was interested in attending, since her parents were insisting. Rachel seemed to clam up every time she was about to speak, her eyes on Seth.

They talked more about colleges, and teachers, and sports and the Spring Formal in a week. Seth wasn't planning on going. Angela and Shevaun teased him about it. He didn't seem to care.

CHAPTER

56

"Hi Jimmy. Could you give Karen her phone back?"

"Angela, I don't know where Karen is. I got home from Berkeley and her phone was here ringing."

"Okaay, that's odd. I rode back in the car with Seth, and she was going to be on the bus. She should be home by now, even if she left her phone at home."

"Then I don't know what to tell you

<Seth, where's Karen?>

<Karen? At home, I suppose. It's not like she checks her activities with me. We almost never speak to each other.>

<You scry her.>

<If I pick something up through the resurrection bond that she might need help. Otherwise I don't anymore. Dawn and Jennifer said I was being stalkerish.>

<Seth, she's missing. I tried her phone, and I saw her check it earlier today, but her brother found it on the table. So's Carmen; I tried calling her too and it went straight to voicemail. She never does that. Can you crank up the magic sonar and find them?>

<Them? I don't have a connection to Carmen. Karen…> his telepathic voice went distant. She sensed the darkness of his power coalescing. After several moments, *<She's alive. I can get that much. But I'm being blocked… Karen? Can you hear me? This isn't your imagination.>* He waited a full minute, then, *<I don't think I'm getting through, not to a conscious mind or even into a dream. She's in the hands of a practitioner.>* His telepathic voice became subtly louder as he broadcast to the rest of the Nine. *<Meeting at the Headlands. Tonight. Tell them whatever you have to, Teddy. A practitioner is going after our friends The last school bus from Stinson. Yes, I'm sure. I wouldn't be calling in the justice league if it were that simple. Teddy, if it were that simple the bad guys would already be dead.>*

<If our friends are being targeted, we need to respond,> Alex put in.

<Oh, shit,> Bridget said. *<Karen's one of the people grabbed, isn't she?>*

<If Karen's been taken, Seth's going in hard fast and mercilessly. Got your back, dude. None of them live.> said Teddy.

<Breathe deep, Seth. Let's get them back in one piece,> Alex said. *<Does anyone know who else was on that bus?>*

<Carmen Burns, Dave Clebourne, Ivan Polikoff, June Ito, Susan Ericssen, Samantha Reilly, Teresa Llewellyn, Roxy Hansen, Sarah Ulrich, Valentina Solotov, Kristina Lee, Sara Hong, Michelle Wong, Natasha Yertensky, Juliana Bolen, Heather MacAllister… >

<That's a lot of girls. You don't think…> Dawn said.

<White slavers?> Keisha asked.

<Here?> Malcolm asked. *<If that's what they are, I'm not even going to try to restrain Seth's lethality.>*

<Neither am I,> Dawn said.

<We need to trace where they went. Keisha?>

<I'm on it. Jennifer, I'll need you at the Opera. If you can keep calm and focused, Seth, I'd like you to join us. You've scryed Karen more than the rest of us combined.>

CHAPTER

57

It was just after dinner that her cellphone rang. "Angela. Keisha's finally found Carmen, Dave, and Karen. Malcolm's friends are keeping an eye on it, but we need to go now. Do you want in on this? You're ready." Seth asked.

"Where would we be meeting up?" she replied, while thinking at him, *<Where's Carmen?>*

"The ship's already reached Chinese territorial waters. Do you want me to come get you? Dress for battle."

"Let me ask," she said into the phone, while thinking at him, *<Can Alex or Bridget get me?>*

"They're both busy. Alex is checking over the ship with Keisha and Bridget whipping up a storm in the South China Sea. Jennifer's helping them. Malcolm's in communication with his friends. Solly and Teddy are working on the illusions to cover us. Dawn's figuring out how to send the ship, once we take it, towards a US Navy ship. Which leaves me. Or, if you feel ready, I can give you the image and you can teleport here." Seth seemed to have no doubt about the ability of ten teenagers to take the ship. Of course, given what those ten were capable of...

"Where's *here?*"

"Inferno, Teddy's lair. They're going to freak when he arrives, but he needs his prop," Seth replied. "It's this massive, glittering throne with torches burning and blood flowing down it. It's really impressive."

"It's not really a *lair*," Teddy protested. "I don't live here."

"But it is set up for you to do that if you need to. She can make her own mind up when she sees it." Keisha put in.

"Come get me. I've never been there so..."

"The defenses might not recognize you. We'll be there in a minute." She put on her white dress and broad belt, her heavy fold necklace and earrings. She looked at herself in the mirror. "I'm ready for this. I can do this. My friends need me. Carmen, Karen, Dave, we're coming. Just hold on. We'll get you out of there. Time for the Mistress of the Elements to join the battle."

She came out to see Seth in his usual flat black, mounted in Orcinus' black saddle, his gaze locked on her father... who was pointing his target pistol at Seth. The pale gold horse snorted and pawed the ground, ears folded back. Orcinus wasn't exactly in Marshmallow's league when it came to brains, but he knew what a gun was and what one could do, and didn't take kindly to someone threatening Seth. Then there was the Death Goth himself...

"Daddy, please, put the gun away," she said, voice cracking in fear. "Before he decides he needs to defend himself."

"Angela, go on inside, he won't be staying, or do I need to call the police?"

Seth rolled his eyes. "You never told him?" All the same, she felt his power wrapped around him, saw the scythe on Orcinus' saddle, noted the flowing, hooded robe. The gun was no real threat to him, not when Thantoris was armed, armored, and ready for battle.

"Dad, I misunderstood his actions last year. I wouldn't be here now if it wasn't for Seth." She needed to defuse this. She stepped between them right in front of the gun.

"You think he saved your life?"

"Yes, he did. I know of three occasions where he stepped in to save me. And..." she paused. Discussing Seth's secrets was his right, not hers.

"Oh, go ahead and tell him. He won't believe it anyway. Not yet. But he might put that away before he gets hurt." Seth sounded more bemused than anything else. But if he decided to…

"Get out of the way Angela!" her father shouted.

She shook her head. "No, Dad. I'm not protecting *him*. I'm protecting *you*," she said. "He's already protected himself against a gun. For goodness sake, Daddy, look at him. Take the blinders off and *look* at him. He carries a scythe and rides a pale horse! He says the word and you die. I died in that bus crash, Dad. Seth *brought me back*. You're not putting him in any danger with that gun, but I watched him rip apart the guy who kidnapped me last May. He's been tutoring me all year. Why do you think I've got a four oh?"

"Your own intelligence and improved study habits," Seth said. "I may have helped with the latter, but it's not like school work is what you're learning from me." Damnit, why couldn't he have stayed quiet? "Angela, Carmen and Karen need us, and they're not being held alone. We need to get going before that ship docks. You're ready to join the rest of us. Orcinus and I need to suit up. Are you coming or not?"

'Butterflies in her stomach' was such a mild, poetic phrase for what she was feeling. But she nodded. "Carmen and Karen need my help, and I'm going to give it. Let's go." She turned to her father, and spoke two words. "Fiat lux." A ball of teal light appeared in front of the barrel. "Seth has been teaching me *magic*, Dad." Her father let the gun slip out of his grasp.

"Since you're coming, I have a gift for you," Seth said. "I know the saber is gone, so…" He handed her two elaborately wrapped hilts, decorated with elemental symbols from around the world. Once in her hands, they blazed forth in teal light as katana and wakizashi. She deactivated them and tucked them in her belt as Seth switched to Ainu, "Come, Goddess of the Elements." He leaned down from, Orcinus' saddle, and leaned down to help her up, then pulled the hood down to show the skull of Death. The pale gold palomino took four steps into the air before she felt Seth's power coalesce to transport them elsewhere. She shot a glance back to see her father bug-eyed and gaping, unable to believe what he was seeing.

*A*lex stepped up to the front, his breastplate gleaming and the purple cloak flowing around him. A hologram of the ship floated next to him, the yellow sections flashing lavender as he mentioned them. "Here's the plan. We go in pairs. Watch each other's backs. Strong as we've made this stuff," he said as he knocked his knuckles on his breastplate, "they could get lucky. Angela, stick close to Seth or Jennifer. You're newest at this."

"Um, if it's OK with everyone else, I'll pair with Seth. We know each other best." She couldn't have imagined saying that a year ago.

"No problem," Jennifer said. Jennifer was wearing an indigo robe spangled with stars, crescent moons, and ringed planets in gold.

"Right. You two take the crew quarters; hopefully you'll scare them into surrendering. Yes, we take'em alive if they surrender, but they don't get to threaten the kidnap victims, and we don't waste energy restraining someone. Bridget, you and Keisha go for the cells. The prisoners might find girls less threatening than Seth." Given Seth's attitude, she doubted any of their opponents would survive.

"With the possible exception of me, EVERYONE'S less threatening than Seth," put in Teddy. His skin was blood red, his hair, goatee, hooves, and horns were black, and his three-tined fork already looked like it was dripping blood. He got a round of chuckles as he wiggled his horns.

"True enough," Alex replied. "Dawn and Malcolm take the engines. Solly and Jennifer, you're on back up; Teddy and I will take the bridge. Keep an eye out for hostile practitioners, and send up a batsignal if you find any. Remember they're likely to be older and more experienced than us. Any questions?"

"Where do we dump any prisoners?" Malcolm wanted to know. "We'll let the Navy have them. Anything else?"

"No, I think we're good," Seth said, pulling his skull mask down and hood up. With the long gloves, he appeared a walking skeleton, covered only by an open robe. Orcinus, in his black and bone livery, snorted and fire seemed to come from his nostrils. Seth mounted the high backed knight's saddle, and called to his dogs. The big black bloodhounds appeared immediately, tongues lolling out. One of them--Cerberus--came over to Angela and licked her face while the others eagerly sought pets and skritches from the others, even as Alex's huge spike collared mastiffs appeared in answer to his summons. The big, happy dogs wagged their tails and pressed against legs. Lions and tigers and wolves appeared next to Bridget. Growls began filling the room even as the big cats curled themselves around Chiomara like so many tabbies. Teddy took his seat to a chorus of Gregorian chanting. Malcolm called his friends to the fight as Keisha ignited her torch and Dawn infused herself with light, glowing almost too brightly to look at, almost as bright as the sun. Jennifer's indigo robe gleamed as she drew her wand from her sleeve, while Solly's hair grew and grew until he looked more like the common perception of a sasquatch than a teenage boy... and Angela suddenly realized he was naked—and aroused. When she blushed, he wiggled his eyebrows at her.

"Problem, Angela?"

"No, I just didn't realize you'd be quite so, ah, ready."

He smiled. "One of the reason's I'm on backup. Shout if you need extra help."

They transported themselves invisibly. Seth was a mile or so away from the rest of them, Orcinus galloping, the bloodhounds baying as he charged towards the ship. The barks from the Dogs of War and the howls of Nature's Wolves answered the baying of Death's Hounds. In the water below him, Angela saw the dorsal fins of killer whales break the surface. Then Malcolm rose above the waves on the head of a sperm whale, his trident in hand, and she heard the clicking of the cetaceans' sonar. The powerful synchronized sound waves from the sperm whales made the ship ring like a bell.

As they got closer, they could see flashes of gunfire from the crew who saw the approaching agents of supernatural vengeance. A cluster of them by the bow exploded in a sunburst of yellow flame as Grianne made her presence felt with a few choice words in Tsalagi. Angela flew low on the deck as Toranos landed lightly up near the bridge, and lightning fried the ship's communications tower. The Gregorian chanting began and Teddy's throne seemed to rise up out of the deck. The dogs and big cats swarmed over the deck and the only thing that stopped them were the closed hatches. Thantoris and Orcinus landed beside her, and every hoof beat on the deck sounded like a death knell as Seth swung down to join her. A ship's crewman came out of one door with an assault rifle and was buried from above by a tiger.

They headed for one of the hatches. It wouldn't swing open at Thantoris' command, so Angela melted it. They could hear the sounds of running going both directions, so they split up. *<Keep in contact,>* they thought at each other at the same time. She sensed his amusement as she grinned at him. If he was grinning the skull didn't show it.

She headed down the corridor with her flaming wings beating behind her, melting tracks in the walls. Sealed hatches made no difference to the heat of her blades, and she floated down a flight of stairs. Crewmen with whatever they could grab as makeshift weapons charged her, to find the floor wet under their feet and their weapons melting in their hands. But the door to the crew quarters was just in front of her now. Five men stood in front of it with those funny Russian guns with the forward curving magazine whose name she could never remember

The hatchway was barred from the other side. The crewmen fired their guns as they faced her. A few words in a language they couldn't understand, coupled with the deliberate distortion of a triple toned musical voice, and the pointing of her fiery teal sword led to guns melting in their hands and prevented bullets from even getting near her, and they desperately tried to tackle her. Their panic was complete when a black blade cut down the hatch from the other side and Death Himself came through. She smiled at Seth's dramatic entrance. They could face the scythe or her twirling, flaming swords, but this time no one was restraining Seth, and the slavers died as he touched them, just a touch, from the same hands that had returned life to her. Of course, they were soft, cold, and clammy when he touched her… not dry bones.

"So this is where you've gotten to," he said. "Good move trapping them like that."

"Thanks," she replied. "Everyone else?"

"Doing as well as you are. But don't get cocky. Turn on your eyes," he suggested.

She shifted her vision, and she saw what he was talking about: residues of power were all over the place. They weren't the only practitioners on the ship. "Who's the enemy?"

"We're not entirely sure. We were tracking the kidnapped, not other practitioners. But odds are it's a woman, so be on the lookout." He stiffened. "Karen's down those stairs. Two crewmen, plus Carmen."

"Let's go."

They floated down the stairs, to find their friends being dragged through the halls. The crewmen had guns on Carmen and Karen, dragging them different ways. <I'll save Carmen. You can be Karen's hero.>

<Even if you told her she wouldn't believe it, but works for me.> They parted, each pursuing their own rescuee. She melted the hatch the sailor desperately closed behind him and listened to the panicked screams behind her as Thantoris floated towards them implacably. She spoke a

few words in Ainu as she advanced with spinning swords. In a flash of blinding purple she turned the atmospheric nitrogen around her target's head to plasma. He screamed and collapsed.

Flying down the passageway, she saw Thantoris between Karen and the crewman. A steel-jacketed slug fell to the deck, and the crewman toppled bonelessly after it as she felt Thantoris draw on his power, killing the man threatening Karen. "Are you injured, Miss MacLeod?" she asked.

Karen was staring at them, particularly Thantoris. Cloak open, she could see through the ribcage. An illusion of his garb, true, but knowing that didn't lessen the impact for Karen. She backed against the bulkhead.

"'I didn't keep you in Golden Gate Park, Miss MacLeod, and I will not harm you now," Thantoris said gravely. Angela winked at Karen over his shoulder.

Karen somehow managed to keep her face straight when she caught the wink, even as Thantoris turned to leave. "Ah, thank you," she said. "May I know your name, oh rescuer of mine?"

He paused, head bent in the hood. He wasn't casting a spell, just considering. "I am Thantoris." That surprised Angela. The secret names had power.

"Thank you, Thantoris."

"Can you make your way to the control room and call the Navy, Miss MacLeod?" she asked.

"Sure."

"It should be safe enough." She noticed Seth get distant for a moment. "Our team knows you're coming. They have your image." All they'd really needed was her name, of course. "Call my name if you need help."

"I will. Thank you."

They turned out that hatch and kept going. They searched the rooms they found, and the few crew or guards they found died under Seth's gaze. She was starting to think that they could probably accept surrenders, but Seth was still in a lethal mood and never gave them an opportunity to offer their surrender. The fact that they appeared to be supernatural made a lot of the opposition run from them or fire in a random panic, but their carefully enchanted outfits turned aside the bullets. Suddenly Seth stopped short and cocked his head, listening.

"Karen needs help," Seth said right before he vanished. She continued into the crew quarters, opening hatches as she went. Sometimes she found an imprisoned girl. Most of them just stared at her. A few started praying; one of them even fell to her knees before her! She wasn't entirely sure what the girl was saying—she was speaking French—but it sounded like she was being addressed as an angel. She freed the captives—melting their bonds—and moved on.

The next room's hatch was locked. This lock proved no more proof against her than the others; it melted just as easily. The quarters beyond, however, contained a pair of the guards and Dave, bound naked with plastic zip ties to the steel frame of a bed. A word in Ainu sent their heads smashing into the ceiling.

"Angela?!!" Dave said wonderingly, before sliding himself to the deck. As she sent bursts of high-pressure air to remove his bonds, she heard a scream and a shot. She flew down the corridor to find Seth hovering over another girl, another guard dead on the ground.

"Are you alright, Miss Hansen?" she asked. Roxxy was backing away from Seth with a terrified look on her face. She glanced at Seth. "He's not here for you, Miss Hansen."

"I'm not?"

"Not in the sense you're here to take her life," catching Seth's amusement. She continued in Ainu. "Felarie, Bestarion, we found another."

<Okay, send her towards the main deck,> Solly responded.

<Everyone, there's a major power point near Fawedea and Thantoris. In the crew dining area, I think,> Jennifer said. *<Converge there.>*

The dining area was large, crowded with large tables and chairs. The aromas from the kitchen were alternately amazing and disgusting—the crew's food vs. the captives'. A woman in a business suit stood at the center of a protective circle. Seth sent a wave of blackness and the circle turned it aside. A buzzing in her ears was very distracting.

"She's warded against necromancy," Seth said in Tsalagi.

"I wasn't going to try it," she replied in the same tongue, melting the deck under her feet. Their opponent screamed before levitating and turning the air to chlorine. They choked before Angela returned the air to normal… except inside the circle. That forced the woman to change it back herself…but she couldn't. Angela didn't let her, retaining control. The woman suddenly looked scared at Angela's mastery of elements, and pulled air into the circle to disperse the chlorine.

Angela also stayed off the ground, but her melting of the deck appeared to damage her protective circle. Angela froze the oxygen around her enemy. The frigidity pained her, and the woman in the circle suddenly started speaking rapidly in Tagalog. Angela felt her enemy's power reach out to control the world around her. But she'd forgotten Seth in her defense against Angela…and wasn't prepared for the scythe taking her head off. Angela shrieked at the sudden physical violence, just as Bridget arrived.

<Our enemy is dead.> Angela bespoke everyone. Then Seth spoke a word in Coptic, and a dark wave spread out from him. Angela noticed the dark and deadly spell he'd cast…to wipe out all the crew and guards.

"I couldn't risk doing that until she was down," he said. "Good work Fawedea. You've come a long, long way. <Any further problems?>" <Not now. All the bad guys are dead, Seth. Let's meet on the bridge.>

<We encountered another practitioner, guys. She fled rather than face us. We'll have to face her again.> Teddy said.

<See you there.>

They'd gathered on the bridge, and Karen took the microphone. Then she looked at the dead remnants of the radio and arched an eyebrow. Kara shrugged, and with a few words in Cushitic repaired the set.

"SS *Pelewan* to US navy. Please come in. This is a mayday. I repeat, mayday, mayday."

"*Pelewan*, this is USS *Sampson*. Please advise of your reason for declaring a mayday."

"We were kidnapped in California, thrown on this ship, and have taken the ship. The crew is…" she glanced at Thantoris, who's bony hand sliced across his throat, "dead. But we don't exactly know how to sail this thing."

An older voice took over. "Miss, I'm Captain James Merkul. Calm down, we're on our way. What's your name?"

"Karen MacLeod."

"Can you tell me how they died?"

"Dammit Jim, I'm a cheerleader, not a coroner." They heard a sputtering of laughter over the radio.

"Well, they haven't broken your spirit. That's something. Stay on the line, and help's on the way."

"Whoever you guys are, I won't mention you," Karen said to the ten people sharing the room with her, not transmitting. "Thank you, all of you."

"We'll be withdrawing now. Speak my name if you still need help, but the navy's got a helicopter on the way now that the storm has quieted down," Thantoris said. Karen nodded.

"Will I ever see you guys again?" she asked.

Fawedea looked at her. "Like this, all together, probably not. Not that many problems we're all needed for. In disguise, quite possibly."

Angela powered down her glowing swords and dismissed her wings. The heat dissipated instantly as she massaged her biceps. At least the magic of the flaming wings didn't cause her pectoral muscles to ache! Teddy was flexing his ankles. He really had had hooves. "I keep thinking maybe I should just use an illusion."

"Why don't you?" she asked.

"Illusions need to be carefully built if they're to be believed. A detail missing can be the difference. In this case, the sound is important, and when I'm not sure what sort of surface I'm going to be on I can't plan for it in advance. I'm trying to figure out a way for the illusion to automatically take care of that, but I haven't found it yet."

"And," Jennifer put in, "us showing up in full garb is pretty fucking unbelievable as-is, you know."

Angela gave her a tired smile. It was true after all. Solly was putting his clothes back on and pulling his hair back in as Alex took off his helmet.

"Hey everyone, I just learned that the navy's met up with the ship, and they'll be taking them to Manila and then home!" Alex shouted. A ragged cheer went up.

"Um, that's great Alex. But I need to bring up a potential problem. Dave Cleburne identified me, and I didn't get a chance to alter his memory."

That quieted everyone. "Will he talk?" Keisha asked. At her expression, she shrugged. "I don't really know him. I think I've had maybe four or five conversations with him, and we've never shared the same classes."

"That is the question," Alex said. "The other one is 'Does he know enough to identify anyone else?'"

"He might. I don't think he does, but he might."

"Not the end of the world," Teddy said. "But that makes dealing with him your job. I'll come along as back up if you want; I've got the most experience modifying memories to keep the secrets."

"Ok. I guess that will work."

"If you'd rather work with someone else that's fine, too. I know you're still a little uncomfortable around me." At her look, he said, "When you're modifying someone's memory, it's best to have someone else distracting them, so they aren't paying attention to what you're doing. It's not really hard, given the human difficulties with memory in the first place."

"Okay. I haven't done much of that."

"Like I said, I'll be there if you want me there."

"Sure Teddy. Can you be in disguise?" she asked

"Naturally," he said with a smile. "Dave will never suspect I'm there. There are benefits to being concentrated in illusions."

CHAPTER

59

She teleported herself back home. No need for an ugly scene between Dad and Seth, after all. She found the porch light still on, despite it being almost daybreak. Opening the door, she walked in to find Dad sitting in his easy chair, Mom at the table—neither of them changed out of the clothes they were wearing earlier—and the TV on. CNN— the overnight reporter was commenting on how the US Navy had intercepted a ship with American citizens who had overpowered their captors and taken the ship. The reporter was lauding their courage. Oddly enough, none of the crew survived.

"Of course not," she said, appearing in the room. "Seth is far too lethal." She sat down on the loveseat. This wasn't going to be fun.

"Is Carmen OK?" he asked.

She nodded. "So is Karen, now."

"Karen? She was on that ship, too?" Mom asked.

"They grabbed that missing bus. Bad guy dragged her off as a hostage. Thanks to Seth, she's better now."

Mom exploded, rising in fury. "Angela, seeing that... that... boy behind our backs, after what he did to you last year..."

Angela raised a hand and it glowed brightly as she raised nitrogen to plasma. She let some of the heat escape. "Brought me back to life, when

242

I died in that bus crash? Saved my life repeatedly? Warned others with power my life was in danger so *they* could act? Came alone to White Hill to rescue me? Taught me to access my own power? And, for the record, he's my tutor. Not my boyfriend. We don't date among ourselves."

"Could you explain this to me? Please?"

"I'll try." She hesitated, marshaling her thoughts, then, "A few years ago, Seth and some of his friends stumbled onto magic. Real, functional magic, and they've been studying like crazy to enhance their skills. Studying everything they can get their hands on, from fantasy novels to physics textbooks. Practicing in deserted, lonely areas where no one else will know. When he resurrected me, a bond formed between Seth and I. If we're both paying attention we can telepathically communicate. It—my resurrection—mystified and enraged the guy who'd caused the crash in an attempt to kill me, and he kept trying. It saved my life last June, because I was able to reach out to Seth and call for aid."

"Who are the others?"

"Sorry, Mom, but those aren't my secrets. I'm free to tell you mine, and Seth gave me permission to tell his, but no one else has. At least one of them fears a violent reaction from his parents if they knew. Or, more precisely, what he might have to do to defend himself." She paused for a moment to collect her thoughts, then resumed. "At the start of school this year, I asked him to teach me. As we worked, my emphasis turned out to be the manipulation of states of matter. This," she waved her hand, still glowing purple, "is atmospheric nitrogen raised to a plasma state, under my control. Seth's emphasis, by the way, Daddy, is necromancy. Death magic. If he'd felt threatened by that gun, he could have induced a stroke or cardiac arrest before you even knew he'd taken action. As it was explained to me, he's not the most powerful of us, but he is the deadliest."

"You mean he's killed people? He's a murderer? We should report him…"

"In defending me from a vampire at White Hill Christian. Where the autopsies said what, Mom?" She paused, looking intently at her parents.

"The causes of death were "natural", dear. I remember the police telling us. They aren't going to reopen any of the cases."

"And proving he did it would be impossible, wouldn't it?" Mom asked rhetorically, deflating.

"Not impossible. We could do it, if we wanted to. But it would involve betraying a friend and publicly revealing what we are capable of doing. We're not ready to do the second and don't want to do the first."

"But, honey, he's a killer! Someone needs to stop him!"

"He has killed. He's a walking harbinger of death. But, as far I know, he's killed no one who wasn't actively trying to hurt someone else. Him. Me. Karen. One of the kids on the ship. And against that is that unlike most people, he's capable of reversing death. I watched him resurrect extinct species, from bones. There isn't a "relict population" of sea cows in the Bering Sea. He brought them back with knowledge, imagination, and power.

"We're in charge of telling our parents, or anyone else. I know not all of us have decided our parents are trustworthy enough to tell. Some of them have parents who rely on them and their abilities to keep them safe all around the world. We have power. As Seth told me early on, we have a responsibility to use it as wisely and responsibly as we can. Tonight we went to the rescue of our classmates and some other kids. We're terraforming Mars and Venus and debating doing the same with the moon. So, Dad, Mom, tell me. Are you going to spill the secrets?"

They looked at each other, and sighed. "Every parent faces the moment when their child no longer needs them to make the decisions, and is making her own. I thought we had at least two more years. But I think we need to talk some more. We love you and will support you, even if we don't really like all your friends."

"From what we've seen, and what you've told us, you're going to be making your own decisions, and the best we can do is advise you. We certainly can't stop you! I was looking forward to teaching you to drive, but do wizards drive?"

"Seth doesn't—he doesn't have a license yet—but he prefers to ride or teleport anyway. I'm looking forward to learning to drive."

"No taking the car without permission?"

"No need, really. One of the things about learning from Seth was that we practiced teleporting a lot. If I really need to get somewhere, it's more about concealing my arrival than anything else. I can beat you to Hawai'i this summer."

𝒜ngela met Karen in the mall's food court, getting themselves hot dogs and chips. They smiled at each other and hugged, since they hadn't had the chance on the ship. They grabbed a small table and sat down.

"Thanks for coming after me, Ange. Can you pass that on to the others, whoever they are?" she grinned conspiratorially and winked.

"Positively." She grinned back.

"So how's Thant…"

"Unless you want him listening in, don't use that name. He's attuned to it."

"What?"

"Speak of the devil. We all have secret names we're attuned to, if anyone speaks them, we can hear what's being said. Mine's Fawedea," she smiled wryly at her friend. "I know you don't think much of him at all. On the other hand, it speaks volumes about how much he likes you that he'd tell you his name. Given the bond that formed when he resurrected you, you could probably…well, no probably about it…talk to him mind to mind if you want to, initiate it yourself rather than wait for him to. But it's a lot more under his control than yours."

"It is?" she asked, pondering. "What can he do with it under his control?" She seemed nervous.

Angela shrugged. "I'm not entirely sure. He didn't do a lot with it with me, but I can't be sure if that was his restraint or a limit on capability. He kept track of where I was. At White Hill, I deliberately reached out to him and begged his help, and that apparently strengthened the connection. The more it gets used, the stronger. We've been talking mind-to-mind a lot over the past year.

"That said, though... he made me eat a sardine once. That was really, really disgusting." She gagged in memory.

"What a pig! I can't believe you still have him as a tutor after that. Surely someone else would have been better!"

She looked at Karen out of the corner of her eye as her friend continued to sputter, "It was no big deal. A test. We were seeing what he could do, the others were standing by to help if it went too far, and I'd agreed to the test before hand. He specifically cautioned me about the things I did that might strengthen it. Like I said, I'm not sure whether him not doing much wasn't just him choosing not to. I think we should work on your mental defenses, though. I was able to build on the martial arts discipline."

"Believe it or not, cheerleading isn't just for airheads. We put a lot into it." She smiled. "So bring it on, baby."

"Ok, just a warning, though. At least for a while, he can blow past your defenses without any difficulty. He specifically suggested I work with some of the others on it, and it's still easier for the two of us to communicate telepathically than for either of us and one of the others."

"Can he not break your defenses, or did he just not try?"

"Hmph. We haven't worked on it much. He's really good at controlling dead things, not so much what's happening with a living body—or mind. That doesn't mean he can't, though. I'm inclined to think it was just his restraint."

"Wonderful. The God of Death can take control of my body whenever he wants to."

"Karen. I've never told him you know. I don't think he does know. But I've come to know my sensei. He's not going to. He's never taken control of mine."

"He's not…"

"I have taken control of his, once, remember? That was WEIRD."

"Oh, yeah," she laughed.

"He's got you seriously on the brain, from what I saw in his mind. But every image I saw of you, you were wearing clothes. I'd say he'd be ecstatic if you wanted to date him, but he thinks you're not interested, he's not going to make you, and he's not going to waste his time by asking."

CHAPTER

61

$\mathcal{S}$he was sitting in her room catching up on her homework—actual schoolwork for once, algebra. She heard a quiet knock on the door and looked up to see her mom at the door. "Hi sweetie," she said.

"Hi Mom. What's up?" She settled back in the chair.

"I wanted to know if you'd like to start driving lessons this weekend," she said.

"Sure, but I have a history paper and several pages of math due on Monday, plus the swim meet, so I'll have to get the homework done first."

"You've become quite the scholar the last two years, sweetie. I'm very proud of you. Straight A's all year. Maybe even valedictorian."

"Wizards of the Round Table. Right now Morgan le Fay is the odds on favorite to be valedictorian. And the rest of us are right at her heels. I've still got those B's from last year, though, and the others don't."

"Are they cheating?"

"No. Not when it comes to their grades. They've cursed cheaters with inevitable discovery. They're competitive, though. Very. I've fallen in with the smart kids, Mom. Best GPA in a month doesn't chip in to the monthly party, and gets to name which secret base it's at." Mom laughed. "I'm being serious. There are three—one on Earth, one on

Mars, and one on Venus, plus we all have our own little hidey-holes here."

"You do? How'd you afford something like that?"

"They're are secrets, created with our magic. Seth's is an abandoned mausoleum in a graveyard. The others all worked on the big three bases, which they'd mostly finished by the time I started learning from Seth." She scribbled a few more notes. "They helped setting mine up."

"You have one? Can you tell me where it is?"

"A dead volcanic seamount in the middle of the Pacific. Would you like to see it?"

"How do I get there?"

"I'll have to take you. Not even the others can enter it without my permission," she replied.

"And the off-world bases?"

"We've got a… secret on Venus. I'd need to check with the others before taking you there. Mars should be okay once I've got someone on safety watch."

"What sort of secret?"

"When Seth resurrected me, and this past October Karen, no one knew either of us had ever been dead. On Venus, he resurrected someone who is publically known to be dead. As I mentioned, we're not ready to go public with our abilities. So… he's alive, but safely put somewhere that can't be learned."

"That's… I don't know if it's terrible you're keeping him confined or wonderful he's alive."

"We don't either," she admitted.

"Why'd you bring him back, if you didn't know?"

"I think we're getting into territory of secrets I need to keep. Other people's secrets, the ones I'm not free to share."

Mom nodded. "What was that about safety watch?"

"We go up in pairs with someone else monitoring us and able to bring us back if there's a problem. Just in the bases we relax that rule, since we've already ensured they're safe. But if I take you up, I want back up ready and waiting." Her lips quirked. "Who might well be Seth, since you already know about him."

"I'm not really comfortable with that arrangement, Angela."

"You know, the rest of the group thinks your animus against the guy who brought your daughter back from death is rather ridiculous. So do I."

"Honey, he put his..."

"Mom. You're holding a grudge over him performing CPR on me." Mom blinked at that.

"I..." She stopped, considered, and nearly started again, then shook herself. "I guess I am, aren't I? I hadn't thought of it like that."

"Resurrection is easiest when there's skin-to-skin contact at head and heart, takes the least amount of our own energy. But since death is his specialty, he can do things on either side of the death line that would put me in a coma. My focus is manipulating states of matter."

"What do you mean put you in a coma?"

"I watched him resurrect the Stellar's sea cow from sub-fossil remains. I know he's resurrected at least one mammoth. The only thing keeping him from resurrecting some other species is our inability to hide a relict population somewhere. I know how to bring back the dead—I've done it myself in practice. But the quantities he's capable of, in as quick succession, from prehistoric or fragmentary remains... not safely."

"What have you brought back?"

"Plants. Animals killed on the side of the road. A fish in one of the tanks at school. Our foci are what we're best at, what takes the least out of us. The others tell me that so far, everyone can do everything the others can do."

"You haven't brought back any people?"

"From what he tells me, there's no real difference in the process. The biggest differences with people are the post resurrection complications. We bring an animal or a plant back, no one's likely to wonder what happened. I didn't know I had died. I just thought I'd hit my head. Karen rapidly figured out that she died, but he and I were the only ones that knew it. But someone known to be dead is a different story, which is why he's stashed on Venus. It would expose us, and that would make us do things we don't want to."

"So what do you guys want to do?"

"Save the world."

"How?"

"We're still discussing that. The one we're preferring at the moment is to make the Moon habitable and getting a bunch of people to move there. They'd already discussed and, for now, rejected, the awful options before I joined them."

"Awful options? Like what?"

"Global pandemic. World War Three. Ragnarok. Zombie apocalypse." Mom laughed at the last one. "I'm being serious. When they were discussing them, they worked out how."

"You ARE serious. Could they actually do it?"

"I wouldn't bet against them, especially if they're all agreed. So far they've been unanimously voting against doing anything like that. They're doing all they can to not perpetrate a holocaust. What we're worried about, though, is that we may not have an option, that the only way to relieve the stress is to sacrifice a substantial portion of the human population so that the rest can survive."

"Heavy stuff for some teenagers."

"Yeah, heavy. Problem is, it's not a philosophical discussion like the ones the teachers like to have in class or you hear talked about at lunch. We've already worked out HOW. It's a serious debate on whether we should pull the trigger."

Mom looked at her horrified, and left the room a little unsteady in her tennis shoes. Angela went back to her English paper.

62

Angela was lunching with Seth, behind his privacy shield. Seth's shield could either just keep people away or slowly kill them as they got closer and closer; at school he just kept people away (not that there were many seeking him out) and let the shield interdict sound and scramble vision. Almost anyone he normally talked to already knew how to counter the shield. They took turns providing the shield; she'd do it next time, with the one she was working with Solly on. They were practicing Tsalagi, discussing whether they should send out interstellar probes in between talking about how to refine her own privacy shield. She was surprised to see Karen MacLeod walk right up to them and sit down with her lunch. *<Seth, can she do that? Did you leave Karen out of the interdict?>*

<No.> He did, however, break off the conversation and start gathering up his orange peels. *<But it's designed to shunt people away, not completely prevent access. If she's decided to grit her teeth and come through, it won't stop her.>*

"Wait, Seth," Karen said. He glanced at her as he stood up, his eyebrows raised. Karen stood too, reached out and took his hands in hers. She looked into his face for a long moment, then hurriedly said, "I didn't fight my way through all that fear and disgust and nausea just to have you run away. I know you want me, and I'm only going to say this once. I can't say that I feel the same way about you that I know you feel about me, and I think you know that too. But I also know that when I was lying dead on the grass in Golden Gate Park, you came and gave me my life back. When I was taken by white slavers and thrown on a ship for who knows where, I felt when you reached out to me to find me and you came for me. When I was dragged at gunpoint away as a hostage you came to my rescue and put yourself between the gun and me and kept me safe and I've been told that you'll never ask me for more or make me do anything and I just wanted to say, where we're protected by your power from anyone eavesdropping who doesn't already know the secrets, *thank you.* Thank you, Seth, from the bottom of my heart. Thank you for my life, for my freedom, for protecting me as only a living breathing god of death can. Thank you, Thantoris." She released his hands, but kept gazing into his eyes.

"You're welcome, Karen." He walked away, both girls watching him go.

The silence didn't last much longer before Angela broke it. "For a second there I thought I was in some romantic movie and you were going to surprise the hell out of him and kiss him."

"I considered it. Just a peck on the cheek, you know, but I thought he might get the wrong idea."

"It's good you let him down easy. What did you mean he put himself between the gun and you? You never mentioned that before."

"He was coming closer and closer and the guy pointed the gun at my head, and he said something suddenly he and I had switched places. The gun fired, and the bad guy died." She took a drink. "I figured I owed him an easy let down after all that. Creepy, scary, but not a bad guy."

"Must have been really weird for the thug, to suddenly be gripping bones." Karen's eyes widened. "Yeah, that outfit of his includes disguising touch. When we were working on mine he told me his covered all five senses, but I've never tried taste, so I have to take his word on that one. He did let me feel his hand in those gauntlets, though. Dry bone."

"You do bony too?"

"I do great flaming wings. You may have noticed them?"

"Those are really flaming? How do you stand the heat! I thought they were illusions!"

"Controlled plasma, actually. I fly with magic, not the wings." She sipped her water. "Since it's under my control, I control how much heat gets out, and where."

"Really? How do you do that?"

Angela looked at her bemusedly. "Karen, repeat after me: it's *magic*. If you really want to learn, I suppose I could see if someone's willing to teach you. Granted, that *would* mean you'd be getting to know Seth a lot better." She grinned at Karen's dismay. "But that doesn't mean he'd be your tutor. I can ask someone else, if you're interested."

"I dunno. Can I study with you guys and not learn magic? Just schoolwork? Mom and Dad have really been on me to improve my grades." She made a face. "That or drop the squad. My grades aren't that bad, but they've taken something of a hit this year. They want A's and I'm getting B's."

"Last year, I was studying with at least one of them and didn't even know it, so sure. And it's not like there's no one who doesn't. Julian and Shevaun study with us and don't know about the rest of it."

Karen arched a brow. "You sure about that?"

"They don't know. They've probably gotten enough around the edges to suspect something more is going on, but how much more I don't know. I haven't probed their minds."

"Who has?"

"Lady Liberty, Morgan Le Fay, Asmodeus, and Pan have that task."

"Some pseudonyms!" she laughed.

Angela shrugged. "Using their secret names lets them listen in, and they wouldn't like this conversation. I won't use their real ones. So... I came up with a few that lets you know who I'm talking about without violating confidences."

"Gotcha." She pondered a moment. "Maybe I should learn magic. Do you really think I can?"

"No idea, really. I know you've got the brains if I do. I think I need to check with Morgan le Fay, she'll know."

Dave sat at the table in Kaiser's Hof Brau, his roast beef sandwich in front of him, the smell of the hot meats and pickles redolent in the air of the hof brau. Angela got her pastrami, a fully loaded Coke, and a custard desert and joined him, drawing a privacy sphere around them. Dave looked at her apprehensively. "Thank you. Where do you put all the calories?"

"Do you get why I wasn't answering, now?" she asked after taking a bite, savoring the sandwich. Delicious as always, especially with the spicy mustard and aus jus dip. "As for the calories… the energy for magic has to come from somewhere, and drawing it from the environment is harder than supplying it from my own cells."

"Yeah, I do, and I guess that makes sense," he nodded. He played a bit with his pickle spear, then asked, "Who are they?"

"Friends of mine, and that's all I'm going to confirm. I'm the newest member of the group. They're my teachers. I'm not the strongest, or most powerful, or the leader. That was the first time I really joined the others in a rescue and battle. There's some discussion about whether we should fudge your memory, to keep the secrets. We're not ready to publicly reveal ourselves and what we can do." She paused for bit of thought. "One of them gave me back my life once. Literally."

"So what is this? A warning to keep my mouth shut?" he waved at the two of them sitting and eating lunch.

"Some outsiders know, or at least have an idea. If we can trust them, we don't need to take any steps. This, basically, is figuring out how trustworthy you are. Do we need to take steps?"

"And they assigned my ex to make the determination?"

She smiled tightly. "You IDed me. That makes you my problem. If you hadn't, we probably wouldn't be having this conversation."

He bit his lip. She reached out and put her hand over his, teal nail polish gleaming. "Dave, believe it or not, I'm not trying to scare you. As one of my friends says, fear is a weakness. We can't rely on it to get you to keep the secret. You need to want to. It needs to be your decision, not ours."

"What happens to me if I don't?"

"Well, first we laugh at the story. On the surface, it's ridiculous." She took a bite. "If we need to, though, we can take more direct steps. Human memory, we've discovered, is malleable. We can adjust it if necessary."

<Angela?>

"In the middle of something here, Teach," she replied, noting Dave's completely confused look. She held up a hand to keep Dave from asking more questions just then.

<Fawedea, Grianne has noticed a large meteor. She's already crunched the numbers and it will impact dead center of Beijing. The trajectory is somewhat suspicious. We don't have a lot of time to act. How quickly can you suit up and get here?>

"What was that, Angela?" Dave asked.

"I need to cut this short, Dave. I'm needed over Beijing."

"*Over* Beijing? Did I hear that right?" He asked, disbelieving. "Yep," she grinned. "I think it will probably be on the news, though you won't see *us*." *<On my way>*, she thought to Seth.

As she was striding out the door, Dave called out to her. "Angela, I'm sorry. I was an asshole. Can you forgive me?"

She smiled. "Sure, Dave. You pissed me off, but we're good."

"Any possibility you'll give me another chance?"

She stopped, blinking at the question. She couldn't help it. She took his hand in hers and spoke a verse in Ainu, giving her access to his mind. It wasn't like entering Seth's mind, with its' slick shields and pyramid fortress and only a small antechamber for a visitor, or intruder. Dave's mind was open to her probe. A stunned look came over his face, and there was recognition of what she was doing.

"Are you…"

<*Peeking inside your head, yes.*> His jaw dropped. But as far as she could tell, he was sincere in his repentance, in his desire to be with her again. She dropped his hand and kissed him. "I need to go. You wanted to know where I was, when I wasn't answering my phone?"

"Um, yeah, but I can guess "busy" covers it."

She gave him a crooked smile. "Mars. Or Venus." She flashed her eyebrows at him.

"Leave it to me to fall in love with a goddess," he said somewhat ruefully, smiling. She smiled shyly at him. "We're not gods, Dave. We're just… powerful.

"I'll call you," she said as she subtly increased her speed to get somewhere concealed. She made her way around back, went invisible, put on her wings, and teleported to join Seth.

In the Chinese sky, the ten of them hovered invisibly. The cities glowed beneath them in the darkness, but they could also see the contrails of jets scrambling to meet the unexpected meteor. They were all there: Alex in his chariot, Seth on Orcinus, Bridget sitting serenely on Gomph, Angela's plasma wings beating, Teddy on his burning throne, Jennifer on a broomstick, Malcolm on a waterspout, Keisha on a cloud, Dawn seemingly balanced on a sunbeam, and Solly on his carpet. They couldn't see the meteor yet.

"That impacts and we have a dinosaur-level extinction event," Bridget said. "How do we stop it?"

"The Chinese are already preparing missiles," Alex said. "On the other hand, stopping a meteor isn't like shooting down a missile. And they're going to do a lot of damage to themselves. The pulses alone will do a lot of damage."

"They might deflect it, but I don't think they'll stop it. Jennifer?" Keisha asked.

"You're right. Damn, Karen's better at probability math than I am. But… yeah, they aren't going to stop it."

"We need Karen? Back in a moment," Seth said.

"We're on a schedule here, Seth. How will you find her?' Alex asked reasonably.

"She was dead once, and I brought her back. I know where she is, and she knows what I am. I'll be right back." He and Orcinus vanished.

"And he didn't think to discuss this with us because...?" asked Teddy coldly. No one else seemed to think it was a problem, though.

"Teddy, really," Malcolm said. "We all know Seth feels about Karen. We also know what it would take to stop him. Since neither she nor anyone else has been talking about someone coming back from the dead, we're still good. Does she know what happened?"

"Yeah, she does," Angela put in. "I was with her when she was shot. I called in Seth..."

"Let go of me you perverted ass!" Seth and Orcinus reappeared in a swirl of blackness with him holding Karen's arm. She was dressed for cheerleader practice. Bridget stepped in.

"Karen, at the moment his hold is all that's keeping you from falling. If I may?" The skull nodded, once Gomph's trunk was securely around Karen. She stared at the mammoth, at the ground below, the clouds around them, the huge meteor coming at them, her eyes widening at each impossible sight. "I understand you're good at probabilities. We're planning to stop that," she motioned at the meteor. "We'd like to do so with minimum damage to Beijing." She gestured at the city.

"Wow, China? Um, okay. Sorry, Seth, er, Thantoris. What are the parameters?" Her brow furrowed in concentration.

They told her, she and Jennifer leaving even the rest of them behind as they did the calculations in their heads. Teddy stepped up by putting their calculations into visible illusions as they spoke, written on a cloud where all eleven could see. "Um, unless you've got some impressive power those missiles are not going to do it."

"What about going nuclear?" Angela asked.

"Um, that would work, delivered in the right place. I don't think those missiles will get to the right place, though. Are you going to take some Chinese uranium?" Jennifer replied.

"Don't need it," Angela replied.

"Yeah, we do, Fawedea," Malcolm replied. "We don't have the juice to protect us and the city and simultaneously create a nuclear detonation. Two of the three, yes."

"Don't worry about it. I don't need it to set off a nuclear blast. You guys crunch some water and methane for the hydrogen, shield the city from the blast, and I'll take care of the rest."

"Fusion?" Teddy asked incredulously. "That's a lot harder to do. My head aches even thinking about what it would take."

"It's easier than turning *that* into a critical mass of uranium," Angela replied.

"Nuclear fusion, because you would have it so." Karen was flabbergasted, but she could still see the calculations flashing through her mind and coming up with how to make it work. Cuan looked closely at her, his eyes glowing blue.

"Felarie, could you check Miss MacLeod?"

She looked at him. "You think...?"

"Come on, Cuan. What are the odds?" Keisha said.

"None of us had thought she," he nodded at Angela, "has the potential she did before Thantoris raised her, either, and we all know her brains; she just gave us another demonstration. Maybe the application of his power triggered something. She could be another of us."

"You think it might just take time to manifest?" Kara asked hopefully.

"Possibly. It's just possible that he awakened a latent potential they have and he doesn't, though," Cuan replied.

"Oh, enough, Malcolm! Angela, Teddy, Alex, Bridget, Seth, Keisha, Jennifer, Dawn, Solomon," pointing at each in turn. Angela got the impression Seth was amused at their discomfiture. "Only person I got wrong was Dani. Once someone knows who one of you is, the others sort of fall into place." She looked apprehensively at Bridget. "You're, um, not going to push me off the furry elephant are you?"

"Columbian mammoth. No." She shook her head. "That would be pointless." She suddenly grinned. "Seth likes you far too much for that to be an option. He'd just bring you back again."

Karen rolled her eyes at that as the rest chuckled. "This won't hurt," Felarie said, maneuvering the carpet closer. Her eyes glowed indigo as she looked Karen up and down. "You're right, Cuan. She definitely has the potential. Karen, we're going to send you home; it's easier than having to protect you from the blast."

"What's with the names, anyway?"

"Not now. Thantoris, would you do the honors?" To Karen, as Seth came forward on Orcinus, she said, "I know he's not your favorite person, but thanks to Angela's misunderstanding last year he's the best teleporter among us. Swing your leg over Orcinus's back."

"Orcinus? As in *Orcinus orca*? Taking the theme a little far, aren't you?" she teased as she took Seth's hand and got behind him on the horse. "Don't get excited," she said as she put her arms around him. "I'm just holding on."

"I understand," he replied. Angela sensed his mind going distant, calling up his power, even as he thrilled to her touch, then they were gone in another swirl of darkness.

"Too bad, we could have used her strength," Solly said.

"Bestarion, you're the abjuration specialist. Put the shield in a concave disk half a mile over the city. Kara, Angoral, Cuan, help him. Felarie, back me up. Toranos, Grianne, and Chiomara get to work on that hydrogen, have Thantoris help you when he gets back," Angela started issuing instructions. "Felarie, could you work on shielding us? And keep the Chinese military from being a problem?"

"You got it." The air filled with the sounds of their incantations as she concentrated on pulling in the hydrogen and helium in the atmosphere. She barely noticed when Seth returned and added his power to making more hydrogen.

As the shielding spells took form, Angela felt the tingling of the power welling up within her as she prepared to force the molecules together. She included the helium she'd be making in her formulation, and even the lithium, beryllium, and boron, upping the energy she'd be unleashing. She felt the forceful wills of the others combining as the ones on fuel creation joined the protection team in ensuring that none of the heat and radiation would get through to annihilate the people—all life, really—of Beijing.

The blast was intense, blinding… as at the heart of the sun. But none of that got through to the capital of China, and their protection spells held it off them, too. They were drenched in sweat, breathing heavily, but they had done it, and Angela, drained as she was, knew they were all looking at her in amazement. They gathered close in and listened to Seth's incanting a teleport spell, and they were no longer in China.

The blackness of Seth's teleportation spell brought them back to the room under Battery Wallace. They grabbed their seats and flipped on the air conditioning and the pizza ovens. Granted, it was a lot hotter where they'd just been, but still…

Alex, in his purple chair, spoke up first. "Everyone good job the past week. We stopped the white slavers preying on our friends, rescued the people taken, and saved Beijing. With all that, Thantoris has a few items of business. Thantoris?"

Seth stood. "Ladies and gentlemen, three pieces of business, before we head home. First, I present Angela Fujiwara as a full member of our company, no longer an apprentice. Her name, in case you've been absent from game night, is Fawedea." Everyone clapped and smiled and cheered.

"Are sure about that full member? A lot of what you guys can do is really scary," Angela said.

Alex cocked his head at her. "Fawedea, you just set off a thermonuclear detonation by will and knowledge and power. How are you NOT as scary as any one of us?" Everyone laughed at that.

"Any of us would be on our back for a week just to cause the detonation," Teddy said. "Not only are you up and around, we could all feel you joining with us to strengthen the shields. You are fully one of us, and I'm happy and proud to have you with us."

Seth continued. "Second, Karen MacLeod. She knows who we are, as she just demonstrated. She has the potential to be one of us. This state of affairs is dangerous." The laughing quieted immediately, even the smiles vanished from their faces.

"And you want to take her on as a new apprentice?" Teddy asked.

"We all know what someone who doesn't know what they're doing can do with these abilities. For her own sake, Angoral, we should take steps," Jennifer put in.

"Agreed we need to do something. The question is whether we take the ability from her or teach her what she needs to know. My impression of her isn't very high on the keep things under wraps angle. It might be safer for all concerned if we simply remove the power from her and adjust her memory."

"Karen's figured it out on her own, and she's known for a while," Angela put in. "She's kept the secrets."

"Fawedea, I don't like the fact that you didn't tell us she knew," Alex said.

"Neither do I, Toranos," Dawn said, "but let's stay focused. The fact that she figured it out will make it harder to adjust her memory. Bringing her fully inside would solve the problem."

"I was ready to take action if necessary."

"Karen's brilliant, guys. We just watched her compute probabilities in her head. A little unfocused, but let's be serious. There are enough anomalies out there—Fawedea being so close to, being tutored by Thantoris, for example—that someone who's had the direct experience of his power being applied to her could, and apparently did, figure it out," Keisha said. "And Fawedea has every right to tell anyone she wishes about her abilities. So quit huffing and puffing. I'll be happy to tutor Karen."

"I wasn't saying I wouldn't tutor her. I don't think anyone here would object to taking that on. We just need to consider all the options, including the distasteful or objectionable ones. I'll take on the tutoring task myself, if her parents are anything like mine."

"I've got the widest range, though," Jennifer put in. "And Fawedea's not only her close friend, but the act of teaching can help reinforce the learning she just was doing." With that the argument was off and running. Everyone was arguing about who would be the best tutor, when Bridget cocked her head and stared at the one person who was staying out of the discussion and just concentrating on his double-sugar extra dark hot chocolate.

"Thantoris, why aren't you trying for it? You did a great job tutoring Angela, so why not Karen? It's not like we don't know how much you'd love to be that close to her for so long."

"I would, but I think you're all forgetting something. Fawedea approached me about learning to control her power. I agree that it's best for her if she undergoes training. But if Karen wants training, why not let her decide?"

"Out of mouths of corpses. Kara, can we use the Opera?" Keisha nodded. "Fawedea can you get her there? It's in the Civic Center."

"Why not here? Now?" Angela asked. "Thantoris can get her, since he's got a bond with her from the resurrection, and it would put her on the path to control." There were nods and sounds of agreement.

"I'll ask. No promises," he said, doubt infusing his face and voice. "Karen? Seth. Yes, this is telepathy. I'm sorry to disturb you, but we need to speak to you." He paused. "Privately. And as soon as possible. Now, if you can. Yes, that will work."

He turned his attention back to the room. "She needs to get someplace private."

"You going to go get her?"

"I'll just pull her here without going, just as if she were on Mars or Venus." He wiped his forehead before picking up his hot chocolate. He downed the mug in one go. "Oh, the third thing. I think there are two others we need to keep an eye on, Julian and Shevaun. I'm not as positive of them, and no, Angoral, neither of them has died near me. Felarie?"

She concentrated. "You're right, I think they do have the potential. I don't think either has tapped into it really, though. I'll keep an eye on Julian."

"I was in Brownies with Shevaun. Time to rekindle a friendship," Dawn said. "Is there anyone else? Someone we should keep an eye on?"

"We know about Fawedea, Karen, Julian, and Shevaun because they're friends, people we interact with," Malcolm said. "Someone we never do anything with, who's quiet, could easily slip past us."

"Well put, Cuan," Solly said. "Should we do a survey for others?"

"I think that would be more Felarie's area than anyone else's," Alex said. He looked around and everyone nodded. "It's yours."

They busied themselves with the little grooming spells on Gomph, the horses, the cats, and dogs and sent them home. Then Seth cocked his head. "Karen, my hand is going to appear in front of you. Take it and I'll bring you here."

A few minutes later Karen appeared in a swirl of blackness. Seth stood and went over to the kitchen area. "Can I get you anything? Root beer, cocoa? The pizzas will be ready in a moment, the lasagnas a little later."

"Um, a diet root beer…" she said hesitantly.

"I'll see what I can do."

"Do we have diet?" Angela asked, glancing around.

"Not normally," Alex replied. "Coming back from something like that we need the caloric boost in a big way. But it's not hard to conjure up some." He glanced around, and then said, "Karen, you have the ability to do this. We've screwed up plenty of times, but having nine—excuse me, Fawedea, *ten*—of us has meant we've been able to fix the problems. Fawedea had the benefit of direct instruction, since she only joined us last year. She's made rapid progress, though, and there's no reason you couldn't do the same thing.

"That said, if you don't want this power, we can take it from you. If you want training, we can do that. We think it's better for one person to be the primary tutor, though we all provided some form of instruction to Fawedea and would be happy to do the same for you. We were discussing which of us should take on the task. But as Thantoris reminded us, Fawedea picked him to be her primary tutor. In the same tradition, if you want training, you might as well be the one to select your tutor, and we'll fix it with school. Fair enough?"

"Do I have to decide right now? This is kinda sudden, guys."

"No, of course not," Dawn said. "We're all exhausted from stopping that meteor. It is better, safer, to get it started as quickly as possible though. Safer for everybody, especially you. Our first forays into the magic were accidental, and we think that most people who do develop these abilities kill themselves with them by not really knowing what they're doing."

"At the moment," Seth said quietly as he telekinetically put eleven pizzas on the table, "in order to reach someone quickly, I'm probably your best option. Thanks to the resurrection bond, you can reach me with your mind or by intention. If you need help, you can call on me. That will, however, strengthen the bond."

"What do you mean, 'by intention'?" she asked.

"With most of us," Bridget answered for him, "someone would have to speak our secret names for us to pay attention, and we usually follow it up with "I beseech thine aid" so we know to pay serious attention. For you—and Fawedea—you can just say 'Seth' if you're intentionally trying to contact him."

"Really?" at her expression, Jennifer snorted.

"She's known she's had the ability for less than a day and she's already planning on pranking the guy who can set off the zombie apocalypse." Karen laughed.

"Karen, she's serious. I watched Seth zombify the corpses of the people he killed at White Hill," Angela said. "And that includes any dead tissue, including that wooden chair you're sitting in." She smiled at Karen's expression of chagrin and slight pleading look at Seth.

Teddy piped up. "Something to know, Karen, is that we're all capable of immense damage if we choose. The differences are more a matter of method, and any of us can do what the others do. Angela just whipped up a nuclear fusion explosion. When fully trained, you will be, too. We learn and practice control to keep from accidentally causing damage. We act, as necessary, to restrain each other from causing too much damage. We restrained Toranos earlier this year when someone put roofies in Dani's Sportyade. That said, are you in?"

Karen looked at each of them, haggard from stopping a meteor that might have killed a billion people. She tried to catch everyone's eye, and nearly succeeded. Only Seth wouldn't meet her gaze. He played with his mug, checked on the lasagna, and stared off into space. "What's wrong, Seth?"

"Nothing."

Angela reached up and squeezed his shoulder. She could guess what it was, after being in his mind.

"Well, then I think I'll join you. Angela, would you be my tutor? Can you be my tutor?"

"To answer the second question," Jennifer said, "Yes, she can. Seth just graduated her from apprentice to full member."

"I'd be honored, Karen. As my teacher told me, we have no idea what your particular bent for this might be."

"If you need help, Angela, just ask," Teddy said.

"You all helped teach me. I hope you'll all help me teach Karen." They nodded. Seth vanished.

"Oh, dear."

"Should we go after him?" Karen asked.

"We don't know where he went," Malcolm responded. "Teleporting doesn't really leave a trace."

Angela and Karen looked at each other. "We know where he is," Karen said.

"He's at the Mausoleum."

"Which still means we can't follow," Solly said. "Not with the defenses he has in place."

"I'm not understanding," Karen said.

"Our personal lairs—hidey-holes, whatever—are warded to keep others out. Given his necromantic focus, Seth's wards are likely to simply kill anyone trying to force their way in," he replied. "And I doubt we could resist his power long."

"I'll go," Angela said. "He gave me a pass while he was training me. It should keep me alive long enough to talk to him."

"I'm coming, too," Karen said.

"You don't have a pass, Karen," Jennifer pointed out.

"If it's set up to be lethal, you won't survive long enough for Angela to teleport you out of there."

"I know. But you said if you pushed me off the elephant he'd just bring me back, so I'm betting he won't hurt me."

"Karen, understand that if you die from Seth's power, we can't override that," Bridget said. "Only he can. And while ordinarily he'd never hurt you, we don't really know what he's feeling right now."

"Understood," she said in a slightly shaky voice.

Angela spoke in Ainu and they stood before the Mausoleum. It was overgrown with ivy, a neoclassical white marble tomb with a bronze door. The ivy nearly covered it. Fog had rolled in, and they could barely see anything. The moon wasn't visible.

"Not too late to wait for me here, Padawan," she told Karen. "No. Something about this is related to me. I'll brave the mummy's curse."

"Okay. Stay behind me." She reached up to her neck and pulled out the ankh. Placing her middle finger through the hole, she approached the doors. The ivy rustled in the evening breeze, but didn't animate and attack. The bronze doors swung open when she put the ankh in a slit and turned it.

"There isn't a mummy. It broke in some earthquake or other, and the bodies were reinterred elsewhere, but the structure was left up." They entered the small chapel. Seth had redecorated; no crosses or angels. A flight of stairs led down, into complete blackness.

"Dark as a tomb down there."

"You're surprised?"

"I thought he'd need light."

"Well, he doesn't, not here. Follow me." She adjusted her sight to include the infrared and ultraviolet and boosted her hearing and sense of smell. He was down there, all right.

"Angela, I can't."

"Yes you can. This is no time to get cold feet."

"The mind is willing. The body is blocked," she said.

"Okay then. I go on alone. Keep your ears open." She went carefully down the stairs, letting her enhanced vision guide her. As she expected, she found Seth in the main room. She wasn't expecting to see him lying on the bier, his eyes closed. His face was wet.

"Are you okay, Teach?"

"Not really."

"What's wrong?"

"Dreams die hard, Angela. Even impossible ones."

"She's upstairs. I'm sure you can sense her presence."

"I'd rather be alone."

"She insisted on coming with me, Seth."

"You wouldn't be here now without the key, Angela. Desires aren't really relevant at the moment."

"Seth? Can I come down there please? I'm not leaving until we talk," Karen called out. *<Karen, here in the Mausoleum, he can eject you.>*

<He hasn't yet.>

Seth was silent for several minutes. "Alright." She felt Seth's power reach out to cancel the barrier.

"Thank you, Seth." She slowly made her way down the stairs, feeling with her foot for each new step. "I know it's your place, Seth, and you're not exactly happy to see me just now, but if you don't mind… fiat lux." A light in the darkness appeared, glowing pink. It came from Karen, highlighting her as she walked confidently forward. Seth's face was dry. "What's wrong, Seth? It's not like we just broke up."

"Never mind. It's my problem. I'll deal with it." Silence hovered in the crypt for several long seconds before they realized Seth wasn't going to continue.

"It's a little weird talking to you on a slab meant for a coffin. Would you mind sitting up?"

"Talking to me was your idea," he said, his eyes still closed. Her lips tightened, and her hands didn't seem to know what to do. More seconds passed as the silence got a little more oppressive.

"Seth, whatever's wrong has something to do with me. I'm trying to think of what I might have said or done to make you vanish from that meeting, retreat to your cathedral in a graveyard. I can't come up with anything. I have an inkling of what you're capable of. I really don't want to face your opposition to me learning magic. I'd thought everything was clear between us."

"It is. You have nothing to fear from me."

"Then what's the problem? You won't even look at me!" Seth just lay on the bier, not answering. He barely seemed to be alive, by sight; it was only the connection between them that stopped Angela from checking his pulse. Then Angela made the connections between what she'd seen in his mind and what he'd said.

"You can tell her, or I will."

"It doesn't matter. It's my problem, not hers. I'll deal with it myself, without bothering her," he repeated. "She doesn't need to know."

"I'm not having my apprentice worried about enmity from the master of necromancy, Seth. This stuff is daunting enough without that sort of confidence killing worry hanging over her." When Seth didn't respond, she sighed and put a hand on his shoulder. "He knows you're not interested. He was clear about that even before your little speech last week, and he was leaving you alone. But he still had the hope, the dream, that you'd change your mind and come to him. When you asked for training, that dream died."

"I thought you went to the Valentine's Ball with Bridget," she said to him. He let Angela answer for him.

"She had to call in a favor to get him there, and that was to clean up the mess I made last year. We don't date amongst ourselves."

"Oh, right, you told me that once I think." She seemed to be considering something, then she held out her hand and said, "Lord Thantoris, I'm Lady Fawedea's apprentice, Karen Indira MacLeod. I hope that we can be friends." Her hand shook even as she looked directly at him.

Seth rose from the bier, sitting straight up and swinging his legs down to the floor. The black robe hung about him like a shroud, but his eyes opened and he took Karen's tremblingly outstretched hand. "Of course we can."